TURNING THE TIDE

Early Los Angeles Modernists 1920-1956

TURNING THE TIDE

Rico Lebrun *Woman of the Crucifixion (Mourning Woman)*, 1948, brown conte crayon and ink, 24 x 19". Collection of Mrs. Constance Lebrun Crown, Santa Barbara, California.

TURNING THE TIDE

Early Los Angeles Modernists 1920-1956

Paul J. Karlstrom

Susan Ehrlich

Curators: Susan Ehrlich and Barry M. Heisler

Santa Barbara Museum of Art 1990

The Santa Barbara Museum of Art

BOARD OF TRUSTEES

OFFICERS

Arthur W. Schultz, *President*
Mrs. William C. Henderson, *Administrative Vice President*
Kent M. Vining, *Second Vice President and Chief Financial Officer*
J. Hewes Crispin, *Third Vice President*
Mrs. Earnest C. Watson, *Secretary*

TRUSTEES

Thomas C. Amory
Richard Reed Armstrong
Jill Goodson Bishop
Mrs. Terry George Bliss
Mrs. Ernest A. Bryant III
Ernest M. Clark, Jr.
J. Hewes Crispin
James E. Davidson
Henri Dorra
Robert W. Duggan
David Dvorak
Mrs. Robert B. Eichholz
Dr. Robert J. Emmons
Paul Gray
Jeffrey Harding
Mrs. E. Walton Hedges
Mrs. William C. Henderson
Mrs. Harry Hovey
Harris Huey
Mrs. Burke Kaplan
Eli Luria
Mrs. Frank W. Norris
Herbert Peterson
Arthur W. Schultz
Kent M. Vining
Mrs. Earnest C. Watson
Mrs. S. Robert Weltz, Jr.

LIFE HONORARY TRUSTEES

Mrs. Eugene Davidson
Wright S. Ludington
Miss Margaret Mallory
John Rex
Robert K. Straus
Mrs. Edward R. Valentine
F. Bailey Vanderhoef, Jr.

MUSEUM STAFF

Richard V. West, *Director*
Thomas R. Mathews, Jr., *Assistant Director for Administration*
Peggy Stevens, *Personnel and Office Manager*
Elizabeth Bradley, *Executive Secretary to the Director*
Julie Senn, *Administration Department Secretary*
*Karen McGinnis and Martha Emmanouilides, *Receptionists*

CURATORIAL

Robert Henning, Jr., *Assistant Director for Curatorial Services*
Nancy Doll, *Curator of 20th Century Art*
Susan Tai, *Curator of Asian Art*
Terry Atkinson, *Designer*
Sharen O'Riordan, *Curatorial Administrative Assistant*

COLLECTIONS MANAGEMENT

Cherie Summers, *Registrar*
Elaine Cobos, *Assistant Registrar*
*Silvia Tyndall, *Preparator*
*Kim Kosai, *Art Handler*

EDUCATION

Deborah Tufts, *Curator of Education*
Ron Crozier, *Librarian*
*Beverly Decker, *Museum Educator*
Frances Thorpe, *Assistant to the Curator of Education*

DEVELOPMENT AND MEMBERSHIP

Barbara Luton, *Director of Development*
Shelley S. Ruston, *Director of Special Programs*
Virgina Cochran, *Grants and Public Relations Director*
Kathy O'Leary, *Events and Volunteer Coordinator*
Cathy Pollock, *Publications Manager*
Kelly L. Cretti, *Membership Manager*
*Libby McCollum, *Programs Coordinator*
*Delta Giordano, *Programs Assistant*

Joan Enasko, *Development Assistant*
Adis Morales, *Development Secretary*
*Christine Steele, *Grants and Public Relations Assistant*

BUSINESS OFFICE

Gale Poyorena, *Controller*
Sharon Beckett, *Accounting Supervisor*
Marilyn Skiold, *Accounting Clerk*
Kurt Angersbach, *Admissions and Information Clerk*

MUSEUM STORE

Penny Mast, *Manager*
*Lauren Baldwin and Evelyn Harley, *Sales Assistants*

MAINTENANCE AND INSTALLATION

John A. Coplin, *Facilities Manager*
Jerry Travis, *Building Technician I*
Dane Goodman, *Building Technician I*
Alfonso Bravo, *Building Technician I*
Gene Brundin, *Building Technician II*
Raul Matamoros, *Custodian*
John Morales, *Custodian*

SECURITY

Walter Hildbrand, *Chief of Security*
Noel Assayech, *Deputy Chief of Security/Security Control*
Alexander Grabner, *Senior Security Guard*
Security Guards:
  Steven Bissell
  Bert Espinoza
  Philip Liddicoat
  Micheal Woxell
  *Kurt Angersbach
  *Michael Caulfield
  *Mansour Matin
  *William Miserendino
  *Mario Munarolo
  *Ann Skiold
  *Peter Stettinius
  *Brad Wright

*Part-time employee

Contents

7	FOREWORD	Richard V. West
8	INTRODUCTION	Barry M. Heisler
13	*Modernism in Southern California, 1920-1956 Reflections on the Art and the Times*	Paul J. Karlstrom
43	THE ARTISTS	Susan Ehrlich

    Karl Benjamin
    Ben Berlin
    William Brice
    Hans Burkhardt
    Grace Clements
    Jules Engel
    Lorser Feitelson
    Oskar Fischinger
    Frederick Hammersley
    Peter Krasnow
    Rico Lebrun
    Helen Lundeberg
    Stanton Macdonald-Wright
    John McLaughlin
    Knud Merrild
    Lee Mullican
    Agnes Pelton
    Henrietta Shore
    Howard Warshaw
    June Wayne

97	COLOR PLATES
161	CHECKLIST
164	BIBLIOGRAPHY

Helen Lundeberg *The Portrait*, 1953, oil on canvas, 30 x 36". Santa Barbara Museum of Art, Santa Barbara, California. Gift of Mr. and Mrs. Thomas C. McCray.

Foreword

Richard V. West
DIRECTOR

When I was a child growing up in the early 1940s on the fringes of Hollywood, I was an *Angeleno*. I knew this because the newspaper my parents read—Mr. Hearst's *Examiner*—told me so. Angelenos were apparently something special (according to the paper), certainly different from those snobbish folk up north in San Francisco. I was unaware of it then, but I guess Los Angeles had a terrific inferiority complex. In those pre-smog days, Los Angeles boasted of a wonderful climate, orange trees galore, and Hollywood. San Francisco, however, had Old Money, Sophisti-cation, Culture—and History. Of course, Los Angeles had a history—it just seemed that no one could find it. It had been mislaid somewhere along the line during the invention of Hollywood and (so it seemed to me at the time) simply been interred at the Forest Lawn cemetery along with the giant reproduction of Michelangelo's *David*.

Living and going to school as I did with the children of film folk (and having a landlord who was one of the original Keystone Kops), it was easy to believe that the history and culture of Hollywood was, in fact, the history and culture of Los Angeles. Even as an art student at UCLA in the fifties, where Annita Delano and Frederick Wight, among others, were my teachers, I was only dimly aware of a Los Angeles art history and of the art scene even then evolving. What I do recall is how abashed and apologetic we all seemed to be about it. Our eyes were fixed on New York and we read every word of Clement Greenberg's ringside account (as reporter *and* referee) of the unfolding drama of Abstract Expressionism. It made Angeleno art seem provincial.

Now, thanks to the research of art historians Paul J. Karlstrom and Susan Ehrlich, we can get a much clearer picture of Los Angeles' role in the international modernist movement, before the "big bang" of the early sixties. I want to thank them, and curator Barry Heisler whose hard work and devoted attention brought the exhibition together, for showing us that Los Angeles in the twenties, thirties, and forties was the arena for a number of highly talented artists drawn from all over the world.

Introduction

Barry M. Heisler
GUEST CO-CURATOR

Modernism in America has received much critical study and attention during the past decade. Exhibitions devoted to artists such as Arthur B. Carles, Georgia O'Keeffe, Arthur Dove, Charles Sheeler, and Marsden Hartley, as well as broader studies such as *Images of America: Precisionist Painting and Modern Photography* (San Francisco Museum of Modern Art, 1982) or *The Machine Age in America* (Brooklyn Museum of Art, 1986) have done much to further the study of this vital and important aspect of American art history. In addition to introducing a new generation of scholars to American modernism, these exhibitions and their accompanying catalogues have also brought back into public view many works which have lain neglected in museum vaults for years.

However, these exhibitions and most of the others dealing with American modernism approach the subject solely from the East Coast point of view, as though no other region in the country could have produced art of any worth. This has little to do with the quality of art produced in such places as Illinois, the Pacific Northwest, or Northern and Southern California, but rather is an indication of the ever-eastward gaze of art historians and curators.

The art of California has suffered further neglect as very little attention has been devoted to the study of the state's artists before 1955. Most scholars and museums have dealt primarily with the art of the past thirty years, feeling that only then was the art of California really able to measure up, to sustain any long-term interest, and to be compelling enough to inspire a generation of younger artists. To the contrary, as Paul Karlstrom so aptly points out in his essay, the successes enjoyed by many contemporary California artists are undoubtedly linked to prior developments in the history of California modernism.

While this dearth of material and exhibitions devoted to the art of the state is evident, some exceptional projects should be mentioned. The most noteworthy is the programming at the Oakland Museum, begun by former Santa Barbara Museum of Art Director Paul C. Mills and continuing to this day, which seriously presents and interprets the art of the region. To a lesser degree, important exhibitions have been mounted, by the San Francisco Museum of Modern Art, Laguna Art Museum, Santa Barbara Museum of Art, and most recently, Wight Art Gallery at the University of California, Los Angeles, featuring individual artists ranging from Arthur and Lucia Mathews to Beatrice Wood, Hans Burkhardt, and Howard Warshaw. While there have been several exhibitions dealing with some of these modernists as a group (for example, the seminal *Painting and Sculpture in California: The Modern Era*, organized by Henry Hopkins at the San Francisco Museum of Modern Art in 1976, and *Forty Years of California Assemblage*, organized by Wight Art Gallery in 1989), detailed discussions of Los Angeles painters have been left to later scholars.

Turning the Tide surveys twenty artists, who between the years of 1920 (the year that Stanton Macdonald-Wright organized *Exhibition of Paintings of American Modernists* at Exposition Park in Los Angeles) and 1956 (the year preceding the opening of the Ferus Gallery, whose artists, among them Edward Kienholz, Joe Goode, Ed Ruscha, and Billy Al Bengston, gained Los Angeles its first international reputation) actively created modernist art in a climate of frighteningly conservative aesthetic taste. Unlike their East Coast peers, they struggled for public understanding, for galleries, and for patrons. Confrontation, frustration, and even political opposition were familiar obstacles to these artists as they attempted to turn the tide (so to speak) of aesthetic taste and support from blind acceptance of the prevalent Eucalyptus School landscape tradition to an understanding and appreciation of modernism.

The exhibition's concept and direction resulted from a meeting with Paul J. Karlstrom, West Coast regional director of the Archives of American Art, in the summer of 1986. Both Dr. Karlstrom and I became fascinated with a group of artists who had lived and worked in Los Angeles during the first half of the twentieth century, but were little known outside a few small circles. While we were aware that there was a growing interest in the artists and in the art history of Los Angeles, we also noted that no exhibitions had yet been offered on this topic.

We began making plans to present an exhibition which would, for the first time, examine in depth this group of artists, and, equally important, would also explore the relationship of the artists to the urban environment which was to become modern Los Angeles. Dr. Karlstrom, who has been an invaluable source of advice and information throughout the project, agreed to act as consultant, and also to contribute a catalogue essay which would provide an overview on the art and times of Southern California during the twenties, thirties, forties, and fifties.

We soon realized that the project should include Susan Ehrlich, a Los Angeles art historian who had devoted many years to the research and study of most of these artists. Dr. Ehrlich graciously accepted my invitation to act as co-curator to the exhibition and has been an immense asset in planning the exhibition and selecting works; she also contributed detailed biographies of each of the twenty artists included.

Clearly, any long-range worth of the exhibition and its catalogue will be due to the diligent efforts of Dr. Karlstrom and Dr. Ehrlich, who have faced a vast number of challenges in preparing material and planning the many details involved in a project as complex as this one. They both deserve a great deal of thanks.

I am also grateful for financial assistance from the National Endowment for the Arts, a federal agency, and from Bente and Gerald Buck of Laguna Hills, California. Without their generous support, the exhibition and catalogue would never have attained its current scope and magnitude.

Thanks must also go to the Santa Barbara Museum of Art's Board of Trustees and Director Richard West for their support. Robert Henning, Jr., Nancy Doll, and Dane Goodman made themselves available for numerous discussions regarding this exhibition, and their input and suggestions have been much appreciated. Registrar Cherie Summers has ensured that all of the details of physically organizing the show were taken into account. And finally, I would like to thank Patty Ruth and Cathy Pollock for their able editing of the catalogue essays, and Nancy Zaslavsky for her creative and sensitive design.

A special acknowledgement goes to the Archives of American Art, Smithsonian Institution, for making its files and records, and, in particular, oral histories of many of the artists, so accessible. In addition, Tobey C. Moss and Jack Rutberg must be commended, not only for their assistance in planning this show, but also for their dedication to many of these artists during the past twenty or more years. The efforts of these farsighted gallery owners and others like them have enabled many of these artists and their works not only to survive the basic neglect of past years but now to be re-examined in the light of history. I fervently hope that *Turning the Tide* will serve as only the beginning for further study of this fascinating period and its diverse group of artists.

AKNOWLEGDEMENTS

The authors and curators wish to thank the following people for their assistance during this project:

Will Ameringer of André Emmerich Gallery; Ms. Susan Anderson, associate curator, and Mr. Bolton Colburn, registrar/associate curator, of Laguna Art Museum; Professor Karl Benjamin; Mr. and Mrs. Edward Biberman; Tiska Blankenship, curator of the Jonson Gallery at the University of New Mexico; Professor William Brice; Peter Briggs, chief curator of the Tucson Museum of Art; Maudette Ball and Janet Dominik of the Buck Collection; Mr. and Mrs. Hans Burkhardt; Mr. and Mrs. James Byrnes; Kay Koeninger, Marjorie Harth Beebe and Mary MacNaughton of the Galleries of Claremont College; Ron and Rocky Dammon; Mr. and Mrs. Mort Dimondstein; Kevin Donovan, curator of collections of the University Art Museum at the University of New Mexico; Ms. Christine Droll, librarian/associate registrar, Terry St. John, associate curator, and Harvey L. Jones, senior curator, of the Oakland Museum; Dr. Charles Eldredge; Jules Engel; Tom Enman; Mrs. Elfreide Fischinger; Ilene Susan Fort, associate curator for American Art, Los Angeles County Museum of Art; Hal Gebhardt; Dr. Barbara Gilbert and Director Nancy Berman of the Skirball Museum; Peter Goulds of L.A. Louver

Gallery; Naomi Sawelson-Gorse; Frederick Hammersley; June Harwood; Lise Honshour; Josine Ianco-Starrels, senior curator, Long Beach Museum of Art; Mr. and Mrs. Herbert Jepson; Ann Heath Karlstrom; Peter and Rose Krasnow; Felix Landau; Professor Susan Larsen of the School of Fine Arts, USC; Pamela Ludwig of Goldfield Galleries; Helen Lundeberg; Ruth Maitland; Dean Lynn Matteson of the School of Fine Arts, USC; Mr. and Mrs. Robert McIntosh; Lauren Mellon; Dr. William Moritz; Tobey C. Moss; Nancy Dustin Wall Mouré; Professor Lee Mullican; Pamela Nask; Kathy Clewell, registrar, and Katherine Plake Hough, curator, of Palm Springs Desert Museum; Robert Perine; Penny Perlmutter of Perlmutter Fine Arts; Martin Petersen, curator, San Diego Museum of Art; Phyllis Plous, curator of University Art Museum, UCSB; Dr. Aimée Brown Price and Dean Monroe Price; Vincent Price; Dr. Michael Quick, curator of American Art, Los Angeles County Museum of Art; Victoria Ricciarelli; Jan Rindfleisch, director of the Helen Euphrat Gallery at De Anza College; Amy Rule, archives librarian at the Center for Creative Photography, University of Arizona; Esther Robles; Kenneth Ross; Jack Rutberg; Kristin Selby; Laura Shirley; Tom Silliman, director of the Vincent Price Gallery, East Los Angeles College; Margaret Stainer; Alfred Stendhal; Irving Stone; Dale Trevelan, director of the Oral History Program, UCLA; Betty Turnbull; Steve Turner and Victoria Dailey of Turner Dailey Fine and Applied Arts; June Wayne; Jane Welton; Rita Wiener; Nicholas Wilder; Dr. Dolores Yonker, chair of the Art History Department, California State University, Northridge.

We are also greatly indebted to the following private and institutional lenders to the exhibition:

Edward Albee and Jonathan Thomas; Albuquerque Museum; Ruth Bachofner Gallery; Karl Benjamin; Adrea and Sandy Bettelman; The Buck Collection; Mr. and Mrs. Hans Burkhardt; Columbus Museum of Art; Mr. and Mrs. Harry Carmean; Mrs. Constance Lebrun Crown; Detroit Institute of Fine Arts; Jules Engel; The Lorser Feitelson and Helen Lundeberg Feitelson Arts Foundation; Dr. Frank M. Finck; The Fischinger Archive; Fred and Freida Fox; the estate of Thomas A. Freiburg; 609 Gallery; Mrs. Joni Gordon; Solomon R. Guggenheim Museum; Nora Eccles Harrison Museum of Art, Logan, Utah; Dr. Lillian Carson and Sam Hurst; The Jonson Museum at the University of New Mexico; Mr. and Mrs. Albert Kallis; Fannie Hall and Alan Leslie; Long Beach Museum of Art; Los Angeles County Museum of Art; Judah L. Magnes Museum; Tobey C. Moss Gallery; Museum of Modern Art, New York; Lee Mullican; National Museum of American Art of the Smithsonian Institution; Newport Harbor Art Museum; Oakland Museum; Palm Springs Desert Museum; Herbert Palmer Gallery; Charles Pollyea; Mr. and Mrs. O.P. Reed, Jr.; Jack Rutberg Fine Arts; The Sadoff Collection; San Diego Museum of Art; San Francisco Museum of Modern Art; Sheldon Memorial Art Gallery at the University of Nebraska; Skirball Museum of Hebrew Union College; David J. Supino; Syracuse University Art Collections; June Wayne; Whitney Museum of American Art; Wight Art Gallery at UCLA; and other anonymous lenders.

Authors

PAUL J. KARLSTROM, regional director of the Smithsonian Institution's Archives of American Art, helped to establish the Archives on the West Coast in 1973. With research centers at San Francisco's M.H. de Young Memorial Museum and the Henry E. Huntington Library in San Marino, the Archives has assembled the most comprehensive body of information documenting the history of visual arts in California. Dr. Karlstrom, a graduate of Stanford University, received his Ph.D. in American art history from UCLA. The author of several books (*Louis M. Eilshemius*, *Fletcher Benton*—with Edward Lucie-Smith) and numerous articles, he has an abiding interest in the art and culture of California.

SUSAN EHRLICH, a George Page and Amy McClelland Fellow, received her Ph.D. from the University of Southern California where she wrote her dissertation on Los Angeles pioneer modernists. Her essays on early Southern California modernists have appeared in the *Los Angeles Institute of Contemporary Art Journal* and in exhibition catalogues published by the Laguna Art Museum, USC, and the Wight Gallery at UCLA. In addition to lecturing and participating as a panelist at many conferences, Dr. Ehrlich teaches art history and criticism to film and art students at USC.

John McLauglin Untitled, 1951-1952, oil on masonite, 24 x 28⅛". Collection of Mr. and Mrs. O. P. Reed, Jr., Malibu, California.

Modernism in Southern California, 1920-1956 Reflections on the Art and the Times

Paul J. Karlstrom

The most serious obstacle to approaching a history of art and culture in Southern California is the commonly encountered perception that there has been none. Art historians may be aware of general cultural activity in the Los Angeles area during the years 1920 to 1956, the period covered in this exhibition, and some may even be familiar with the names of a handful of artists associated with the area. But even those few scholars specializing in California art seem to have neglected, until recently, this extraordinarily rich place and time in American cultural history that has been understood only in fragmentary ways.[1]

The literature on the subject of California art is so thin, and attention paid so new, that a clear profile has yet to emerge. Although we now see the period in broad outline, the details need to be interpreted in context. Identifying a few key artists and describing their artistic environment gives recognizable features and personality to an anonymous silhouette. Once these main characteristics are identified and we determine what is unusual or unique about Southern California as a creative center, it is possible to see how the visual arts either reflect or contribute to that broader cultural environment. Then we can consider Los Angeles art as a phenomenon within the broader development of twentieth-century modernism and begin to evaluate its relative significance and possible contributions.

Enormous attention has been devoted to Hollywood and the movies as Southern California's main contribution to American culture, yet there has been little effort to relate fine art to the entertainment industry.[2] It is revealing in this connection that in an important recent study of Los Angeles in the 1940s, only one visual artist is mentioned: Salvador Dali.[3] The famous Spanish Surrealist was hired by Alfred Hitchcock to design the dream sequence for *Spellbound*, and in so doing he represents one of the few direct collaborations between a prominent international modernist and a major Hollywood studio, in this case MGM and David O. Selznick. Despite their presence in Los Angeles and, in several cases, their periodic employment by the film industry, completely ignored are artists of the stature of Rico Lebrun, Man Ray, Stanton Macdonald-Wright, Lorser Feitelson, Eugene Berman, Millard Sheets, Granville Redmond (who worked with Charlie Chaplin), Albert King, and—an extraordinary oversight—Oskar Fischinger. In fact, none of the artists in the present exhibition are included in the aforementioned study, nor are they in most others that purportedly deal with Southern California culture. Of the several reasons for this, the most vital is unquestionably the cultural dominance of film in the Los Angeles region. As the art form of the twentieth century, cinema overshadowed the traditional expressions of painting and sculpture—at least in the community with which movie production became most identified. And for many, the big business potential and mass audience appeal of film further complicated its relationship to art in the modern world. To this day, writers are irresistibly drawn to the lore and legend of Hollywood and tend to overlook individuals and events that were significant parts of broader cultural and artistic developments. The result has been a surprisingly insubstantial, one-dimensional historical treatment of one of America's most influential creative centers.

Almost all writers observing Southern California complained of the lack of serious cultural life and institutions, in which at the time there seemed indeed to be little or no interest on the part of the local population. The frustration of transplanted New Yorkers and others accustomed to the cultural advantages of a more established city was evidently acute. In 1924, Louise Arensberg moved to Hollywood along with her husband Walter and their renowned modern art collection. In the early 1930s she wrote to a friend,

> *We have had a marvelous winter with [Otto] Klemperer as conductor of the orchestra. He has accomplished miracles (plural) magnificent performances of the Beethoven Ninth—and it is to the everlasting disgrace of Los Angeles that he has not been reengaged. We feel ashamed to live in a town where they do not react to such God-given opportunity. . . . Walter is deep in his work and frequently remarks that as soon as he comes to a good stopping place we shall certainly pack up and go East . . . but when?*[4]

As it turned out, both Arensbergs died in Los Angeles some twenty years later, having tried unsuccessfully to find a local home for their collection. Southern California's loss was Philadelphia's gain, and the Arensberg collection was not the only one lost to the area during these "formative" years. Nonetheless, the ambivalence of these would-be donors is instructive in that, despite misgivings about the cultural maturity and prospects of their "temporary" home, they actively sought to improve the situation through their patronage. The history of culture in Los Angeles, at least in terms of support of institutions, is one of a growing number of patrons recognizing that their own cultural lives and well-being are now aligned with the area in which they have settled rather than where they came from. Because of its youth and notorious rootlessness, Southern California had marked difficulty in creating this kind of positive identification, an essential ingredient in developing patronage and a stable cultural base such as that which, despite severe shortcomings in the visual arts, had long been in place in San Francisco.

Presumably, other cultivated visitors and residents felt about Southern California as did Louise Arensberg. This must have been especially true of the artists, writers, composers, and musicians who gathered in great numbers to work in Hollywood. This impressive coterie was richly augmented by European emigrés who began arriving in the 1920s, drawn by opportunities in the film industry, and who appeared in increasing numbers throughout the 1930s as Hitler's troops marched across Europe. Many were Jewish, most were politically liberal (certainly anti-fascist), and almost all had abandoned prestigious positions and successful careers to reestablish themselves in an unfamiliar land and in a foreign language. Among the newcomers were Thomas Mann, Arnold Schoenberg, Bertolt Brecht, Igor Stravinsky, Billy Wilder, Jascha Heifitz, Josef von Sternberg, Jean Renoir, and Aldous Huxley. During these years, Southern California—specifically Los Angeles—attracted one of the greatest concentrations of creative talent in the world. Virtually all the most prominent European emigrés gravitated to either New York or Los Angeles for the obvious reasons of professional opportunities and personal contacts;[5] Southern California had the further appeal of low rents and a Mediterranean climate.

With or without the rise of Hitler and Nazism, many of these Europeans would have found their way to Hollywood eventually. French, German, and especially British "colonies" were already established by 1930. To an extent without parallel in more established cities, in Los Angeles these groups came to constitute the intellectual elite by default. They were joined at one time or another by most of America's greatest writers. Their expectations in terms of an acceptable minimum of cultural activity were not met by what Los Angeles had to offer, hence the often-heard sobriquet "wasteland." Imagine moving from Berlin, Paris, London, or New York to a boomtown somewhat isolated on the Pacific coast where "culture" was dominated by the business of making motion pictures, and the culturally sophisticated were, for the most part, from somewhere else and were in town (no matter how long they stayed) only temporarily.

From this perspective, it appears that most of those who were in a position to comment on Los Angeles and its cultural/artistic environment, namely prominent writers, never felt part of the Southern California community. Apprehensive about compromising their own artistic principles, but unwilling to forego the easy money Hollywood had to offer, William Faulkner, F. Scott Fitzgerald, and Dorothy Parker kept returning to Los Angeles. But the experience of these and most other visitors was characterized by professional uneasiness and intellectual distrust along with undeniable fascination. A distinct ambivalence is reflected in most of the writing about the area—whether Fitzgerald's *The Last Tycoon* (unfinished, 1939), Nathanael West's *Day of the Locust* (1939), Evelyn Waugh's *The Loved One* (1948), Aldous Huxley's *After Many a Summer Dies the Swan* (1939), or the Los Angeles novels of Raymond Chandler, James M. Cain, and John Fante. Running throughout the predominantly negative literary view is a sense of the region's impermanence and artificiality. As much as the sunshine, palm trees, and orange groves, these qualities have become part of the image of Los Angeles and its culture.

Many of the European and especially the East Coast intellectuals seemed to make an effort to distance themselves from this unsettled and unsettling area—as if to maintain a separate and serious identity. Hollywood and its products were decidedly not serious, except from the standpoint of income. This professional ambivalence, misgivings about the appearance of compromising integrity, of "selling out" in Hollywood, extended to attitudes towards the region itself, contributing to a deep-seated suspicion of all aspects of Los Angeles life and culture.

In America, and exaggeratedly so in Southern California, an inevitable tension developed between inherited European cultural values and an unprecedentedly open and youthful society composed of the world's most diverse population. What New York was to Europe, Los Angeles was to America. Nowhere else in the country were the traditional ideas of urban environment and social structure so inoperative from about 1920. It was as if the city were being reinvented to suit the needs and desires of a new, adolescent society. The result was a world distinguished, and to a remarkable degree formed, by a new set of community values: speed, mobility, constant change, and individual choice. In a sense, Los Angeles was the first and remains the archetypal twentieth-century city, with the attendant problems and opportunities associated with growth, experimentation, and license. Under such anti-historical circumstances, the continuity required for the orderly development of cultural institutions is almost entirely absent.

Apartment Buildings, 9th and Hobart Streets, Los Angeles, 1936. Milton J. Black, architect.

This lack of social stability and cultural underpinnings was understandably disconcerting and profoundly distasteful to newcomers—

especially visitors from the more established eastern cities who, to this day, find Los Angeles anomalous among major urban centers. It was the Europeans, not the natives, who first recognized in the vitality of Los Angeles what was most interesting and indeed unique in American culture and society: a dominant indigenous expression drawn from popular culture, entertainment, and advertising imagery. Whereas the East was attached to ideas of age, history, and tradition—looking to Europe for cultural models—Europeans were attracted to what was new, colorful, and different. Perhaps for this reason a number of Europeans, especially the English, from Aldous Huxley to David Hockney, have more readily been able to adjust to and enjoy life in Southern California.

In the Los Angeles literature, it has also frequently been foreigners, like Franz Werfel, who acknowledge the beauties of the landscape, the virtues of the climate and life-style, and even the charming distinction of being the home of modern fairy tales:

These snobs slanderously call California a desert covered with artificial luxuriance, whose rouged roses, bougainvilleas, poinsettias, and other flowers have no fragrance, whose fruits and vegetables have no savor, whose inhabitants are good-looking but somehow—Lemurian. . . .The Lemurians [ancestors of present Californians] seem to have been a shadowy, trifling race, white sepulchers, in a word, actors, who deceived the world with gay and false pretenses with nothing true and tested behind them. And so the snobs of today . . . turn up their noses at California, chiefly because a certain famous city in that state produces films, those fantastic, photographic tales that have become the vogue of their time. . . .[6]

The author goes on to praise the natural beauty of Southern California, the very quality that had with varying degrees of success inspired several generations of landscape painters.

It may well be that, lacking the prevalent American cultural self-consciousness, Europeans were free to respond positively and with genuine enthusiasm to the imagination and spontaneity they found in Southern California. Nonetheless, European and American visitors alike frequently shared the perception of Los Angeles as superficial, an image factory where art in the service of truth and ideas was replaced by a monumental deception created to sell everything from real estate to the insubstantial products of the Hollywood studios. For many observers in the 1930s, everything about Southern California was as much illusion as were the films exported by its leading industry.

There is admittedly some basis in truth for this point of view. However, it entirely misses the true character of Los Angeles as a vital creative center. Southern California has an enviable record of contribution in design, architecture, music, dance, and the visual arts. In a community that has—more than any other—created itself, the possibility and example for invention and experimentation with a minimum of risk is greatest. The distinction between fine art and popular entertainment/commercial art is probably more blurred in and around Hollywood during these years than anywhere else in the world and, for that matter, at any time in history. Los Angeles provided the perfect environment for the emergence of what have now been identified as postmodernist ideas and attitudes. It is entirely possible that, at least in terms of an absence of "requirements" for producing art, Southern California offered an unprecedented freedom to creative individuals. The price the artists in this exhibition paid for this freedom was distance from the New York art world and a corresponding lack of professional opportunity, support, and stimulation.

Barnsdale Lodge, Griffith Park, Los Angeles, 1920. R.M. Schindler, architect, for Frank Lloyd Wright.

This, then, was the creative environment in which California's early modernists sought to establish themselves as serious contributors to international contemporary art. And, even in the early years, their isolation from colleagues in the east and in Europe was actually less than might be expected. In 1929 Annita Delano, a founding member of the UCLA art faculty, wrote to her friend Sonia Delaunay in Paris concerning the situation in Los Angeles:

> *He [Stanton Macdonald-Wright] said to tell you he was hiding away in a cave in Santa Monica by the sea. I will tell you he's painting some splendid things . . . he is still interested profoundly in oriental art. . . . In architecture here in Los Angeles there are a few leaders. Quite a number of buildings by Frank Lloyd Wright and some by his son. There are two men, R.M. Schindler and Richard Neutra who represent tendencies similar to Corbusier & Gropius. . . . So you see we have a miniature group pounding at the conservatives. The architectural clubs and the painters and the sculptors are all debating about the modern trend—but they are so slow. I believe the greatest influence felt here is that of the Orient, and I suppose next to that the great raw country—so new, so provincial in some ways—but waking up.*[7]

The efforts of these artists were not always or entirely successful and certainly were not as well-received as they might have been in the east.[8]

However, they created a distinguished body of work, much of which stands up to what was being done elsewhere in America and deserves to be acknowledged as part of our national art history. Furthermore, they provided a foundation—a "tradition" of serious artistic activity and inquiry—upon which the more famous Los Angeles artists of the 1960s could build and against which they could react. When we discuss these pioneers of the twenties, thirties, and forties, we are really talking about the art history of a region that we have been told never really had one. This is inaccurate and, furthermore, does a grave disservice to the diversity and richness of American art of the period.

Particularly in discussing Southern California, the question is to what degree, and in what specific ways, does an emerging popular culture—one that appeared quite spontaneously and at an early date in this locale—affect traditional fine art ideas, expressions, and forms? What is the relationship between the two and how has it operated in American sociocultural life? These questions now occupy a new generation of critics and Americanists and are changing the ways in which we view art and culture.[9] One approach to the topic is to describe briefly the existing artistic situation and suggest a few points where the boundaries between high and low art, between traditional and popular culture, are blurred, if not eliminated entirely. What was the cultural environment in which Southern California art developed? Was there something special about it that might account for the appearance of a local aesthetic?

Lovell House, Los Angeles, 1929. Richard J. Neutra, architect.

T*hen suddenly the car plunged into a tunnel and emerged into another world, a vast untidy, sub-urban world of filling stations and bill-boards, of low houses in gardens, of vacant lots and waste paper ... Mile after mile they went ... To right and left, between palms or pepper trees, or acacias, the streets of enormous residential quarters receded to the vanishing point.*
CLASSY EATS.
MILE HIGH CONES.
JESUS SAVES.
HAMBURGERS.
Five or six more turns brought the car to the top of the hill. Below and behind lay the plain, with the city like a map extending

indefinitely into a pink haze. . . Before and to either hand were mountains—ridge after ridge as far as the eye could reach, a desiccated Scotland, empty under the blue desert sky.[10]

The art of Southern California was being created in an environment determined by explosive growth and continual change. In the boom decade of the 1920s, California's population increased by over two million, of which almost 1,300,000 settled in Los Angeles County. These newcomers, many of whom arrived by automobile, constituted what has been described as the greatest internal migration in the history of the American people.

Stimulated by oil, the motion picture industry, tourist trade, and the related real-estate bonanza, the boom—and the millions of dollars that accompanied it—had serious and far-reaching consequences for the social and institutional structure of the region.[11] Los Angeles's population more than doubled in less than ten years, and the urban environment came to be shaped by the requirements and opportunities of the automobile. The future development of the region was determined accordingly.

The look, form, and character of Los Angeles and environs can be explained only in part by geography and climate, the natural features to which artists ordinarily respond and which contribute to a "sense of place." Perhaps more relevant was the mass influx of humanity that overwhelmed the existing community, still little more than a very large village. In the view of historian Carey McWilliams and other astute observers, the formation of urban Los Angeles is the direct consequence of heterogeneous transplanted populations attempting to recreate the familiar on an accommodatingly neutral and expansive landscape. Hence the sprawl of architecturally incongruous residential neighborhoods that greeted Jeremy Pordage, Aldous Huxley's fictional British visitor to Los Angeles in *After Many a Summer Dies the Swan*. The general image of the area has, in fact, grown directly out of this physical setting stamped by "highly imperfect cultural adaptations, the general unrelatedness of things, the everpresent incongruity, and the odd sense of display."[12] In the words of Willard Huntington Wright, "Culture in Los Angeles is not indigenous, but rather an elaborate transmutation."[13]

Whatever the cultural disadvantages of this situation, the lack of structure provided a unique urban ambience for the stimulation of innovative creative activity. Los Angeles must be understood as a singular phenomenon, a product of the twentieth century embodying the American

Wilshire Boulevard, Los Angeles, looking west, 1949.

quest for open space, mobility, and freedom of individual expression. This was the environment in which these artists and their colleagues labored to establish a sense of community while exploring ideas and themes within a modernist idiom. Judging from their work, there was sufficient local support and inspiration for them to succeed.

Southern California was created by combining, often audaciously, disparate elements and imported styles. In the fields of architecture and design, this has long been recognized as a distinct virtue. The Los Angeles area embraced some of the world's most innovative design talent and, as we are consistently reminded, under the California sun "there was a flowering of new forms and designs, a combining of materials in a fresh, spirited way."[14] From the symbolically complex fantasy projects of Robert V. Derrah (e.g., the Coca Cola Bottling Plant, 1937) to Stiles O. Clements's stylish commercial Moderne and the superb International Style homes of R.M. Schindler and Richard Neutra, the Los Angeles area abounded with stimulating examples of stylistic diversity. Perhaps the most picturesque evidence of local faith in the efficacy of free invention were the extravagant theaters created as architectural expressions of Hollywood. S. Charles Lee and other designers imaginatively combined ideas, motifs, materials, and light (neon virtually became another "building" material in the 1930s) in an effort to embody the film world's drama and calculated effect.

Pan-Pacific Auditorium, Los Angeles, 1935-38. Wurdmann and Becket, architects.

Lovell Beach House, Newport Beach, CA, 1923-26. R. M. Schindler, architect.

Though Southern California is certainly more than Hollywood, the film industry nonetheless has exerted an enormous influence on the region and its culture. Carey McWilliams describes the impact of movies arriving at the moment the community was assuming the dimensions of a city: "Lacking deeply rooted social traditions, Los Angeles quickly adopted the motion picture elite as its arbiters of taste and style... Los Angeles imitated Hollywood."[15] As the center of the most highly publicized industry in the world, Hollywood quickly was transformed into a state of mind that still affects the image and the reality of Southern California. It was inevitable that the art of the region—whatever its other influences and origins—reflect this potent sociocultural environment, an integral part of the creative ambience.

Far more than an indigenous aesthetic tradition (which, to the extent it existed at all, was a fairly conservative reflection of developments elsewhere) the psychology of the area provided the sense of place to which artists eventually responded in quite unfamiliar ways. More than anything else, including the famous California light and expansive horizontal landscape, it seems to be the psychology of change, incongruity, and impermanence that underlies what is most original in Los Angeles art of the period. These dual qualities, evidence of ideas and forms drawn from elsewhere and their free combination expressive of a distinctive aesthetic and social point of view, distinguish Southern California's most interesting art. This has certainly been the case since 1960, and in the work of some of the best earlier artists—among them those in this exhibition —it seems to be equally true. Frank Gehry, Robert Irwin, Ed Moses, Larry Bell, Ed Ruscha —none of these well-known artists developed in a creative vacuum. Certainly, in retrospect, it seems no accident that it was at the Otis Art Institute where, from 1954 to 1958, Peter Voulkos's abstract expressionist ceramics destroyed one barrier between art and craft. This breakthrough could have occurred elsewhere, but nowhere more appropriately than in an environment with a strong crafts tradition and a fortuitously weak notion of the categories and boundaries of fine art. In a sense, international recognition of these artists of the 1960s acknowledged the continuity of an already established tradition of experimentation. So to the extent that we can identify a unifying principle in Southern California art history, it is surely its relationship to this unique American environment and the unusual forces and circumstances that shaped it, not the least of which is Hollywood and the popular culture it represents.

Academy Theatre, 1938. Charles Lee, architect.

The cultural situation in Southern California made of Los Angeles—almost from the beginning—a *post*-modernist, rather than a modernist, city. Without proposing a complete definition of the elusive and by now much-abused term *post-modernism*, I would call attention to the eclecticism, fantasy, sense of humor, colorism, and random "grazing" among historical styles that characterize an approach to architecture and design that had been established for decades in the Los Angeles urban environment. The L.A. "fantasy" style, highly imaginative and symbolic, is epitomized in the notorious commercial establishments fabricated in the shapes of hotdogs and hats, giant doughnuts and pumpkins. This picturesque and eccentric fairytale quality, as exemplified in the whimsical Spadina house in Beverly Hills (Henry Oliver, 1929), persisted as a local aesthetic, one echoed in more serious "high-art" structures such as the wonderful Art Deco Richfield Building (demolished: Morgan Walls and Clements, 1928) and Frank Lloyd Wright's California period houses, the most theatrical of his career. As architectural historian David Gebhard has pointed out, no other region in the country was as open to the "imagery of the new."[16]

Ennis House, Los Angeles, 1924. Frank Lloyd Wright, architect.

Fantasy and the picturesque are essential parts of Hollywood film, popular culture, and the Los Angeles ambience. Revivalism, playfulness, incongruity, illusion, impermanence, eccentricity, and color are basic qualities of post-modernism. They also have contributed to the spirit and physical appearance of the Southern California region from the boom decade of the 1920s, if not before. This non-traditional aesthetic could, and did, take any number of forms in Los Angeles. In connection with painting and related imagery, no city seemed better suited to spawn an unself-conscious reaction to doctrinaire European modernism with its ethical imperatives and commitment to high culture.

In New York, or even San Francisco, Abstract Expressionism gives the postwar period a strong stylistic identity. The same period in Los Angeles, on the other hand, has been treated as a creative lacuna, sandwiched between the government arts projects and the emergence of the internationally acclaimed "L.A. School." Critical attention devoted to the achievements of the late 1950s and 1960s has overshadowed consideration of earlier developments and even discouraged investigation of cultural continuity. In one of the few books on the subject, *Sunshine Muse*, Peter Plagens states that "pre-war Southern California produced little important art, and the main gain was the hard-won beginning of modern art's cultural acceptance."[17]

Presumably, the same would be said of the 1940s and early 1950s, which is generally viewed as a conservative period with the figurative expressionism of Rico Lebrun at one extreme and the reactionary Society of Western Artists at the other.[18] In any event, the accepted view is that art in Southern California came of age with the Ferus Gallery group and the art boom of the 1960s. Everything that went before was mere preparation. But is that really the case? Is it not possible to identify trends and patterns that, at least in retrospect, constitute an art history uniquely suited to this region?

It is true that, in comparison to developments in Northern California, art activity in Los Angeles seemed to be fragmented, conservative, and devoid of ideological underpinnings and stylistic direction. Bay Area art of the late 1940s has a major figure (Clyfford Still), an important venue (California School of Fine Arts), and a significant "movement" (Abstract Expressionism), all of which give the period a single identity and historical coherence lacking farther south. Los Angeles seemed to enjoy a great deal of artistic activity, but no art-historical personality emerged from this pluralism. Furthermore, no individual or movement seemed dominant enough to impose a single personality, despite the presence of prominent artists such as Stanton Macdonald-Wright, Man Ray, Lorser Feitelson, and Rico Lebrun. A number of explanations for this situation are possible, from the area's lack of a strong visual arts tradition and supporting institutions, to its urban sprawl and the absence of a true bohemian center in which ideas are generated and exchanged.[19] But of these explanations, the most fruitful for the purpose of this discussion have to do with the *positive* aspects of the very factors that would seem to inhibit the emergence and growth of traditional forms of "high-art" culture: community indifference, rootlessness, flexible standards, and indistinct boundaries.

Watts Towers, Los Angeles, 1921-54. Simon Rodia, inventor.

As a matter of fact, these so-called negative characteristics were not limited to Southern California. They have played a role in the development of American culture in general. Los Angeles was but a more recent and, because of Hollywood, more visible example of the phenomenon. However, in at least two ways the situation in Los Angeles may well have been unique. First, there existed a young society that put an unprecedented premium on entertainment and recreation as a way of life. Second, as the paradigm of the modern city, Los Angeles by this time had come to embody, both physically and psychologically, change, freedom, and mobility—the very ingredients essential to modernist sensibility and the rise of an art based upon popular culture. A value system developed, contributing to and fed by "the industry" built on illusion, artifice, and the interchangeability of levels of experience. Inevitably, along with a clearly associated life-style, it informed the attitudes and work of a generation of local artists. This is best seen by the 1960s in the work of Ed Ruscha, Billy Al Bengston, and David Hockney. And, in a far subtler way, it is as evident in the light pieces and environments of Robert Irwin, DeWain Valentine, or James Turrell.

The impact of the industrial and social Southern California environment on these artists, all of whom display a healthy disregard for traditional categories, has been documented and extensively discussed.[20]

There are, then, two unusual aspects of the cultural ambience of Southern California in the decades leading to the 1960s. Given the relationship of movies and the entertainment industry to the area's life and economy, the role of popular or mass culture takes on a greater significance than it might elsewhere. Furthermore, the demographics of this rapidly expanding region, especially after the war, and the reasons for settling in Southern California, would tend to reinforce a basic leveling of cultural values. Most of the population did not come from the art centers of the East; and when they did, they were seldom representatives of those levels of society that were accustomed to, and presumably would demand or require, the cultural amenities.[21] Despite pockets of distinguished musical, theatrical, and related intellectual activity, popular culture and disposable aesthetics—manifested in architecture and other aspects of the urban environment—came to dominate the Southern California scene, providing it with a lowbrow image that for many it still has.

Edward Ruscha, *Hollywood,* 1968, silkscreen, edition of 100.

The second unusual feature paradoxically stands in dramatic contrast to this general cultural environment: the presence of the spectacular group of European artists and intellectuals fleeing Hitler and the Nazi occupation, along with the group of both Europeans and East Coast Americans who were in Hollywood to sell their various literary, dramatic, and musical skills. This remarkable creative community, which at one time or another included a disproportionate share of the world's talent, has often been treated as an historic anomaly[22] though it seemed perfectly appropriate for a similar community to appear simultaneously in New York City where European-style tradition and high culture were already well established. In contrast to New York, the emigré presence in Los Angeles is viewed as having had little lasting impact on the cultural life of the community. The assumption has been that the soil was barren, the climate inhospitable, and the population transient.

The actual results of this presumed incompatibility may be more complex and surprising than has been acknowledged. Many of the artists and literati who settled in Southern California during the 1940s actually liked their adopted home and pursued productive careers there,[23] and the interaction of the traditions they represented and the lively world of mass culture in which they found themselves ultimately created an idiomatic Los Angeles art. Each, in a sense, was modified by the other, opening up and pointing the way toward new possibilities, producing a unique mixture of social and creative forces.

Because of a lack of fixed boundaries, traditions, and the paucity of institutions (Hollywood was undeniably the most important of these), the open and expanding community of Los Angeles in the 1930s and 1940s provided an unusually rich and fresh creative environment for those artists who made their way west. That is not to say that they appreciated it as such.[24] However, the high seriousness and moral obligation that was part of the European heritage had negative as well as positive aspects, and Europeans who found themselves in America, and particularly on the West Coast, were relieved of some of this burden, allowing them to consider sources and subjects that might not have occurred to them previously. Outside the arts, the best examples of this phenomenon are probably found in the area of the social sciences in the work of Theodor Adorno and his colleagues. Europeans seemed far more able to appreciate, or at least be fascinated by and exploit intellectually, American culture at the popular level.[25]

The 1940s were, of course, dominated by the war; and for the duration, art activity in Southern California, as was the case elsewhere, decreased or was redirected. Most of the area's artists served in the armed forces or some related activity.[26] Temporarily, issues of conservatism versus modernism were set aside as the arts were enlisted in a common cause. Unable to participate directly, modernists such as Peter Krasnow, Knud Merrild, and Hans Burkhardt recorded the great conflict through changes of content and style in their work.[27] The war affected the development of the fine arts as surely as it determined the content and mood of Hollywood movies. The painters responded to global upheaval through highly personal expression. In contrast, the filmmakers reflected direct and indirect pressure to serve national ends by forming public opinion. Herein, of course, lies one of the great differences between the two art forms, between traditional and popular culture.

Still, neither was exempt from the political forces that so dramatically shaped the creative climate of the period and infused American society with a regrettable degree of insularity, intolerance, and paranoia. As Stefan Kanfer chronicles in *A Journal of the Plague Years*, Hollywood was singled out as a particularly fertile arena for "red-baiting."[28] Congressional investigative focus on the entertainment industry was, in effect, an acknowledgement of its power to affect American thought and life. Los Angeles, through the movies, projected an image that contributed powerfully to America's self-conception. Distributed throughout the country and the world, the image was also consumed locally. And for this reason, the House Un-American Activities Committee was correct to turn its attention to Hollywood as an effective mechanism for the dissemination of ideas, Communist or otherwise. In part as a result of this unwelcome attention and the environment it created, postwar Southern California became a fairly heated battleground for the war on Communist-inspired art and "subversive" abstraction. The art world of Los Angeles in the 1940s and early 1950s was basically conservative, and, in alliance with anti-Communist crusaders, the dominant landscape school and academicians mounted an attack on the outnumbered and struggling modernists. The nature of the charges was absurd enough to, in retrospect, to be laughable.[29]

Obviously, circumstances were, in several important traditional respects, less than ideal for experimentation in the fine arts, and indeed other expressions fared much better. It has been argued that Los Angeles' important contribution from the 1930s was in the areas of architecture, design, and other "applied" arts, not in painting and sculpture.[30] It has also been suggested, despite frequent claims to the contrary, that Los Angeles absorbed and developed rather than created new forms in architecture and design. For example, Modern and Moderne were not invented in Los Angeles, but few, if any, cities can boast such imaginative examples. Somehow, architecture and design, more naturally than painting and sculpture, bridged the gap between fine-art tradition and Southern California imagery based on lifestyle and popular culture. Architect Richard Neutra blamed Hollywood for lowering standards of taste, but Hollywood film simply drew upon what it had at hand, thereby reinforcing rather than creating current taste and fashion.[31] In this respect, Hollywood "distributed" Southern California imagery (architecture and lifestyle) to a receptive international audience.

Lauritz Melchior residence, Los Angeles, 1941. Frederick Monhoff, architect.

Though most creative folk who marketed their skills in the film industry went west, painters and sculptors, almost without exception, congregated in New York City. Novelist Leon Feuchtwanger's advice to Brecht that Hollywood was cheaper than New York and one could make more money there, did not apply to the likes of Mondrian, Ernst, and other artists who gravitated to New York at the same time.[32] Nevertheless, a respectable and thoroughly sophisticated community of modernists developed in and around Los Angeles despite the odds. Most, in fact, were well-established by the thirties and some even earlier. For example, when Ben Berlin arrived in 1919, he could already join forces with others of similar interests. In 1923 he exhibited with Stanton Macdonald-Wright, Boris Deutsch, Nick Brigante, Morgan Russell, and Max Reno at the first Group of Independent Artists exhibition. The modernist "tradition" in painting and sculpture did not arrive with the emigrés but in fact was represented by this small group of advocates two full decades before the war. By 1940,

Los Angeles had a population of one-and-a-half million, the freeway system was mapped out and the Arroyo Seco leg under construction, architecture and design were at their high points, and a dedicated coterie of progressive artists was struggling to find a place in the sun for international modernism.

The importance of Los Angeles as an early modern art center is frequently overlooked. In the person of Stanton Macdonald-Wright the city had one of the founders of Synchromism, introduced in Paris by Americans. In 1934, Lorser Feitelson, Helen Lundeberg, and Knud Merrild founded Post-Surrealism as a home-grown Southern California (soon state-wide) art movement that attracted national interest and attention. They drew upon international Surrealism, one branch of which led to Abstract Expressionism in New York, but theirs was a literary and theatrical expression (akin to the illustrative style of Dali) that in retrospect seems appropriately related to the cinema. In a similar manner, the romantic Surrealism of Rico Lebrun and Eugene Berman (another set designer), which dominated the decade of the forties in Los Angeles in terms of influence, provided another challenge for the indigenous Eucalyptus School.

At any rate, despite differences in forms, directions, and current art-historical stature, a number of Angelenos were sophisticated participants in the evolution of modern ideas. From this vantage point, the chief players seemed to have been Macdonald-Wright, Lorser Feitelson, Rico Lebrun, Man Ray, Knud Merrild, Hans Burkhardt, Oskar Fischinger, and, by the very end of the forties, John McLaughlin. Also, in retrospect, the work of Peter Krasnow, Helen Lundeberg, and Agnes Pelton assumes greater prominence and significance. Each practiced a form of modern art that, in varying degrees, reflected something of the creative environment in which they worked. It would be convenient to be able to say that the work of these and a handful of others shares certain characteristics and stylistic features that define a Southern California modernist school. That was not the case. However, there are several themes that seem to emerge in connection with progressive Los Angeles art of the period. A preoccupation with light and movement, for example, informs the work of several key figures, suggesting an attractive connection to the Hollywood film.[33]

Although the link is well worth noting, it would be a mistake to try to understand Los Angeles art entirely in terms of the cinema. A far more fruitful line of inquiry involves an increasing openness to nontraditional sources *(including* film), materials, and combinations of elements. The result of distance from the artistic centers—chiefly New York—and relative immunity to current stylistic and ideological influences, this "freedom" took several forms. As early as the 1920s (and concurrent with the first appearance of the modernists), there arose a group of conservative landscape painters whose work, especially in watercolor, showed characteristics that came to be associated with the California School.[34] An explanation suggested by one of the school's leading representatives, Millard Sheets, is that what made the art distinctive was precisely the lack of traditions and stylistic movements in Southern California. The artists had to resort to nature and their environment rather than other art for their inspiration and subjects.[35] This quality was apparently recognized by eastern critics at an early date. Sheets, who enjoyed a national reputation, reflects the best of the California landscape style. Although not part of the story of modernist experimentation, his high-level professionalism and example as a successful artist in Los Angeles were important contributions.

Although the California School represented a powerful indigenous presence by 1940, a more fecund response to the freedom offered by Los Angeles' distance from the entrenched art establishments of the east and Europe is seen in the efforts of those who developed their art with an eye to international modernism. Macdonald-Wright and Feitelson should share credit as *the* pioneering figures in California art. As has been pointed out, both established movements which were based on modernist thinking and goals. Macdonald-Wright's notions of color harmony, developed with Morgan Russell in Paris about 1913, actually had much in common with Symbolist correspondences between the arts (music and painting), not to mention the contemporary work of the Orphists and Futurists.[36] This, of course, had little to do with art in California. However, it may be significant that, after returning to Los Angeles in 1919, Macdonald-Wright experimented with color wheels and a color machine, collaborating with ceramist and movie special effects pioneer Albert King. For Macdonald-Wright and other artists working in and around Hollywood, the technical innovations of filmmaking and the medium itself may have affected their work more than has been realized.

As was the case elsewhere, Cubism and Surrealism were the modern trends, and Los Angeles had its followers of each. Along with Macdonald-Wright, Lorser Feitelson was the best-known California modernist, and the two of them helped pave the way for local acceptance of modernist culture (although neither could be described as radical). Feitelson and his wife, Helen Lundeberg, founded in 1934 what turned out to be America's first organized response to European Surrealism. The California variety differed considerably by emphasizing the rational, the classical union of form and content, over the irrational dream imagery of Surrealism.[37] Feitelson was attracted to the Italian metaphysical paintings

Millard Sheets, *Spring Street-Los Angeles*, 1929, watercolor. Santa Barbara Museum of Art. The Dicken Collection.

of Giorgio de Chirico and Carlo Carrà, which exhibited a sense of theatrical narrative and stage-set space. The degree to which this type of vision is related to cinema in the Post-Surrealist work of Feitelson and other Angelenos has yet to be determined, but the connection at certain other points seems quite probable. For example, Susan Ehrlich finds in the *Magical Space Forms* series—in the strong black and white contrasts, eccentric perspectives, off-balance shapes, and figure ground reversals—an instability that recalls *film noir*. According to Ehrlich, the artist was aware of these expressive cinematic devices which effectively communicated the tensions of the McCarthy era. A similar echo of *film noir* may be encountered in the work of June Wayne and others, such as Jules Engel, working in and around the film industry.[38] At the very least, a strong element of romantic surrealist fantasy occurs in both visual art and film of the time. The influence of *film noir* specifically on painting would be a tantalizing area of investigation, but at this point it is premature to draw conclusions about general stylistic correspondences. However, film as a popular medium has influenced, and been influenced by, fine art. The interaction between the two is especially evident in the creative world of Southern California: films aspiring to be art; painters irresistibly attracted to the impact of mass-audience movies.

Rico Lebrun was a major figure in Los Angeles art who, through his own teaching at the Jepson School and through his students Howard Warshaw and William Brice, set the tone for the late 1940s and 1950s. This "tone" was highly moral and subjective, involving a strong narrative quality in which drawing and other academic devices are enlisted in the service of humanism. Lebrun, too, had contact with Hollywood and was even engaged to teach animators at Disney to draw animals for *Bambi*, another example of how artists in Los Angeles moved from one world to another, from traditional to popular culture, with relative ease. Although Lebrun's lofty conception of art would seem to preclude an unholy alliance with film, in fact he produced at least one important work with cinema in mind (as did Huxley, Brecht, Schoenberg, Man Ray, and other famous Southland residents). The *Crucifixion* cycle (completed in 1950) was, in fact, designed to be filmed, and the specific ways in which these cinematic goals affected the work's execution and style appear in other works as well.[39] However, despite these significant and revealing digressions, the work of Lebrun and his circle clearly reflected art-historical precedent, and we must look elsewhere for a more meaningful dialogue between traditional and popular attitudes and forms as evidence of a peculiarly Southern California aesthetic expression.

One artist to look to is Danish emigrant Knud Merrild. A member of Feitelson's Post-Surrealists, he went further than either Feitelson or Lundeberg in terms of freedom of invention. Merrild supported himself as a house painter and decorator, and his abstractions incorporated both the colors and material of commercial paint. Although no one will press the point of art-historical precedence, Merrild deserves recognition for anticipating Jackson Pollock with his "flux" paintings of the late 1930s and 1940s. Equally interesting, however, was Merrild's assemblage activity in which he selected and combined various materials to create three-dimensional constructions. Both these constructions and the poured paintings created with commercial material owe something to the freedom and openness of the Los Angeles creative environment.

A more sophisticated disregard for rules or conventions was the hallmark of Man Ray, an internationalist and American founder of Dada who spent the forties in Hollywood as a refugee from occupied Paris. Because of his prominent position in the history of modern art, Ray's presence in Southern California must be noted here despite what first appears to be a minimum of influence in either direction. The critical question surrounds what effect Los Angeles had on an artist who was already open to popular culture and delighted in incorporating the most unlikely elements in his work. In fact, there was a perceptible response in Ray's ironic comments on Southern California physical culture and other oddities, but in balance, the impact was negligible; Man Ray returned to Paris in 1950, having enjoyed the company of some very interesting people while waiting out the war in a comfortable climate. From the standpoint of the development of art in Los Angeles, Man Ray is viewed simply as a casual visitor who left no mark. In fact, the attitudes he represented—breaking down barriers between media and combining ideas and materials in new ways—were precisely those that stimulated later art in Los Angeles.

Perhaps the time has come to reevaluate Man Ray's years in Southern California and his connection to the unique cultural world that grew up around Hollywood. It may be that Ray, in certain respects, was as much Californian (or at least American) in his creative worldview as he was Parisian. An important step in reclaiming Man Ray for American art was taken in the recent exhibition and catalogue *Perpetual Motif: The Art of Man Ray*. It may well be that the chapter on Ray's years in Hollywood makes the strongest case for his Americanism.[40] Man Ray himself was quoted as saying, "[T]here was more surrealism rampant in Hollywood than all the surrealists could invent in a lifetime."[41]

As Merry Foresta has pointed out, Ray's decision to settle in California to reestablish his reputation as a painter was based, at least in part, on the success of his 1935 exhibition at the Los Angeles Art Center.[42] Unfortunately, Ray's show at the Frank Perls Gallery (March 1941) was a critical and financial disappointment. Nonetheless, in the following years he enjoyed six important museum exhibitions in both Northern and Southern California. And his friendship with William Copley, which led to an important 1948 show at the Copley Gallery, brought Man Ray into direct contact with the Hollywood art world.[43]

Man Ray's California work—paintings such as *Infinite Man* (1942)—had a poignancy missing in the more secure European oeuvre upon which much of the imagery was based. During the forties, Ray recapitulated themes and compositions from the past. *The Wall* (1938), for example, became *Swiftly Walk over the Western Wave* (1940), presum-ably a personal reference to flight from Europe to California and, perhaps, the emptiness of life in exile. Among the Hollywood period works, many of which were narrative, *Night Sun—Abandoned Playground* (1943) seems most clearly to reflect the California experience. The entire scene has the artificial quality of a stage or movie set, with sun, ocean, sky, cypress, and vaguely Spanish architecture evoking the Los Angeles environment. Despite the geometric order and stability of the chessboard foreground (an allusion to the perceived game-like quality of life and work in California?), the uprooted cypress suggests a basic instability, unreliability, and impermanence—all qualities ascribed to Los Angeles and its culture. Ray's California images also seem to contain specific autobiographical references. The tree may well be the artist himself, supported by the house—the reality of a new home in California. Additional stability is provided by a new mate (wife Juliet, the bedsheet) and friends (Linus Pauling, the molecular presence in the house).[44] Interest in the tension created by unstable (and ambiguous) forms is, as we shall see, important to the work of several prominent Californians, among them Lorser Feitelson and John McLaughlin.

Man Ray, *Night-Sun Abandoned Playground,* 1941, oil on canvas. Private collection.

Night Sun and some other paintings contributed imagery to an unfinished novel that may have been intended as a film. Describing a world of fantasy and sensual pleasures, the manuscript seems clearly based upon Southern California and the hedonistic freedom that was associated with it in the popular view. It was a fascination with this aspect of California life and an awareness of American scientific and technological innovation (for example, the molecular arrangements in *Night Sun* and *Optical Longings and Illusions*, 1943) that informed much of Man Ray's art in the 1940s. Whether or not the response was one of significant and sustained impact, it was nonetheless a specific response.

During Ray's sojourn in Hollywood, he moved on the periphery of the movie industry. Given the opportunity, he no doubt would have happily participated in a more active way. As it was, some of his works were included as props in movies, and he contributed a script entitled *Ruth, Roses, and Revolvers* for a segment in the 1946 film *Dreams That Money*

Can't Buy.[45] Rather than direct involvement with film, however, it may be Ray's shifting back and forth between media—as in the photo-derived *Equations for Shakespeare* series—that best demonstrates his conceptual relationship to the aesthetic experimentation taking place at the time.[46] Although Southern California cannot take the credit for Man Ray's ideas and art, it provided a most sympathetic and stimulating locale for their development in the 1940s, particularly as they touched on certain implications of abstraction.

Abstract Classicism, Feitelson's second major "movement," was introduced to an international audience in 1959 by Jules Langsner's exhibition in Los Angeles and London.[47] John McLaughlin was another Southern Californian working by the early 1950s in a related, reductive manner that Langsner identified as an indigenous form of geometric abstraction. Rigidly controlled imagery based on the rectangle firmly locked within a horizontal-vertical matrix would seem to place McLaughlin's work at the opposite pole from some of the characteristics introduced here as representative of a developing local aesthetic. Almost everything about McLaughlin and his highly conceptual paintings, in fact, was far removed from notions of style, change, motion, popular imagery, color, light, specificity—those "concerns" that seem to suggest at least the possibility of some unity of expression in Southern California art. However, McLaughlin is now widely acknowledged by critics and artists alike as the leading "old master" of California modernism. Looking beyond style to more fundamental issues of artistic position and creative independence, John McLaughlin may well be the exception that proves the rule.

What the younger generation of California artists—among them Tony DeLap, Ron Davis, Ed Moses, Fletcher Benton—came to admire about McLaughlin, who worked by choice in semi-isolation on the coast south of Los Angeles, were his extraordinary independence and total commitment to an art developed on its own terms. Like David Hockney, Richard Diebenkorn, and a score of others who chose to work in California in part because they would be left alone,[48] McLaughlin charted and maintained an independent course with relatively little regard for contemporary developments outside his small Laguna Beach and Dana Point studios. In this, McLaughlin was more uncompromising than most.

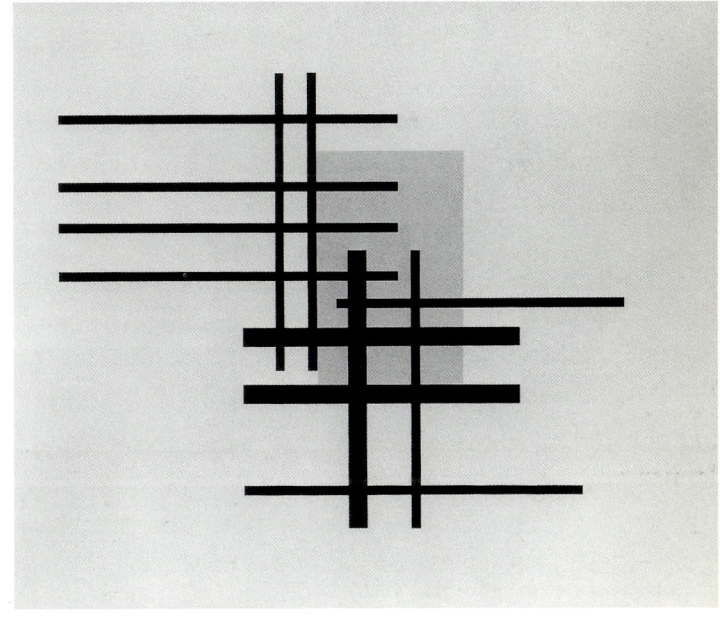

John McLaughlin, untitled, 1951, oil on masonite. San Francisco Museum of Modern Art. T.B. Walker Foundation Fund Purchase.

And the extent to which his rigorously controlled imagery evolved independent of geometric abstractionists such as Barnett Newman or Ad Reinhardt, to whom he is often compared, is admittedly open to question.[49] Nonetheless, although his exploration of geometrical forms places McLaughlin within a Western tradition (Constructivist/de Stijl), the philosophical basis for his art—and its ultimate goal of neutrality and emptiness—seems to be largely Eastern.[50] The clarity of conceptual focus and consistency of stylistic development that distinguish McLaughlin's work may have been, at least in part, reinforced by his distance from the pressures and distractions of the contemporary art world. A letter from Stanton Macdonald-Wright suggests that McLaughlin was indeed working at some remove even from the Los Angeles art community:

You are most kind to send me the S.F. paper clipping of [critic Alfred] Frankenstein—I hadn't seen it but he has been nice to me for some time—I'm looking forward to meeting him sometime in San Francisco—Let me add that Mrs Wright & I are sorry you two don't live nearer this center of contagion (or is it "infection") I'm sure we have much in common.[51]

Just how important geography was to McLaughlin's intellectual and creative independence is impossible to determine. But it is certain that his unique achievement, an effective and uncontrived joining of Western imagery and Eastern thought, took place in an environment unusually free from outside influence and interference. Patiently, and with unrelenting concentration, McLaughlin planned and fabricated an art that provided the visual "terrain" for the individual's confrontation with himself and his relationship to nature. It is entirely possible that Southern California provided just the right balance of freedom, opportunity, and professional encouragement to nurture the independent vision of an "outsider" such as John McLaughlin. That was demonstrably the case with Oskar Fischinger, an artist who may have more in common with McLaughlin than their very different work would at first indicate.

One of the paradoxical things about the early critical view of McLaughlin (and for that matter Feitelson) is its characterization of the work in terms of geometric order and stasis. In fact, as Susan Larsen points out, McLaughlin's painting is "profoundly anti-classical. He creates disequilibrium and virtually subliminal visual and psychological motion out of stasis and symmetry."[52] In this respect, McLaughlin appears to move closer to a general Southern California aesthetic that acknowledges change and impermanence as conditions of existence.

Despite the admirable contributions of McLaughlin and some of the other hard-edge painters, Los Angeles area artists as a whole had yet to produce a body of truly influential work. But, as a number of critics have claimed, the innovative contributions of Los Angeles may well be outside the area of painting in its traditional form.[53] Ceramics, assemblage, and design in general come to mind. Light, the use of new media, and matter-of-fact Pop imagery (distinct from the self-conscious New York variety) are all part of what amounts to a portrait of a place. One should add to the list movement and illusion, both from film and auto culture, along with commercial-industrial tools and process.

If this is the case, the most important artist of all may well be Oskar Fischinger, who arrived from Germany in 1936 with a reputation for abstract film animation. Fischinger is just now beginning to receive the attention he deserves beyond film critics and historians, recognition that ironically may have been delayed by his identification with art cinema.[54] Fischinger's films and paintings are both experimental and eclectic, resulting in a body of work that critic William Moritz calls "one of the most important and distinguished achievements in modern art."[55] Whether or not this assessment is justified, Fischinger's artistic accomplishment becomes increasingly impressive the more closely it is examined and it does so in precisely those areas that have been suggested here as characteristic of the creative situation in Los Angeles.

After a frustrating experience at Disney Studios creating abstract sequences for *Fantasia*, Fischinger turned to painting and invention while continuing his film experiments under the difficult patronage of Hilla von Rebay and the Guggenheim Foundation.[56] The Guggenheim grants and local support from Galka Scheyer allowed Fischinger the freedom to pursue experimentation, which was the basis of his art. Two factors seemed to make possible a development that went beyond conventional expectations: societal breakdown caused by the war and a lack of structure in Los Angeles. A delicate balance of isolation (independence) and support seemed necessary for radical imagery and ideas to unfold. For Fischinger and a few others at the time, Los Angeles offered this balance.

Given the proximity of the film industry, it should not be surprising that abstract film constituted much of the important visual activity in Los Angeles. Artists moved back and forth between animation and painting, carrying influences as bees transport pollen—an image that is entirely appropriate. An underlying attitude of exploration, seeking new and different means to express ideas about sound, color, shapes, and movement, is seen in a variety of artists of the 1940s—ranging from Stanton Macdonald-Wright to Fischinger and the Whitney brothers, James and John. Fascination with just this sort of union of the arts provided the basis for an unusual body of theoretical writing and inventions by the artists involved.

Fischinger's film *American March* (1941), done immediately after his work on *Fantasia*, is particularly relevant in its high art/low art fusion of painting and animation techniques. This conscious stylistic statement carries the theme of the film: America as the melting pot. Hard-edged, outlined figures painted on animation cels become part of the meaning of the work as the outlines and other elements melt.[57] In painting, a similar melding of categories occurs in *Motion Painting No. 1* (1947), a major work about motion and change which fuses (literally: each figure is hand-drawn in an eleven-minute filmic synthesis) painting and film. Fischinger's experimentation knew no bounds. Entirely open to ideas, he tried every material and device available to achieve his abstract and humanistic ends. Free from tradition and working alone in relative isolation, he could attempt anything. As a result, he elevated methods of commercial/popular art to fine-art status and, in so doing, was one of the few artists who took full advantage of a creative climate conducive to breaking down barriers.

James and John Whitney, in some ways, wandered even further from tradition in creating their audio-visual music. Feeling that music was too dominant in Fischinger's non-objective films, they invented a "pendulum system" to transcribe sounds directly. This optical printing and pendulum composition was the basis for their revolutionary *Five Abstract Film Exercises*.[58] When first screened in Los Angeles and New York, the films, seen as shockingly radical, were described as electronic music and neon images "from the science fiction future."[59]

This science fiction (film fantasy) aspect of Los Angeles modernism, combined with an almost total disregard for convention and tradition, seems in retrospect among the salient features of abstract filmmaking activity. After further investigation, we may find that experimental film, in the hands of painters such as Fischinger, constitutes the most noteworthy contribution of the war decade. The abstract combination of shape, color, movement, and sound represents a kind of cinematic fusion of traditional and popular art. Furthermore, it employed the technical and commercial devices readily available in the film industry. This innovative disregard for categories, a hallmark of our time, came to characterize subsequent developments in Los Angeles.

Among these developments is a post-modernist sensibility that seems particularly well suited to Southern California. An interesting recent observation is that "modernism's asserted distinction between high culture and popular culture is regarded as untenable. . . . Post-modernism recognizes that ideology has now secreted itself among the images we consume, and that it is no longer worth the effort to hold ideas separate from the daily practice of life to which they supposedly refer."[60] The ideal environment for the cultivation of such attitudes existed from the beginning in youthful, free-form, non-traditional Los Angeles. They began to emerge in the 1940s in the work of a few independent artists who indicated some of the directions that were followed by those who established the L.A. School. Post-modernism, then, with its eclectic openness to diverse sources, affection for "low-brow" popular culture, and willingness to enjoy unashamedly the decorative and sensual, may well be the genuine Los Angeles "style" and contribution.

In the final analysis, the most remarkable cultural feature of Los

Angeles, especially during the period covered by this exhibition, was the city's ability to absorb and reflect the diverse characteristics that make America and its people what they are. It was a city constantly being formed and formed again by newcomers and changing times. This phenomenon has been noted by most observers of American society, and Farnsworth Crowder's observation of earlier years is equally valid today:

> *What America is, California is, with accents, in italics. National currents of thought, passion, aspirations and protest, elsewhere kept rather decently in subterranean channels, have a way of boiling up in the Pacific sun to mix in a chemistry of queer odors and unexpected crystallization: but it is all richly, pungently American and not to be disowned, out of embarrassment and annoyance, by the rest of the nation which is in fact its parental flesh and blood, its root and its mentor.*[61]

Today, as the end of the twentieth century draws near, Southern California constitutes one of the world's great urban regions. The state of California has become an economic colossus blessed with an unusually diversified economy, one that—despite the meteoric rise of some of its Pacific neighbors—still ranks among the top ten nations. Southern California boasts over sixteen million people (a thirteen-fold increase from 1920), and Los Angeles is home to one of the world's most ethnically diverse populations. It is no longer possible to speak of the Los Angeles area as socially undeveloped and culturally deprived. During its rather short history—and despite the "subversive" influence of Hollywood and the entertainment industry—Los Angeles has established for itself an undeniable position of cultural leadership. Throughout Southern California new museums are being built, the performing arts are thriving, art galleries proliferate. At last it seems likely that the great collections formed in the area—Simon, Weisman, Hammer—will, unlike the Arensbergs', remain. Reflecting a new level of maturity and stability, the area's enormous wealth is finally being channeled into local cultural institutions and programs. The far-reaching impact of the J. Paul Getty Center, for example, is only the most dramatic example of the new patronage. Although these are relatively recent developments in the cultural history of Southern California, the seeds were sown decades ago, and they were planted in unexpectedly fertile soil. The "wasteland" turned out to be, like so much else that has come out of this storied region, just another myth. Part of the story is that of the developing, still youthful West in which Los Angeles increasingly plays the central role. For much of this century it has served as the melting pot for the people of America, much as New York City was the port of entry for Europe. With its recent wave of Asian immigration and the continuing influx from south of the border, Los Angeles has assumed the role of the new Ellis Island. These patterns of immigration and settlement will determine the Los Angeles of the future, including its artistic life and culture. But this is how it has always been in Los Angeles, the main laboratory for the great American experiment during the twentieth century.

With the establishment of solid cultural institutions, some of the notorious impermanence of Southern California has receded. The region seems to have achieved new stability and substance. However, as greater Los Angeles becomes more respectable and "permanent," even developing some contours and physical features of a "true" city—indeed, as it begins to lose some of its unique character—one should keep in mind its main historic role and contribution as a social and cultural testing ground for the rest of the country. The visual arts in Southern California and the activities of these selected artists should be approached squarely within this framework, a unique regional context within the broader historical sweep of American art and culture.

NOTES

1. Among those who have turned their attention to the visual arts in Southern California through the 1940s, Susan Ehrlich is the leading authority. Dr. Ehrlich was kind enough to share with me parts of her dissertation on the subject, including important information that will appear in a book now in preparation and will provide the foundation upon which other studies will be built.

2. This oversight, quite surprising in light of the role played by the movie industry in Southern California, is being remedied in the work of Ehrlich and William Moritz, both of whom conscientiously look for those points where commercial/popular forms (i.e. animation) intersect traditional fine art forms (i.e. easel painting) in the work of a single artist. (See, for example, Moritz's "The Films of Oskar Fischinger," *Film Culture* Nos. 58-59-60 (1974): 37-188). However, neither has yet examined these developments within the total cultural picture of a unique urban environment.

3. Otto Friedrich, *City of Nets: A Portrait of Hollywood in the 1940's* (New York: Harper & Row, 1986), 225.

4. Louise Arensberg to John Davis Hatch, 24 April, (1934?), John Davis Hatch papers, Archives of American Art, Smithsonian Institution.

5. Recent years have seen a number of important studies of the World War II European emigration and its impact upon American culture. Particularly useful in connection with the subject here is Anthony Heilbut's *Exiled in Paradise: German Refugee Artists and Intellectuals in America, from the 1930's to the Present* (New York: The Viking Press, 1983).

6. Franz Werfel, *Star of the Unborn* (New York: The Viking Press, 1946), 16. Author of *The Song of Bernadette*, Werfel had the dubious pleasure of being married to Alma Mahler, formerly the mistress of Oskar Kokoschka and wife of Gustav Mahler. Alma conducted a somewhat volatile salon for the German emigré community; her recollections in *And the Bridge Is Love* (New York: Harcourt Brace, 1958) provide a fascinating portrait of the emigré experience in Los Angeles.

7. Annita Delano to Sonia Delaunay, 11 March 1929. Annita Delano papers, Archives of American Art, Smithsonian Institution. Roll 2999; frames 238-240.

8. The question of regionalism is receiving a great deal of attention in current art-historical discussion. The issue turns on how the artists would have performed had they been in New York and whether the character of their art, presumably embodying regional qualities, would have changed significantly. An excellent study of Northern California regionalism is Thomas Albright's *Art in the San Francisco Bay Area, 1945-1980* (Berkeley: University of California Press, 1985). For a look at its more conservative aspects see Susan M. Anderson, *Regionalism: The California View* (Santa Barbara Museum of Art, 1988).

9. The central role of "Pop" in American culture has been increasingly recognized over the past decade or so. Certainly its importance became evident in connection with popular music, first jazz and then rock and roll, as an American export, and one of the ways we recognize its visibility as a national characteristic is in the foreign perception of American life. *Time* magazine, in a recent issue devoted to America (see "Pop Goes the Culture," *Time*, 16 June 1986), notes that "Pop" and more serious studies of the intellectual community are becoming more alike than they are different and that divisions between the two once-separate fields are becoming less distinct. As a case in point, both the *Time* article and James Atlas' informative "The Changing World of New York Intellectuals," *The New York Times Magazine* (25 August 1985) quote the California critic Greil Marcus, whose enthusiasm for Chuck Berry as well as for Gustave Flaubert is representative of the democratic approach of his generation.

10. Aldous Huxley, *After Many a Summer Dies the Swan* (New York: Harper & Row, 1939), 4, 7, 9.

11. Carey McWilliams describes patterns of population growth and their sociological impact in his brilliant urban history, *Southern California: An Island on the Land* (1946); reprint (Salt Lake City: Peregrine Smith, 1973), 113-137.

12. McWilliams, 233.

13. Quoted in McWilliams, 178.

14. David Gebhard and Harriette von Breton, *L.A. in the 30s, 1931-1941* (Salt Lake City: Peregrine Smith, 1975), 4.

15. McWilliams, 345.

16. Gebhard and von Breton, 111.

17. Peter Plagens, *Sunshine Muse* (New York: Praeger Publishers, 1974), 117.

18. This group, which evolved out of the right-wing Sanity in Art movement, attempted to promote its own representational conservatism by identifying modernism and abstraction with Communism. In the process they came close to destroying the Los Angeles County Museum's valuable "Annual Exhibition of Artists of Los Angeles and Vicinity" program (see, among others, Plagens, Chapter 2). A general discussion of the phenomenon appears in William Hauptman, "The Suppression of Art in the McCarthy Decade," *Artforum* 12, no. 2 (October 1973): 48-53.

19. Almost every article on Los Angeles art points out the lack of a centralized community, always in a negative way. The assumption is that close and frequent contact between artists is indispensable to creative activity. In this respect, Los Angeles is contrasted unfavorably with New York, Paris, or even San Francisco. In fact, the importance of cafe or "art-bar" society as essential to the production of serious art has never been conclusively demonstrated. Nonetheless, the assumption that social interaction between artists stimulates ideas and work is widely held: Plagens acknowledges that "Los Angeles has no Greenwich Village, Tenth Street, or North Beach--although Venice has become an 'artists' quarter' of a sort. . . " (p. 28).

20. Contemporary criticism devoted to Southern California art of the 1960s and to the "L.A. Look" (often called *finish-fetish*) is as considerable as writing on the earlier decades is scarce. In fact, the L.A. Look is the subject of the pivotal chapter in Plagens' book, and the phenomenon is generally regarded as the high point in California art, that which brought Los Angeles into the international scene. (See, in addition to Plagens, Chapter 8, Jan Leering, "A European's View of California Art" in *Painting and Sculpture in California: The Modern Era* [San Francisco Museum of Modern Art, 1976], 43-56).

21. For a discussion of the patterns of population growth and reasons for immigration, see McWilliams.

22. This view reflects an attitude towards Hollywood/Los Angeles that precludes the presence of serious culture and fine art. A prejudice that dies hard even in the face of evidence, this generally eastern perspective has a moralistic and disapproving side to it, one that protects cultural status quo. The phenomenon is mentioned in several books on the Southern California emigrés, including John Russell Taylor's very readable *Strangers in Paradise* (New York: Holt, Rinehart and Winston, 1983).

23. Among those who adjusted well to their new home were Aldous Huxley, Thomas Mann, Arnold Schoenberg, Franz Werfel, Billy Wilder, and many others in the film community. The prevalent view was that these mostly European intellectuals were fish out of water in Los Angeles, and that they were miserable as a result. However, there is evidence that even the inveterate complainer Brecht was preparing to stay in Southern California at the moment that his summons by, and testimony to, the House Un-American Activities Committee made him decide to leave the country. See Bruce Cook, *Brecht in Exile* (New York: Holt, Rinehart and Winston, 1982).

24. Negative pronouncements on Los Angeles became the fashion among intellectuals, especially writers (Dorothy Parker and Faulkner come immediately to mind), who distrusted the place and the industry that employed them. However, as Tom Dardis points out in his study of five major writers' Hollywood years, despite their complaints, they were often sustained (Faulkner) and even provided with subjects to which their art could respond (Fitzgerald, West). See Dardis, *Some Time in the Sun* (New York: Charles Scribner's Sons, 1976).

25. See Heilbut, as well as H. Stuart Hughes, "Social Theory in a New Context," *The Muses Flee Hitler* (Washington, D.C.: Smithsonian Institution Press, 1983).

26. Susan Ehrlich discusses the wartime activity of a number of prominent Southern California artists in "Five Los Angeles Pioneer Modernists" (Ph.D. diss., University of Southern California, 1985). See also her article "Los Angeles Painters of the 1940s," *The Los Angeles Institute of Contemporary Art Journal* 28 (1980).

27. Peter Krasnow responded to the war by brightening his palette as an antidote. His turn to abstraction, primary shapes, and color was a conscious effort to bring light and order to a chaotic world. At the other extreme, Hans Burkhardt's response took the form of a dark, violent expressionism based in part on the example and forms of Arshile Gorky with whom he was associated from 1927 to 1937, the year Burkhardt moved to California. In her dissertation, Ehrlich describes similar shifts in several other artists' works as well. For a brief treatment of Krasnow and his work, see Joseph Hoffman's essay in *Peter Krasnow: A Retrospective Exhibition of Paintings, Sculpture, and Graphics* (Berkeley: Judah L. Magnes Museum, 1978). See also Jack V. Rutberg, *Hans Burkhardt: The War Paintings* (Northridge: California State University/Santa Susana Press, 1984).

28. Stefan Kanfer's *A Journal of the Plague Years* (New York: Atheneum, 1973) concentrates on HUAC and the entertainment industry. In his prologue he writes, "Show business is not hermetically separated from its national environment. But it does obey laws and bend to pressures that exist in no other stratum of American life, and I believe that performers and writers are frequently more accurate seismographs of their era than politicians and statesmen" (p. 9).

29. Following the lead of Congressman George A. Dondero (R-Mich.), reactionary vigilantes went to considerable lengths to uncover Communist content in abstract and even representational paintings. Among the "un-American" works exhibited at the 1947 Los Angeles County Museum of Art annual exhibition were a painting entitled *Little Red School House* and a still life by William Brice that supposedly displayed a Russian bear and hammer. Such subversive "symbols" were everywhere apparent to members of the Sanity in Art Society and the California Art Club, who picketed the show.

30. See Gebhard and von Breton for an extended discussion of the creative primacy of architecture and design in Southern California.

31. Gebhard and von Breton, 110.

32. Quoted in Cook, *Brecht in Exile*, 39. With the exception of those artists who could work on set design (Salvador Dali did the famous dream sequence in Hitchcock's *Spellbound* in 1944-1945), musicians and writers were far more in demand in Hollywood. New York provided a more traditional and familiar environment for European emigrés.

33. Among them, as pointed out by Ehrlich and others, are Jules Engel, Rico Lebrun, and June Wayne.

34. Among artists of the California School, mostly members of the California Watercolor Society founded in Los Angeles in 1921, were Millard Sheets, Phil Dike, Rex Brandt, Barse Miller, and Emil J. Kosa, Jr. Their work was characterized by regionalism or American scene painting, to which it was also related stylistically. For a discussion of the group, see in addition to Anderson, *Regionalism: The California View*, Janet B. Dominik, *"California School" from the Private Collection of E. Gene Crain* (Gualala, California, Gualala Arts Center, 1986).

35. In an interview conducted by the author for the Archives of American Art, Millard Sheets emphasized the lack of "models" (books, reproductions) available to him and his associates in the earlier years of their development. He believes that this relative innocence of vision contributed to a distinctive quality of art of the California School painters. Interview with Millard Sheets, Gualala, California (28 and 29 October 1986), Archives of American Art, Smithsonian Institution.

36. For a discussion of Stanton Macdonald-Wright, Synchromism, and experiments with color abstraction in general, see Gail Levin, *Synchromism and American Color Abstraction, 1910-1925* (New York: George Braziller in association with the Whitney Museum of American Art, 1978).

37. See Diane Degasis Moran's *Lorser Feitelson and Helen Lundeberg: A Retrospective Exhibition* (San Francisco Museum of Modern Art, 1980) for an account of the development of Post-Surrealism and the fundamental differences between the California version and its European counterpart. Moran points out the superficial similarities along with the widely divergent goals of the Feitelsons' Subjective Classicism of the mid-1930s and the irrational aesthetics of Surrealism (pp. 12-13).

38. Jules Engel's dual roles as fine and commercial artist make him an interesting study in cross-influence. A pioneer animator who founded UPA and worked on *Fantasia*, he was also a disciple of Oskar Fischinger and, like his mentor, moved back and forth between media. Susan Ehrlich has noted, correctly it seems, devices of animation (facets resembling acetate cels, flatshapes, layered backgrounds) transferred from the film studio to his Cubist/Orphist gouaches. This kind of interaction and mobility begins to suggest an L.A. approach.

39. See Rico Lebrun, "Notes by the Artist on the Crucifixion" in *Rico Lebrun: Paintings and Drawings of the Crucifixion* (Los Angeles: Los Angeles County Museum of Art, 1950).

40. Merry Foresta's chapter "Exile in Paradise: Man Ray in Hollywood, 1940-1951" in *Perpetual Motif: The Art of Man Ray* (New York: Abbeville Press for National Museum of American Art, Smithsonian Institution, Washington, D.C., 1988), 273-309, provides an excellent picture of the Hollywood art community and Man Ray's involvement. Foresta's view, contrary to much that has been written, seems to be that the Southern California environment—above all the entertainment industry—was a comfortable one for Ray and his creative perspective.

41. Man Ray, quoted by William Copley in "Portrait of the Artist as a Young Dealer," Archives of American Art, Smithsonion Institution, Roll 2709; frames 451-467.

42. Foresta, 277-278. With a reputation as a surrealist filmmaker, Man Ray no doubt also expected to find work in Hollywood. However, like many other art/experimental filmmakers, he was disappointed in this.

43. Some indication of the makeup of the Hollywood art community is seen in those who attended Man Ray's exhibition at the Copley Galleries (1948): Aldous Huxley, Henry Miller, Thomas Mann, Bertolt Brecht; George Antheil, Igor Stravinsky, Leopold Stokowski; Josef von Sternberg, Luis Bunuel, Jean Renoir, Otto Preminger, René Clair; Edward G. Robinson, Fanny Brice, Harpo Marx; Fietelson, Lundeberg, Merrild, Berman, Krasnow, Henry Lee McFee, and George Biddle. Hans Hofmann, Isamu Noguchi, Matta, Max Ernst, and Dorothea Tanning also attended (Foresta, 304-305).

44. Arturo Schwarz, *Man Ray* (New York: Rizzoli, 1977), 122.

45. See Foresta, 279-280, for a description of *Ruth, Roses, and Revolver*. Other contributors to the project were Duchamp, Ernst, Leger, Calder, John Cage, and Darius Milhaud.

46. For a discussion of the *Shakespearean Equations*, and the significance of the series to Man Ray's interest in the relationship between painting and photography, see Foresta, 300-304.

47. See Jules Langsner, *Four Abstract Classicists* (Los Angeles County Museum, 1959). The concept for the exhibition may have originated with Peter Selz (see letter to the author published in *The Los Angeles Institute of Contemporary Art Journal* 5 [April-May 1975]: 11); in any event, he and Langsner recognized an indigenous form of abstraction counter to that prevalent in the east. In his catalogue essay, Langsner described its characteristics and introduced the term *hard-edge painting*, which Lawrence Alloway picked up when the exhibition traveled to London.

48. In a video interview produced by the author and conducted by Lawrence Weschler for the Archives of American Art, David Hockney was explicit about his reasons for choosing to live and work in California. In addition to light, color, and space, he was attracted by the possibility of living privately: "I needed that kind of isolation—yet you're still in a city. Los Angeles is admirable for that." Interview with David Hockney, 3 September 1984, Archives of American Art, Smithsonian Institution, time code 01:01-05.

49. For a discussion of the similarities, and greater differences, between McLaughlin's methods and those of Reinhardt and Newman, see Sheldon Figoten, "An Appreciation of John McLaughlin," *Archives of American Art Journal* 20, no. 4 (1980): 10-16. The same issue is addressed in an excellent essay on McLaughlin by Susan C. Larsen in *California: 5 Footnotes to Modern Art History*, 72-73. Most critics have agreed with McLaughlin's claim that, among western artists, he is closest to Malevitch and, especially, Mondrian (see Figoten, 11-12).

50. All writers on McLaughlin emphasize the importance of oriental aesthetic philosophy to his artistic goals. His own writings (see John McLaughlin Papers, Archives of American Art, Smithsonian Institution) consistently emphasize his admiration for Japanese landscape painting of the Muromachi period (1392-1568), particularly the work of Sesshu. For a discussion of the role of Eastern painting in McLaughlin's art, see Donald F. McCallum, "The Painting of John McLaughlin," *The Los Angeles Institute of Contemporary Art Journal* 11 (May-June 1976): 13-14.

51. Letter from Stanton Macdonald-Wright to John McLaughlin, 15 July (1958?), John McLaughlin Papers, Archives of American Art, Smithsonian Institution, Roll 1410; frame 167.

52. Larsen, 70. Several other writers have recognized the "Mannerist" (anti-classical) movement and imbalance in McLaughlin's geometric imagery (for example, Figoten, 15). The same phenomenon in Lorser Feitelson's *Magical Space Forms* series (early 1950s) is described by Diane DeGasis Moran, "Lorser Feitelson" in *California: 5 Footnotes to Modern Art History*, 60. The sense of instability in imagery—changing, becoming—emerges as one possible attribute of a Southern California aesthetic.

53. See Leering, 48. Peter Voulkos is the critical figure in breaking down barriers between media and the art/craft hierarchy.

54. The chief authority on Fischinger, the Whitney brothers, and the abstract film avant-garde in Los Angeles is William Moritz. In addition to his "The Films of Oskar Fischinger" in *Film Culture*, see also "You Can't Get Then from Now," *The Los Angeles Institute of Contemporary Art Journal* 29 (Summer 1981): 27-35. Moritz's most recent and comprehensive treatment of "synesthesia" appears in his "Abstract Film and Color Music," *The Spiritual in Art: Abstract Painting 1890-1985* (New York: Abbeville Press, co-published with the Los Angeles County Museum of Art, 1987), 297-311.

55. Moritz, *Film Culture*, 79.

56. For a full account of this fascinating relationship between the artist and Baroness von Rebay, see Moritz's "You Can't Get Then from Now," 28ff. Moritz also describes some of Fischinger's inventions, among them the Lumigraph designed to play light images (color drawing in air), intended as less expensive alternatives to film (*Film Culture*, 74-75).

57. For a full discussion of this and other aspects of Fischinger's innovation, see Moritz, *Film Culture* or *The Spiritual in Art*.

58. The Whitney brothers are discussed by Moritz in "You Can't Get Then from Now," 35ff. The pendulum composition system is described in John Whitney's *Digital Harmony* (Peterborough, New Hampshire: Byte Books/A McGraw-Hill Publication, 1980), 138-150.

59. William Moritz introduction to "Audio-Visual Music: Color Music-Abstract Film," in Whitney, *Digital Harmony*, 138.

60. Denis Donoghue, "The Promiscuous Cool of Postmodernism," *The New York Times Book Review*, 22 June 1986, 37. *Art After Modernism: Rethinking Representation* (New York: The New Museum of Contemporary Art in association with David R. Godine, Boston, 1984), a provocative anthology of recent critical writing edited by Brian Wallis, provides some idea of the confusing variety of meanings assigned to *post-modernism* as a cultural term. Readers will find Chapter IV, "Theorizing Postmodernism" (167-235), especially germane. It is helpful to recall that Charles Jencks has pointed out, in *The Language of Post-Modern Architecture*, 4th ed. (New York: Rizzoli, 1984), 6, that the primary dualism involves "elitism and populism"—or high and low art. The melding of the two is essential to any definition of post-modernism.

61. Quoted in McWilliams, 370.

Karl Benjamin

(b. 1925)

One of the region's foremost abstractionists (and the youngest of the pioneer modernists), Karl Benjamin forged a distinctive style of geometric painting in the 1950s. Chicago-born, Benjamin entered Northwestern University in his native Illinois in 1943 but interrupted his studies a year later to serve in the Navy. After the war, he settled in Southern California and earned a Bachelor of Arts degree from the University of Redlands in 1949. Initially, he wanted to become a writer but, with a wife and child to support, he took a teaching position in an elementary school. Classroom art projects sparked his interest in painting, which he pursued in his after-work hours. Like John McLaughlin and Oskar Fischinger, he taught himself art fundamentals by touring museums and galleries and attentively reading professional journals.[1]

By 1954 Benjamin was awarded a one-man exhibition at the Pasadena Art Museum. *White Figures On A Red Sky* [color pl. 1], done in the year of that solo show, attests to his high degree of accomplishment. Its tangy palette of pale limes, red-oranges, sands, and teal blues delivers a vigorous visual punch. While serving formalist issues of self-definition—by stressing shape, surface, and hue—the work makes extra-pictorial references. Its large curving forms exist at once as abstract ciphers and as evocative personages; indeed, as its title denotes, they were meant to invoke a leaping being, with arms uplifted, legs akimbo, and head afloat in a persimmon sky.

Within two years Benjamin's paintings had dropped their organic allusions and become non-objective. In *Theme and Variation* [color pl. 2], shapes retain their earlier flatness and brilliance but focus more exclusively on their own means, interlocking with one another to stress the pictorial plane and the grid. By the end of the decade, these forms had evolved into jagged, linear strips that covered the field non-hierarchically.

In 1959 Benjamin was selected by art critic Jules Langsner to take part in the Los Angeles County Museum of Art's noted *Four Abstract Classicists* exhibition. Like Frederick Hammersley, Lorser Feitelson, and John McLaughlin with whom he was grouped, Benjamin evinced a measured, clean-lined approach to non-objective abstraction. In his catalogue essay, Langsner observed that Benjamin deftly employed long, serrated forms to create a surface "without beginning or end." Impressed by the artist's subtle palette, he praised its masterful orchestration of fine-tuned hues.[2]

Since then, Benjamin's oeuvre has received wide exposure. Over the years his paintings have entered many museum and private collections and appeared in numerous exhibitions, including one-man shows at the University of Redlands (1956, 1972, 1980), the Long Beach Museum of Art (1958), Occidental College (1958), the Esther Robles Gallery in Los Angeles (1959, 1960, 1962, 1964, 1965), the Lang Art Gallery at Scripps College (1960), the Santa Barbara Museum of Art (1962, 1968), the Laguna Beach Museum of Art (1965), the La Jolla Museum of Art (1970), Chaffey College (1975, 1981), the Tortue Gallery in Santa Monica (1975, 1977, 1978, 1980), Pepperdine University in Malibu (1981), California State University at Bakersfield (1982), the University of California at Santa Barbara (1984), the Hemmerdinger Gallery in Palm Desert (1986), the Los Angeles Municipal Art Gallery in Barnsdall Park (1986), and the Ruth Bachofner Gallery in Santa Monica (1986,1988). In 1989 the artist was honored in a major retrospective which opened at the Redding Museum and Art Center in Redding, California and then travelled to the University of the Pacific in Stockton and to the Art Galleries of California State University at Northridge.[3] He is currently a Professor of Art at Pomona College and at the Claremont Graduate School in Claremont, California.

NOTES

1. Karl Benjamin, telephone conversation with author, 1 December 1989. Further biographical data was obtained from Merle Schipper's essay in *Karl Benjamin: Selected Works 1979-1986*, Los Angeles Municipal Art Gallery, Barnsdall Art Park, 1986.

2. Jules Langsner, *Four Abstract Classicists*, Los Angeles County Museum of Art, Los Angeles, California, 1959.

3. *Karl Benjamin: A Retrospective 1955-1987*, with essay by Merle Schipper, Redding Museum and Art Center, Shasta College Art Gallery, Redding, California, 1986.

Illus. 15. BEN BERLIN, *Bird, Sky, Water, and Grass*, 1938, oil on firtex, 29 x 23". Nora Eccles Harrison Museum of Art, Utah State University, Logan, Utah. Gift in memory of Ralph Wanclass. (not in exhibition)

Ben Berlin

(1887-1939)

Little is known about Ben Berlin. According to art historian Nancy Mouré, he was born in Washington, D.C. on 16 November 1887, and in 1924, while working in Los Angeles as a portrait painter, he married an artist's model.[1] In 1923 he participated in the seminal *Group of Independent Artists of Los Angeles* exhibition to which he contributed eighteen works, some of which bore strange titles such as *Owngz*, *Glaggle*, and *Vudu Futhmique*. In light of his penchant for the eccentric, it is not surprising that he was described by book dealer Jake Zeitlin as "a rather peculiar man who fancied himself a reincarnation of Edgar Allen Poe."[2]

Although by the 1920s he had established an aesthetic based on the tenets of Cubist collage, he may have been influenced later by Post-Surrealists Lorser Feitelson, Helen Lundeberg, and Grace Clements who served as his colleagues on the Federal Art Project. In his 1938 *Woman with a Lute* [color pl. 5], for example, he gives a fantastic edge to the Cubist trope that relates female bodies to musical instruments. Furthermore, he shares with the Post-Surrealists an interest in formal analogies played out in a medley of curves. Thus, the guitar echoes the woman's collar and head while its sounding hole bears analogies with her globular hand and eye, as well as with the moon.

Berlin, however, differs from the Post-Surrealists in his reliance on Cubist strategies, particularly that of synthetic collage. In *Duck, Cannon, and Firecrackers* of 1936 [color pl. 4] and in *Birds, Sky, Water, and Grass* [illus. 15], he joins pictorial elements to an infrastructure based on a rectilinear grid. With an eye for tectonics, he layers the forms and places them parallel to the surface along right-angled axes. Importantly, though, Berlin bends Cubist tactics to his own objectives, invoking outdoor subject matter rather than urban cafés.

These nature studies might have had escapist value for Berlin, who possessed a frail physique. Habitually clothed in basic black, his pale face crowned by a painter's beret, he seems to have nurtured his image as a pensive aesthete.[3] Impoverished by the Depression, Berlin died in Los Angeles on 16 October 1939, one month shy of his fifty-second birthday.

NOTES

1. Nancy Dustin Wall Mouré, *Dictionary of Art and Artists in Southern California before 1930* (Los Angeles: Publications in Southern California Art, No. 3, 1975), 16.

2. Jake Zeitlin as quoted by Lionel Rolfe in "L.A. Arts & Letters: From A to Zeitlin," *Los Angeles Weekly Reader*, No. 42 (13 August 1982), 9.

3. Helen Lundeberg, telephone conversation with author, 7 June 1988.

William Brice

(b. 1921)

A second generation modernist, William Brice emerged in the postwar years as one of the region's outstanding young talents. Born in New York City on 13 April 1921, Brice grew up in a culturally rich environment which revolved around the visual arts and theater.[1] His mother, comedienne Fanny Brice, nurtured his early interest in art by touring European museums with him and arranging for him to have private painting lessons with artist Henry Botkin. From Botkin Brice acquired a conversancy with New York's gallery scene and a lasting appreciation of Cezanne, Matisse, and Picasso. In 1937 Brice moved with his family to Los Angeles, and while attending Kumnock High School, took life drawing classes at Chouinard Art Institute. After high school graduation and a year of work at the Art Students League in New York, he returned to Chouinard where he studied with Herbert Jepson, Lawrence Murphy, and Henry Lee McFee.[2]

Following a brief stint as a studio artist at MGM—he designed sets and reproduced Old Master paintings to embellish their walls—Brice served in the Army Air Corps. Upon his return to civilian life in 1943, he painted independently, honing his technical skills with drawing sessions from the model at Otis Art Institute. In 1947 he won second place in the Los Angeles County Museum of Art's *Artists of Los Angeles and Vicinity* show and also received a one-man exhibition at the Santa Barbara Museum of Art. The following year he accepted a teaching position at the Jepson Art Institute where he formed an influential triumvirate with his fellow artists Howard Warshaw and Rico Lebrun. When Jepson began to curtail its program in the early fifties, Brice left the school, and in 1953 joined the faculty of UCLA on which he continues to serve.

In his works of the 1940s, Brice favored still life objects such as beach rocks and kitchen utensils, which he rendered illusionistically. With a classicist's penchant for order, he carefully plotted his compositions and depicted their contents with fine-tuned precision.

By the early 1950s Brice had moved stylistically from naturalism to semi-abstraction. Intrigued by the roses in his backyard and by their contrasting qualities—delicacy versus tenacity, sensuality versus pain—he tracked their cyclical growth and decay in a series of drawings and paintings that extended over five years. Although not intended as such, his floral suite can be seen as a metaphor of existence, thereby implying human life cycles of birth, maturation, and death.[3]

In *Rose Tree*, which belongs to this series [illus. 16], a region of night on the right contrasts with a daylight realm on the left in which vitalized flowers bloom. Gone is the stasis and sculptural volume of Brice's prior works as images flatten and lend their surroundings an electric energy. With a nod to Cubism, forms begin to fracture and space crystallizes to integrate solid and void.

After five years of work with flowers, Brice, in reaction, sought a more massive and durable subject. Focusing on the landscape near his home, he created *Land Fracture* [color pl. 6] and *Parched Land* [fig. 1], which belong to a 1950s series inspired by the rustic gorges and hills along Mulholland Drive. In both paintings, small irregular forms strewn across massive clumps allude to skeletal fossils, brambles, and twigs. Chameleon-like, some blend with the ground on which they sprawl, suggesting their primal relationship with the earth. Brice observed:

Illus. 16. WILLIAM BRICE, *Rose Tree,* 1950, oil on canvas, 69 x 45". Los Angeles County Museum of Art. Gift of Jerome K. Ohrback. (not in exhibition)

I was attracted to Mulholland Ridge.... It was elemental, primordial. I was intrigued by how a bush roots itself into the side of the hill, how the land eroded from it: the bush's tenacity, its insistence on existing.[4]

Accordingly, in Brice's paintings, burrowing branches and mutable rocks infer a tenacious will to survive. Structurally, these metamorphic shifts freed Brice from the constraints of physical laws. "I could convert a form from rock to cloud," he later observed. "Solid organic things were malleable." Thus, matter and air, land and sky, weave together in these compositions as coequals in an integral field.

Land Fracture is spatially complex as it employs different vantage points and joins near and far on the same plane. It also suggests both a scrutiny of details and a comprehensive scan. "I wanted a combination of the proximate with the distant," Brice explained, "panoramic in scale yet intimate."[5]

These panoramic landscapes invite comparisons with the *Berkeley* series of Bay Area artist Richard Diebenkorn which they parallel in time. Both portray natural landscapes surveyed from above with elements held close to the plane by a rectilinear structure. Subdued in hue and controlled in design, they exhibit a similar stately restraint.

Like Diebenkorn, whose classical approach he shared, Brice offered a West Coast response to Abstract Expressionism. Thus, while partaking of that movement's heroic ambition and grandiose scale, he avoided its theatrics and emotional angst. In contrast, for instance, to Willem de Kooning, he worked with quite cerebral reserve, resisting impulsive gestures and spontaneous splashes of paint. As a result, his works have an aura of studied assessment, of reasoned composure that obviates tempestuous displays.

Brice's oeuvre over the years retained its

Fig. 1. WILLIAM BRICE, *Parched Land,* 1954, oil and sand on board, 40 x 60". Private collection, Beverly Hills, California.

elegance and cool, cerebral stance. The artist achieved distinction early on, meriting one-man shows at the Santa Barbara Museum of Art (1947 and 1958), at the Downtown Gallery (1948-1949) and the Alan Gallery (1955, 1956, and 1961) in New York, and at the Frank Perls Gallery in Beverly Hills (1950, 1955, 1956, and 1960). Additionally, he participated in many group exhibitions, locally at the Angeles County Museum of Art (1947, 1948, 1949, and 1956) and the Municipal All-City Festival (1950 and 1951), and nationally at the Whitney Museum of American Art (1948, 1949, 1950, and 1956), the Museum of Modern Art (1950 and 1956) and the Metropolitan Museum of Art in New York (1950), the Carnegie Institute in Pittsburgh (1947, 1948, 1949), the California Palace of the Legion of Honor (1952), the M. H. de Young Museum in San Francisco (1953), and the Santa Barbara Museum of Art (1953). Brice won a purchase prize at the Santa Barbara Museum of Art in 1955, and the following year received top awards at the Los Angeles County Museum of Art and the Los Angeles Municipal Art Gallery. In subsequent years, Brice's stature continued to grow as his works entered numerous public collections and exhibitions throughout the United States. During the course of the 1960s, Brice soloed at, among others, the Frank Perls Gallery in Beverly Hills (1960, and 1962 to 1966), the Esther Bear Gallery in Santa Barbara (1961), the Felix Landau Gallery in Los Angeles (1966), and the Alan Gallery in New York (1961 and 1968 as the Landau-Alan Gallery). In 1967 the University of California at San Diego celebrated eleven years of Brice's graphic production (from 1955 to 1966) with a publication and exhibition that traveled to the Santa Barbara Museum of Art, the San Francisco Museum of Modern Art, the Dallas Museum of Art, and the Colorado Springs Fine Arts Center. The subsequent year the University of California at Santa Cruz followed suit.

The seventies and eighties likewise witnessed Brice receiving many awards, including research grants from the University of California in 1974 and 1976. At the same time, he enjoyed a string of solo exhibits at, among others, the Charles Campbell Gallery in San Francisco (1976), the Nicholas Wilder Gallery in Los Angeles (1978), the Los Angeles Institute of Contemporary Art (1978), the Smith Anderson Gallery in Palo Alto (1983), and the L.A. Louver Gallery in Venice, California (1984).

In 1986 Brice was honored by a large retrospective at the Museum of Contemporary Art in Los Angeles and four years later enjoyed an exhibition of his 1982 drawings, *Notations*, at the Los Angeles County Museum of Art. Currently, he is represented by the Robert Miller Gallery in New York City and the L.A. Louver Gallery.[6]

NOTES

1. Parts of this essay appeared in the author's "The Jepson Group: The School, Its Major Teachers and Their Drawings," Nancy Mouré, *Drawings and Illustrations by Southern California Artists before 1950*, Laguna Beach Museum of Art, 1982, 44-55.

2. William Brice, interview with author, 30 June 1981 and 26 October 1989. Crucial data for this essay was also obtained from Richard Armstrong's "William Brice's Essential Elements," *William Brice: A Selection of Painting and Drawing 1947-1987*, Museum of Contemporary Art, Los Angeles, California, 1986.

3. In his essay, "William Brice's Essential Elements," Richard Armstrong suggests that Brice's absorption with themes of mortality was reinforced by critical passages in his life -- the birth of his child and the death of his mother--in the opening years of the 1950s.

4. Jascha Kessler, "William Brice: An Interview," *Art International*, 23, Nos. 5-6 (September 1979), 89.

5. Brice, telephone conversation with author, 26 October 1989.

6. For a thorough chronology of exhibitions and bibliography, see *William Brice: A Selection of Painting and Drawing 1947-1986*.

Hans Burkhardt

(b. 1904)

Because life has many facets ... it cannot be contained within a narrow field of subject matter, or even within one mode of expression ... because all is part of life and all life is one.[1]

Expansive in both subject and style, Hans Burkhardt has sought to express in his art the richness of existence. From this intense engagement with life, he developed a body of work that helped to enrich and define the Abstract Expressionist ethos.

Born to an impoverished carpenter and a laundress in Basel, Switzerland on 20 December 1904, Burkhardt was abandoned by his father at the age of three, witnessed his mother die of tuberculosis three years later, and was subsequently placed in an orphanage. After completing his schooling at fifteen, he apprenticed himself to a gardener and spent the next few years in this trade.[2]

In 1924 Burkhardt immigrated to New York City where he worked as a furniture decorator.

Illus. 17. HANS BURKHARDT, *War, Agony in Death*, 1939-1940, oil on canvas, 78 x 114". Jack Rutberg Gallery, Los Angeles, California.

Wishing to further himself in this craft, he took courses in design at the Cooper Union School. Four years later, he began to train with artist Arshile Gorky in private tutorials which intermittently spanned a decade and yielded close personal ties. From Gorky, Burkhardt learned the mechanics of painting and gained an appreciation of modern art. He also absorbed an artistic approach that relied strongly on empathy. By 1937, Burkhardt had grown disenchanted with life in New York and moved to Los Angeles. Supporting himself as a furniture refinisher, he painted evenings and weekends, and built a house on the side of a cliff in Laurel Canyon where he and his wife still live.

During the 1930s, Burkhardt painted in a Cubist vein indebted to Picasso by way of Gorky. Then, at the turn of the decade, he began to create Expressionist works in which he decried the carnage in Europe.[3] In *War, Agony in Death* [illus. 17], he attacks the canvas directly, releasing his strokes with force. Skeletal figures drenched in colors of ash and blood writhe by graves piled with human debris, while a tank, half metal, half bone, emits a tormented howl. This amalgamation of weapon and beast recalls Picasso's *Guernica* horse and looks forward to Rico Lebrun's *Crucifixion* soldiers [page 79].

While Burkhardt frequently railed against social evils, he also applauded West Coast life in a number of handsome abstractions. In *By the Sea* of 1945 [color pl. 7],[4] biomorphic forms, born of Cubist facets and a painterly brush, evoke a casual day at the beach. Two large figures at right and left oversee a welter of shapes that suggest a picnic in the sand. An azure sky, warmed by the sun, greets the cool Pacific in which Burkhardt regularly swam. In the same year that he painted this work, Burkhardt enjoyed a solo show at the Los Angeles County Museum of Art and a purchase prize at that museum's *Artists of Los Angeles and Vicinity* exhibition.

By 1950, Burkhardt, exhausted by the demands of the furniture business which he now owned, was ready for a change. Thus, he sold his shop and traveled to Mexico. In Zapopan and Guadalajara, where he lived part-time for the next three years, he studied with fascination the colorful pageant of village life, the teeming growth of the swamps.[5] In *Farewell to Mexico* [color pl. 9], he conveys his enchantment with the region through sizzling hues and creamy paint that evoke a tropical paradise. Abstract forms in burnished golds, browns, and reds bring to mind torrid thickets seared by perennial sun.

"I wanted to capture the feeling of happiness," Burkhardt explained, "to celebrate the things I had seen—the people, the birds, the trees, and all the living forms of nature—the soul of Mexico."[6] Like Rico Lebrun in his *Mexican Street in the Rain*, he tried to conflate in a single scene the manifold sights afforded the eye in the course of a typical Mexican day.

The Awakening and *Song of the Universe* [color pl. 10 and 11], also hint of biotic life mingling in wild profusion. Inspired by camping trips to the Sierras, they brim with traces of organisms—pinwheel flowers, dragonflies, and fluttering birds. In *The Awakening*, the artist relates, a waterfall gushes down from top center as two lively bugs, responding to instinct or perhaps to the heat, unabashedly mate.[7] This biomorphic whimsy points to the influence of Miró which was prevalent in America during the 1930s and 1940s and surfaced in the collaborative paintings that Burkhardt did in the 1930s with Gorky.

"The time is spring," Burkhardt said of these two paintings,[8] and in response to this season, buds ripen into blossoms and creatures fraternize. Vaguely phallic and ovular shapes, peeping through the loosely brushed ground, extend the work's theme of fertility to the human sphere.

In alluding to the interdependence of nature, Burkhardt, like Gorky, caused his forms to bear a familial resemblance and to partake of the abstract field in which they nest. However, while inspired by his mentor, Burkhardt, as critic Jules Langsner observed early on, assimilated that influence and made it his own.[9] His works, for example, possess a ruggedness that skirts Gorky's exquisite refinement and poignant sense of erotic desire. Produced by a hand accustomed to labor—carpentry, hiking, and gardening, as well as movie set and home construction—they reflect their maker's resilient strength.

In *Studio of Gorky* [color pl. 8] the artist pays tribute to his close friend, who committed suicide in 1948. Rectangular planes set the scene in a loft to which muted hues, here and there dripped like cascading tears, lend a disconsolate air. A soft film of paint, lightly brushed over the surface, invokes the filter of memory. Just right of center the tortured figure of Gorky appears, wrenched by convulsions and splattered with blood. Drawing upon his empathic powers, Burkhardt renders the sorrow that permeates space and touches inanimate objects. Transcending specifics, this plaintive elegy speaks of all human bereavement.

A seminal piece in the artist's oeuvre, *Studio of Gorky*, which also exists in another version, hung in the Whitney Museum's annual of 1951 and was reproduced in *Art Digest* magazine.[10] By that time Burkhardt was already an established figure in the Los Angeles area. Subsequent to his 1939 debut at the Earl Stendahl Gallery, he enjoyed a succession of solo shows during the 1940s and 1950s: at the Circle Gallery (from 1940 to 1945), the Los Angeles County Museum of Art (1945), the Los Angeles Art Association (1950), the Fraymart Gallery (1951), the Paul Kantor Gallery (1952), the University of Southern California (1953), Occidental College (1955), and the Pasadena Art Museum (1957). His work was also included in exhibitions at the Corcoran Gallery in Washington, D.C. (1947 and 1951), the Chicago Art Institute (1948 and 1952), the Denver Art Museum (1949 and 1953), the Metropolitan Museum of Art in New York (1950), the University of Illinois (1951), and the Pennsylvania Academy of Fine Arts (1951 and 1953). On the international level, it was selected for the prestigious *Pacific Coast Art: United States' Representation at the Third Biennial of Sao Paulo, Brazil* held in 1955.

In 1959 Burkhardt began to teach, initiating a distinguished career that included positions at California State University at Long Beach, the University of Southern California, the University of California at Los Angeles, Chouinard Art Institute, and California State University at Northridge.

Meanwhile, he continued to contribute to countless exhibitions. His credits include retrospectives at the University of Southern California (1960), the Santa Barbara Museum of Art (1961 and 1977), the California Palace of the Legion of Honor in San Francisco (1961), the Los Angeles Municipal Art Gallery (1963), California State University at Northridge (1963, 1965, and 1973), the San Diego Art Institute (1966), the Laguna Museum of Art (1966), the San Diego Fine Arts Gallery (1968), the Long Beach Museum of Art (1972), Palm Springs Desert Museum (1979), and Muhlenberg College in Allentown, Pennsylvania (1990). Since 1982 his work

Fig. 2. HANS BURKHARDT, *Woman With a Wine Glass,* 1947, oil on canvas, 37 x 46". Jack Rutberg Gallery, Los Angeles, California.

has appeared in a series of one-man shows at the Jack Rutberg Gallery in Los Angeles.[11]

Through his painterly, impassioned works, Burkhardt has served as a West Coast master of Abstract Expressionism. Not only did he help to forge that aesthetic during its early stages of growth, but he enriched it with his distinctive vision. He extended Action Painting into the realm of political protest where few of his peers, absorbed as they were with ego dynamics, were willing to tread. In decrying the horrors of war and injustice with a somber palette, angst-laden figures, and rough applications of tactile paint, he prefigured the Neo-Expressionist course of artists such as Anselm Kiefer, Julian Schnabel, and Markus Lupertz. On the other hand, his celebratory abstractions of the Southern California scene foreshadowed the bright, geocentric expressions of Carlos Almarez, Frank Romero, Astrid Preston, and Joe Fay. Indeed, it has been Burkhardt's achievement to treat life's many facets with passion, commitment, and force.

NOTES

1. Hans Burkhardt in statement for his one-man exhibition at the Pasadena Art Museum, California, 14 June-14 July 1957 as quoted by Ala Story in *Hans Burkhardt: Retrospective Exhibition 1931-1961*, Santa Barbara Museum of Art, Santa Barbara, California, 1961, unpaginated.

2. Jack Rutberg, *Hans Burkhardt, 1950-1960*, Jack Rutberg Fine Arts, Inc., Los Angeles, California, 1987, unpaginated.

3. For a complete survey of these and later works on war, see Jack Rutberg's *Hans Burkhardt: The War Paintings, A Catalogue Raisonné* with an interview by Colin Gardner (Northridge, California: Santa Susana Press, California State University, Northridge, 1984). Also see Gardner's "War Leaves its Traces," *Artweek*, 16, No. 9 (2 March 1985), 3.

4. This painting is alternatively called *Dance*.

5. Betty Brown discusses Burkhardt's works of the 1950s in "Issues for an Expressionist," *Artweek*, 18, No. 4 (31 January 1987), 5-6.

6. Burkhardt, interview with author, 30 March 1988.

7. Burkhardt, interview with author, 5 February 1987.

8. Ibid.

9. Jules Langsner, "Los Angeles," *Art News*, 56, No. 4 (Summer 1957), 64.

10. Belle Krasne, "Whitney Annual, 1951 Edition:What's New in American Painting?", *Art Digest*, 26, No. 4 (15 November 1951), 6-7.

11. For a complete list of exhibitions, see Jack Rutberg, *Hans Burkhardt: Paintings and Pastels, 1988-1989*, Jack Rutberg Fine Arts, Inc., Los Angeles, California, 1990.

Grace Clements

(1905-1968)

Modern art ... is no longer the experiment, but the vital and creative art expression of our age. That California is becoming aware of this is a hopeful sign. That Grace Clements is a native daughter who has found recognition in Los Angeles is also significant.[1]

An ardent proponent of modernism, artist and critic Grace Clements sought to awaken Los Angeles of the 1930s and 1940s to vanguard modes of expression. Born in Oakland on June 8, 1905, Clements trained in New York from 1925 to 1930 with Kenneth Hays Miller and Boardman Robinson. In 1931 she moved to Los Angeles and shortly thereafter received a solo show at the Los Angeles County Museum of Art.[2] Four years later she joined the newly-formed Post-Surrealist group and participated in its major exhibitions at the San Francisco Museum of Art in December 1935 and the Brooklyn Museum in New York the following summer.

More socially conscious than the other Post-Surrealists, who held art apart from politics, Clements applied the movement's tenets to the contemporary scene. In the March 1936 issue of *Art Front*, a vehicle of the American Artists' Congress to which she belonged, she published an article entitled "New Content—New Form" in which she castigated "ivory tower" formalism and Surrealist automatism and argued for an art that addressed social issues in a language which the public could understand. Post-Surrealism, she contended, could serve this agenda because it clothed ideas in images that were both modern and clear. Opposed to naturalism, which merely mimicked appearance, she advised artists to emulate techniques of the movies such as filmic montage.

Clements did just that in *Reconsideration of Time and Space* [color pl. 12], in which she combined three separate scenes in a single depiction. In echoing motion picture devices, she simulated film splicing, to lend the image an animate feeling of sequential frames in a reel. She also adopted Post-Surrealist tactics by making formal analogies and taking liberties with linear time. Like her colleagues in this movement, she juxtaposed different realities and explored the links that they forge in the mind. Looking to de Chirico, whom the Post-Surrealists admired, she adapted his signature ploys of upended floor-boards, freestanding walls, racing perspectives and dark, distant figures that cast trailing shadows. Importantly, she updated her model with imagery that speaks of metropolis rather than of Renaissance piazzas. Communication in the modern era appears to be the work's theme, with its montage views of an airplane flying in the sky, a figure suggesting alienation, telephone lines transmitting data, and a bridge spanning a placid bay like the one in the artist's hometown of Oakland.

During the years of the Depression, Clements served as a painter and muralist on the Federal Art Project of the Works Progress Administration. With Helen Lundeberg she painted murals in Venice High School and fashioned a series of mosaics for Bancroft Junior High School in Los Angeles and the Municipal Airport of Long Beach.[3] In 1931 she was honored in a one-woman exhibition at the Los Angeles County Museum of Art where her work also appeared in group presentations in 1939 and 1944. After contributing to the aforementioned Post-Surrealist shows, Clements participated in the 1939 World's Fair in New York and in the Whitney Museum of

Art's *Between Two Wars* of 1942.[4] During the 1940s she contributed art reviews and articles to *Arts and Architecture* magazine. According to Peter and Rose Krasnow, who corresponded with her after she left Southern California in the late 1940s, she subsequently became involved with astrology and married an Indian guru with whom she traveled on lecture circuits.[5]

NOTES

1. Merle Armitage, *An Exhibition of Modern Paintings by Grace Clements*, Los Angeles Museum, Exposition Park, July 1-15, 1931, unpaginated.

2. *American Art Annual*, Vol. 28, 1931; *Who's Who in American Art*, Vol. 3, 1940-1941.

3. "Airport with Murals and Mosaics by Grace Clements," *II California Arts and Architecture*, 59, No. 11 (December 1942); 31-33.

4. Data sheets, courtesy of the archival libraries of the San Francisco Museum of Modern Art and the Oakland Museum in California.

5. Peter and Rose Krasnow, interview with author, 23 January 1978.

Fig. 3. JULES ENGEL, *Outdoor Sculpture*, 1945, gouache on board, 20½ x 14". Collection of the artist, Los Angeles, California.

Jules Engel

Painter, filmmaker, sculptor, and teacher, Jules Engel has achieved success in varied artistic fields. A native of Budapest, Hungary, he immigrated to the United States with his family as a youngster in 1930. At Evanston High School in Illinois, he excelled in his art class where he delved precociously into geometric abstraction.

Upon his graduation in 1937, he ventured to Hollywood, hoping to work as an animator in the film industry.[1] Within two years he had secured a position at the Disney studios on the film *Fantasia*. Assigned to the Russian and Chinese dance sequences of Tchaikovsky's *Nutcracker Suite*, Engel, inspired by Kandinsky and Klee, inventively placed his dancing sprites against a stark black ground. By means of his boldly simplified settings which heightened contrasts of figure and ground, Engel spotlit movement and developed an abstract ambience for the balletic flowers and fairies.

While working on *Fantasia*, Engel met and befriended avant-garde filmmaker Oskar Fischinger who shared his respect for Klee and other European moderns and encouraged his work in abstract animation. Although Fischinger's tenure at Disney was brief, Engel's lasted three-and-a-half years, during which time he also created color work for the feature film *Bambi*.

With the outbreak of the Second World War, Engel resigned from Disney and enlisted in the Motion Picture Unit of the Air Force. After his tour of duty, he joined three members of this filmmaking corps—John Hubley, Bill Hurtz, and Herb Klynn—in 1947 to develop the United Productions of America (UPA) studio. Beginning as a filmic designer, Engel served as an art director during the 1950s, and in this capacity supervised the studio's entire production. At the same time, he helped create such UPA films as *Gerald McBoing-Boing*, *Madeleine*, and *Mr. Magoo*. Legendary in the annals of filmic animation, UPA is credited with bringing concepts of abstract art into commercial film. With Matisse, Kandinsky, Klee, and Dufy as their models, UPA artists conveyed to a broad audience the tenets of formal abstraction via flat figuration placed within a simplified mise-en-scène.

While supporting himself as an animator, Engel devoted weekends and evenings to his easel paintings. In these abstractions of the 1940s, to which *Interior* [color pl. 13], Untitled [fig. 4], and *Outdoor*

Fig. 4. JULES ENGEL, Untitled, ca. 1947, gouache on paper, 10¼ x 13". Collection of the artist, Los Angeles, California.

Sculpture [fig. 3] belong, he reveals his strong feeling for tectonic design. The way that he structures his compositions with flat shapes pressed to the plane reveals his roots in Synthetic Cubism. Within this constructivist mode, he lends his works an architectural air. In *Interior*, for example, he conjures up a vestibule with windows, doors, stairways, and halls.

Comparably, in the untitled gouache [fig. 4] he evokes an abstract cityscape seen through fractured glass. Reminiscent of the *Windows* series by French Orphist painter Robert Delaunay, it suggests a panoramic view of a town through fragmented panes.

Curiously, however, these works relate less to the poised, cubistic structures of Neutra, Schindler, Soriano, and Ain which then dotted the local terrain and more to the brash, asymmetric constructions of latter-day architect Frank Gehry. Indeed, their tilting conjunctions of angular planes seem to portend the Deconstructivist ethos of the 1980s.

These planes which shift in vision reflect a cinematic sensibility. More often than not, Engel's paintings suggest a camera tracking through movie sets, as in *Brilliant Moves* [color pl. 14]. Specifically, they bear a strong a relation to the then-contemporary *film noir*. Their labyrinthine structures compare with *noir*'s complicated plots, while their fractured scenes recall flashbacks in movies which intercut linear time. Passages slant and convolute, ending, as they do in *noir*, in detours and cul-de-sacs. Nowhere is the territory simple and clear, the turf easily read. Vision is fraught with digressions, proceeding as characters do in *noir* movies, with frustration and confusion.

The affinities that these works bear to *noir* films seem to stem from allied responses to Existentialism. Thus, both art forms suggest entrapment through a claustrophobic compression of space, with images squeezed within the frame, and through angled vectors that race toward the distance but find no release. In *Interior*, tilted panels jostle and crowd, while checkerboard patterns and free-floating wedges in *Brilliant Moves* engender anxiety. Chess, to which the latter piece refers, serves as a frequent leitmotif in *noir* narratives. Its tactical ploys are enacted by characters who usually become victimized pawns when they try to circumvent fate. Connoting survival strategies, chess functions in this painting, as it does in *noir* films, as a metaphor for existence.

Brilliant Moves was included in the Art Institute of Chicago's *Abstract and Surrealist Art in America* of 1947-1948, two years after Engel had made his Los Angeles debut in a duo show at Fred Kann's Circle Gallery on Sunset Boulevard.[2] Subsequently, Engel participated in numerous group exhibitions at the Los Angeles County Museum of Art, including its *California Centennials* of 1949 and *Contemporary Painting in the United States* of 1951. During the 1950s he contributed to major national surveys—at the San Francisco Museum of Art and the M. H. de Young Museum in San Francisco and at the Whitney Museum of American Art and the Metropolitan Museum of Art in New York City—and to the international *Pacific Coast Art: United States' Representation at the Third Biennial of Sao Paolo*. At the same time he earned a succession of one-man shows at the Paul Kantor Gallery in Beverly Hills.

As the years progressed, Engel enjoyed critical acclaim from numerous retrospectives in painting and film, both in the United States and abroad. His awards include first prizes from film festivals in Venice, Edinburgh, Mannheim, and Atlanta, and grants from the American Film Institute and from the Andrew W. Mellon and Ford foundations. Under his guidance as art director, UPA films earned three Academy Awards and eleven nominations. Meanwhile, his paintings and drawings entered many private and public collections including the Chicago Art Institute, the Hirshhorn Museum and Sculpture Garden, the Museum of Modern Art in New York, and the Los Angeles County Museum of Art.

Since 1969, Engel has served as founding chair of the Department of Animation and Experimental Film at the California Institute of the Arts in Valencia where he continues to produce abstract paintings and films of distinction.

NOTES

1. Jules Engel, interviews with author, 9 March 1985, 3 June 1985, 30 March 1986, and 7 February 1988. Also Lawrence Weschler and Milton Zolotow, interviews conducted with the artist from 1975 to 1978 for *Los Angeles Art Community: Group Portrait*, Oral History Program, University of California at Los Angeles, California, c. 1985.

2. "Jules Engel, George Barrows," *Arts and Architecture*, 62, No. 9 (September 1945), 40.

Lorser Feitelson

(1898-1978)

Erudite, eloquent, and urbane, Lorser Feitelson served as a fitting spokesman for Modernism when the Los Angeles art scene was very young. In his varied roles as painter, teacher, gallery director, public speaker, and television host, he tried to imbue a conservative public with a respect for twentieth-century art revolutions.

Like Krasnow and Macdonald-Wright, Feitelson learned to paint at an early age, instructed by his father.[1] Born in Savannah, Georgia in 1898 and raised in New York City, Feitelson trained briefly with sculptor Karl Tefft and with anatomical draftsman George Bridgman at New York's Art Students League before venturing into a self-set course of instruction. After seeing the Armory Show in 1913, where the works of Cezanne, Matisse, Gleizes, and Duchamp impressed him the most, he delved ambitiously into abstraction. Extended stays in Paris between 1919 and 1927 placed him in the center of vanguard developments and enabled him to study first-hand the old and modern masters.

Feitelson's career began to take hold with a one-man show in 1925 at the Daniel Gallery in New York and was furthered with his inclusion the following year in the Parisian *Salon d'Automne*. Yet despite his success, Feitelson, like Merrild, Krasnow, and Macdonald-Wright, felt dissatisfied with the quality of life in Manhattan, and thus ventured to Los Angeles in November 1927.

At that time he was working in a Neo-Classical vein indebted to the 1920's work of Picasso, Matisse and Derain. Then, in the early thirties, he became intrigued with the subjective potential of Surrealism and of Giorgio de Chirico's Metaphysical art. With Helen Lundeberg, who earlier had been his student and later would become his wife, he co-founded the Post-Surrealist movement in 1934. Cerebral and classical in their approach, they sought to rid Surrealism of its excesses and lend it a contemplative air. Rejecting spontaneous modes of production, they crafted their compositions with calculated care. Crucially, too, they distinguished themselves from their peers in Europe by their positive image of women. In their agenda women appeared as nurturers and creators rather than as sexual objects servicing male desire.

Feitelson's *Genesis* suite, for example, honors women's procreative powers. Placing his subject matter in a cosmic paradigm, the artist allies human fertility with that of other organisms in the biosphere. His directive approach leads the eye in lock-step progression from one object to the next to help it discern bonds between forms and the theme which they address.

In *Genesis, First Version* [fig. 5], he engages thought with his scheme of analogies while charming the eye with lustrous hues and sensuous curves. By aligning the womb and the moon (a female symbol), he calls attention to their points in common, and by framing them with a looking glass and drape, he lends them solemnity. Nuanced tones of flesh, eggshell, and blue enhance the cosmic symbolism and the pensive mood.

Feitelson's focus on sexuality and analogic form reveals ties with modern psychology. His method of association, linking forms by structure and proximity, relates to Freudian dream analysis, while his objects—eggs, fruit, shells, and moons—serve as psychoanalytical female symbols. Moreover, his attachment of these symbols to a cosmic model suggests an awareness of C. G. Jung. In the context of American art of the 1930s, when Regionalism reigned supreme,

Feitelson's Post-Surrealism, with its aesthetic adaptation of psychological thought, clearly was prescient for its time and place.

Feitelson and Lundeberg officially launched their Post-Surrealist movement in November 1934 with a show at the Centaur Gallery in Hollywood.[2] Their next exhibition, at the Stanley Rose Bookshop on Hollywood Boulevard in May 1935, included works by Knud Merrild, Reuben Kadish, and Philip Goldstein (who later changed his name to Guston), and was accompanied by a manifesto written by Jules Langsner. In his text, Langsner distinguished the California movement from its European model:

Surrealism by exposing the plastic possibilities of the subjective has occasioned the birth of Post-Surrealism; an art that affirms all that Surrealism negates: impeccable esthetic order rather than chaotic confusion, conscious rather than unconscious manipulation of materials, the exploration of the normal functionings of the mind rather than the individual idiosyncrasies of the dream.[3]

In December 1935 the Post-Surrealists—now represented by Feitelson, Lundeberg, Merrild, Lucien Labaudt, and Grace Clements—staged their Northern California debut at the San Francisco Museum of Art. The following May they exhibited at the Brooklyn Museum in New York where they received positive notices from *New York Times* art critic Edward Alden Jewell.[4] They also attracted the attention of Museum of Modern Art curator Alfred Barr who included Feitelson, Lundeberg, and Merrild in that museum's important *Fantastic Art, Dada, and Surrealism*

Fig. 5. LORSER FEITELSON, *Genesis, First Version*, 1934, oil on celotex, 24 x 30". San Francisco Museum of Modern Art. Gift of Helen Klokke.

Fig. 6. **LORSER FEITELSON**, *Magical Forms*, 1948, oil on canvas, 36 x 30". San Francisco Museum of Modern Art. Gift of the Lorser Feitelson and Helen Lundeberg Feitelson Arts Foundation, Los Angeles.

survey of 1936.

At the same time that he participated in these exhibitions, Feitelson tried to develop local forums for contemporary art. At the Centaur Gallery in 1934, at the Stanley Rose bookshop in 1935, and at his own Hollywood Gallery of Modern Art from 1935 to 1937 he mounted a series of modernist shows that included works by the Cubists, the German Expressionists, the European Surrealists and the California Post-Surrealists. From 1937 to 1943, he brought art to the public as Southern California supervisor of the Federal Art Project's easel painting, sculpture, and mural division. In 1939 he began to co-direct the Los Angeles Art Association with Helen Wurdemann and for the next thirty years organized the cooperative's numerous exhibitions.[5]

Feitelson also served the community by lecturing to the public, juring exhibitions, advising dealers, and in the mid-1950s hosting a television series, "Feitelson on Art."[6] Concurrently, he gave private tutorials in his studio, counting among those whom he instructed painters Philip Guston and Reuben Kadish, actor Edward G. Robinson, Mrs. Adolph Menjou, and producers Sidney Franklin and David Loew. In 1944 he joined the faculty of the Art Center School where he taught painting and

Fig. 7. LORSER FEITELSON, *Geomorphic Metaphor*, 1950-1951, oil on canvas, 58 x 82". Los Angeles County Museum of Art. Gift of Mr. and Mrs. Thomas C. McCray.

aesthetics and arranged several shows on campus, including a screening of Oskar Fischinger's films and a Stanton Macdonald-Wright retrospective.[7]

While teaching at the Art Center School, Feitelson ventured into biomorphic Surrealism. With a nod to Tanguy, Picasso, and Ernst, he developed a series of inventive figures he termed "Magical Forms." Painted with flat, opaque hues and endowed with irregular silhouettes, these Magical Forms, like the one from the San Francisco Museum of Modern Art [fig. 6], emerged as strange, eccentric beings. With its bone coloration and pointed horns, this chimerical figure conjures up the skeletal head of an ox and thus gained the name "Skull."[8] Although it calls to mind Georgia O'Keeffe's cow skulls, its shrill demeanor stands at odds with the grace of her lyric depictions. Refusing to soothe, it bewitches with its vacant yet hypnotic stare.[9]

Equally mesmerizing is the Magical Form of color pl. 16 which draws our gaze to the raindrop at center encased in bright red. As we focus on this shape, the planes surrounding it coalesce into a figurative image. Moodily evocative and structurally taut, this Magical Form, like the preceding Skull, blends purist abstraction and fantasy. Both of these works project an eerie, disquieting air, one that was meant to correspond to psychosocial tensions. According to art historian Diane Degasis Moran, the artist referred to these and other postwar expressions as "mean and ominous" and designed them to convey the era's apprehensions.[10]

More than a distant threat, the Cold War hysteria affected the artist directly. In November 1948, the year in which these Magical Forms were conceived, one of Feitelson's Federal Art Project murals and one painted by Lundeberg under his aegis were accused of being Communist-inspired. According to Lundeberg, claims were made that her portrait of Jedediah Smith was subversive because his deerskin outfit looked like a Russian tunic.[11] Although Feitelson rebuffed these attacks, he must have been shaken by them as he increasingly lent his work an anxious edge.

More often than not he expressed this stress in terms of optical flux. In the Magical Space Forms of color pl. 18, for example, smoothly-painted planes cradle one another to compete for the viewer's eye. Granted equal valence, they play a no-win game. Once the reds, for instance, attract our attention, the grays become assertive, and then, as they predominate, the reds reinstate their claims.

While eliciting similar optical shifts, the

Magical Space Forms of color pl. 17 and 19 dispose of curves and utilize pointed shapes as emblems of aggression. Sharply angled planes, shooting in different directions, incarnate distress. As they abut and collide they prompt figure-ground reversals which engender uncertainty. In entering these works one is thrown off balance, denied a visual footing in a slippery terrain. Jostled by shuffling forces that refuse to stabilize, one is set adrift in a topsy-turvy universe.

In *Geomorphic Metaphor* [fig. 7] massive planes in lunging perspectives invoke careening slabs of land, not unexpected in earthquake territory. Set against a dense blue field suggesting outer space, these tumbling shards induce in the viewer a feeling of vertigo. The artist intended these and other restive shapes to signify the tensions in society.

> *I have tried to create a wonder-world of formidable mood-evoking form, color, space, and movement: a configuration that for me metaphorically expresses the deep disturbance of our time: ominously magnificent and terrifying events, hurtling menacingly from the unforeseeable.*[12]

With their precipitous plunge, these Magical Space Forms encode existential dread. In this they resemble contemporary *film noir*. Compared, for example, with a still from Elia Kazan's *Panic in the Streets* [illus. 18] released the prior year, the Magical Space Forms of color pl. 17 seems to employ kindred visual strategies. Its slanted perspectives correspond with *film noir* shots of urban alleys, long hotel corridors, and endless flights of stairs. In a similar way, Feitelson's clash of blacks and whites parallels *noir*'s distinctive play of searing lights on midnight streets, dank interrogation rooms, and smoky, shadowed bars. Additionally, the work's maze-like structure, with its shifting points of reference and out-of-kilter shapes, calls to mind *noir*'s complicated plots. In 1951, the year that he painted this work, Feitelson had cause to be anxious. The municipal exhibition in Griffith Park for which he was a juror was attacked by right-wing factions as being Communistic. Boldly, he defended the exhibition in City Hall and castigated Councilman Harold Harby who had denounced the art as "stinkweed stuff." At a time when many capitulated to McCarthyism, Feitelson courageously resisted the forces of reaction.

Feitelson's assertiveness makes itself felt in his Magical Space Forms of color pl. 19 as spiky

Illus. 18. Still, *Panic in the Streets,* 1950, directed by Elia Kazan. Courtesy of Twentieth Century Fox Corporation.

geometries tear through the field to meet one another tip to tip. Their sleek streamlining and steep inclination suggest velocity, making the piece emblematic of twentieth-century speed. An icon of flight, the boomerang shape with swept-back wings seems to bespeak the marvel of new jet airplanes.

As evidenced by this and the prior three pieces, Feitelson's oeuvre by the early fifties had become highly distilled. Reductive in means and expansive in scale, it engaged a few, simple shapes on the foremost plane. The palette, starkly restricted in hue, exploited bold contrasts of tone. From these economical measures sprung works of laconic concision, proving the Miesian adage that less could, in fact, be more.

These works were included in a Feitelson retrospective at the Pasadena Art Institute in 1952 and at the Marion Koogler McNay Art Institute in San

Antonio, Texas three years later. In 1958 the artist and his wife, Helen Lundeberg, were honored in a joint exhibition at Scripps College in Claremont, California. The following year Feitelson's Magical Space Forms were included, together with paintings by Southland artists Karl Benjamin, Frederick Hammersley, and John McLaughlin in the Los Angeles County Museum of Art's seminal *Four Abstract Classicists* exhibition. In his catalogue essay for this show, curator Jules Langsner coined the terms *hard-edge* and *colorform*, both widely used today, to denote these works' crisp handling and their complementary binding of shape and hue. Likening the colorforms to Chinese Yin-Yang symbols, Langsner noted how they functioned in an interactive way. He also observed how, in Feitelson's paintings, they prompted reversals of solid and void to exploit the "duality of space and form."[13]

By the sixties and seventies, Feitelson's paintings had become strikingly sparse. Simplicity conquered complexity, planarity won over depth. Delicate lines of consummate grace served to define the space and declare the reality of the support. These elegant arabesques of paint assumed the role of the 1950's colorforms in engaging shape and space in a visual exchange.

With these Minimal pieces Feitelson stood eminently of his time, as he had with his notable works of prior years. During the 1930s he interpreted psychological thought in intriguing pictorial structures and tamed the Surrealist ethos with a California calm. Then, in the 1940s, he fashioned Magical Forms which crystallized social tensions and supplied Surrealism with new figuration. When, in the 1950s, he explored the dynamics of visual flux, he contributed to the stream of art that eventuated in Op and furthered the development of non-objective painting. And in the 1960s and 1970s—until his death from cancer in 1978—he refined the terms of reductive painting to a taut Minimalism. It was ultimately his achievement to devise throughout the years structures of compelling strength and cogency.

NOTES

1. Lorser Feitelson, interview with author, 13 December 1977. Primary sources of information for this essay were Diane Degasis Moran's *The Painting of Lorser Feitelson*, Ph.D. dissertation, University of Virginia, August 1979, Moran's "Lorser Feitelson," *Lorser Feitelson and Helen Lundeberg: A Retrospective Exhibition*, San Francisco Museum of Modern Art, 1980. Also Fidel Danieli's interview with Feitelson for *Los Angeles Art Community: Group Portrait*, Oral History Program, University of California, Los Angeles, 1974.

2. Also in this exhibition were Knud Merrild, Etienne Ret, Harold Lehman, and Lucien Labaudt of San Francisco.

3. Jules Langsner, *Post-Surrealists and Other Moderns*, Stanley Rose Gallery, Los Angeles, California, 1936, unpaginated.

4. Edward Alden Jewell, "Brisk Pace in Museums," *New York Times*, 17 May 1936, Section IX, 10.

5. Diane Moran presents a detailed account of these activities in *The Painting of Lorser Feitelson*.

6. Ibid. "Feitelson on Art" made its debut on NBC in 1956 and screened successfully for the next seven years. As described by those who viewed them, these telecasts were signal achievements, richly entertaining and cogently conceived. Their popularity and longevity in the mercurial field of television attest to the artist's communicative skills.

7. Moran, "Lorser Feitelson," *The Painting of Lorser Feitelson*, 111 and 178-179.

8. Feitelson, interview with Fidel Danieli, *Los Angeles Art Community: Group Portrait*, 94, and Moran, "Lorser Feitelson," 16.

9. A seminal piece in the artist's oeuvre, this painting appeared in numerous exhibitions. In 1948 it made its debut at the Los Angeles County Fair in Pomona where, the artist related in interviews with author and with Fidel Danieli, it was reproduced on postcards that sold very well. The following year it was included in the University of Illinois' *Exhibition of Contemporary American Painting* and in 1951 it was presented in the Los Angeles County Museum of Art's *Contemporary Painting in the United States*.

10. Lundeberg, interviews with author, 6 January 1981, 7 June 1984, 17 January 1985, and 2 April 1986, and Moran, "Lorser Feitelson," 16. For analyses of these two paintings, see Moran's essay.

11. Lundeberg, interview with author, 6 January 1981, and newspaper clipping provided by Lundeberg, "Los Angeles Artists Resent Renewed Blast Against Murals in Hall of Records," *The Mirror*, Friday, 12 November 1948, 18.

12. Feitelson in a statement for the *Exhibition of Contemporary American Painting*, University of Illinois, Urbana, 1951, 176.

13. Langsner, *Four Abstract Classicists*, Los Angeles County Museum of Art, Los Angeles, California, 1959, 10-11. A thorough chronology and exhibition history of the artist to 1978 appears in Moran, *Lorser Feitelson and Helen Lundeberg*, 32-35.

Oskar Fischinger

(1900-1967)

Known as a pioneer of abstract animation, Oskar Fischinger was also a talented easel painter who brought his skills in this art to fruition during his years in Los Angeles. The child of a merchant, Fischinger was born on 22 June 1900 in the village of Gelnhausen, Germany. Upon his completion of school at the age of fourteen, he apprenticed himself to an organ maker for a year and then worked as a draftsman for an architect.[1] Relocating to Frankfurt in 1916, he supported himself as a tool designer while studying at night for an engineer's license, which he earned in 1922. Later that year he opened a film production shop in Munich in which he explored filmic techniques. In the process, as Fischinger scholar Dr. William Moritz relates in his authoritative monograph on the artist, he experimented with different media, including paper cutouts, tinted fluids, and multi-colored wax.[2]

By 1928 Fischinger had settled in Berlin and was devising special effects for Fritz Lang at the U.F.A. Studios. The following year he returned to independent production in order to focus on his *Absolute Films* or *Studies*. These were groundbreaking ventures in abstract animation comparable to the works of Hans Richter. To finance them, Fischinger undertook commercial projects on consignment.

During the 1930s Fischinger, now assisted by his wife Elfriede, enjoyed critical and commercial success, crowned in 1935 by his earning first prizes at film festivals in Venice and Brussels. Impressed with his award-winning entry, *Composition in Blue*, Paramount Films invited the artist to California.

The year was 1936. His life and work threatened by Hitler, Fischinger fled to Hollywood with a Paramount contract in hand. A few months later his wife arrived in Los Angeles with a cache of his abstract films, condemned as depraved by the Nazis.

Sadly, however, Fischinger found his relations with Hollywood studios to be problematic. As an abstract filmmaker used to working on his own, he bristled at the industry's bureaucracy and conservative tastes. Frustrated by the neglect of his projects at Paramount, he resigned after a few months. A subsequent venture with M.G.M. yielded a colorful non-objective short, *Optical Poem*, but not another contract.[3]

Troubled by dwindling funds, Fischinger traveled to New York in 1938 with the aim of attracting investors for his abstract movies. Although he failed to secure loans, he won the support of Baroness Hilla von Rebay, curator of Solomon R. Guggenheim's collection and soon-to-be-opened Museum of Non-Objective Painting.[4] (Later, during the 1940s, von Rebay included Fischinger's paintings in two group exhibitions at that museum [1942 and 1945] and awarded him several Guggenheim grants.) Additionally, during his stay in New York, he enjoyed solo exhibits at the galleries of both Philip Boyer and Karl Nierendorf.[5]

Upon his return to Los Angeles in 1939, Fischinger obtained a position at the Disney Studios through Leopold Stokowski. Here, too, however, he found his conceptions out of line with those of his employers, who preferred figurative illustration. His abstractions for the Bach *Toccata and Fugue in D Minor* passage of *Fantasia* suffered so many revisions that he resigned from the studio and withdrew his name from the project.[6]

Expeditiously, a Guggenheim grant arrived soon after Fischinger left Disney. Renting a space on the Sunset Strip, he crafted *An American March*, an animated tribute to his new country, in which abstract shapes synchronically strut to John Philip Sousa's rousing score.[7] A few months after completing this film, Fischinger was invited by actor Orson Welles to join the Mercury Studio staff. Again he met with

Fig. 8. OSKAR FISCHINGER, Untitled, 1942, oil on canvas, 13 3/4 x 16 3/4". The Solomon R. Guggenheim Museum, New York. Hilla von Rebay Collection.

frustration as the project in which he was to participate—a biography of Louis Armstrong—never came to fruition.[8] Happily, though, Guggenheim granted him another stipend which enabled him to create his award-winning film, *Motion Painting #1,* and to devote attention to his easel art.

A self-taught painter, Fischinger learned art fundamentals by studying works in museums, galleries, journals, and books. According to his wife, he most admired Piet Mondrian and Paul Klee, whose mystical views of abstraction he shared. Like these two modernists, he approached his art in a spiritual way, regarding it as an avenue to higher truths. Moreover, like Klee, he conceived it as an evolving process, representative of life's movement and change.[9]

Devout but non-sectarian, Fischinger based his art and patterned his life on a personal set of beliefs drawn from different religions, but most responsive to Theosophy and the mystical East. Presaging New Age devotees, he faithfully followed a yoga routine and tried to keep in harmony with cosmic currents.[10] As a devotional aid, he built an electrically powered prayer wheel which, in turn, served as a model for his artistic logos.[11] In light of his mystical leanings, it is not surprising that Fischinger favored cosmic imagery. Intimations of outer space arise in his films as they do in his oils, which he began in 1937 between studio jobs.[12] Thus, one finds in his paintings a common concern with an infinite void in which circular forms suggesting planets revolve or float in airy suspension.

Although he disliked being compared with Kandinsky, Fischinger nonetheless shared with that master an interest in Theosophy, a conception of the artist as a suprasensible being, and a penchant for non-objective forms that conjured up cosmic realms.[13] Abstraction—or what he termed "concrete" expression—functioned for him as it did for Kandinsky, as a path to a lofty spirituality.

Fischinger's paintings, however, compared to Kandinsky's, are simpler and less cerebrally wrought, more frank and direct in their touch. They also diverge from those of Kandinsky in the cinematic air they project. More often than not, they invoke sequential or rotary motion. By extension, their images tend to suggest progressive movement to the next frame. The circles in the untitled piece of fig. 8, for instance, presume an impulse to roll and thus presuppose an imminent change despite their taut balance on lateral shafts.

Striking in its simplicity, with shapes restricted to circles and bars and hues confined to black, white, and blue, this painting foreshadows the taciturn ethos of Lorser Feitelson and John McLaughlin. Moreover, like the latter, it implies an infinite cosmos inspired by the resonant void of Eastern mysticism.

Fischinger, however, unlike McLaughlin, refused to adopt a reductive agenda or limit himself to a single style. Thus, in *Circles, Triangles, and Squares* [color pl. 21] and *Experiment* [color pl. 20] he increases pictorial elements and spreads them across the field. Inspired by his work with a light machine and with filmic cels, he explores transparent effects. Overlays of translucent planes relate to progressions in his movies and at the same time look forward to the colored beams of his Lumigraph, the light apparatus that he perfected in 1950.[14]

The artist's obvious penchant for discs seems not unrelated to his metaphysics. Dense with conflated meanings, the sphere refers at once to the sun, the source of divine and earthly life, to the mandala of Eastern religion, daily used by the artist in Tantric meditation, and to psychic integration, a notion which Jung had popularized. No doubt aware of these significations, Fischinger used the circle advisedly, hoping, much as did Kandinsky, Krasnow, and Mullican, that it would inspire the viewer toward transcendent thought.

In line with these aspirations, the golden spheres act like mandalas to commandeer sight. Enhancing this mandalic aura, the repetitive strokes of paint in *Experiment* serve in the manner of mantric cantation, to lull one into a quiet state. Behind them shadowy discs can be glimpsed, their spectral appearance suggesting the artist's interest in after-images.

At the same time that he studied the effects of perception and conjured up mystical worlds, Fischinger could, in works such as *Searchlights* and *Yellow Brown* [color pl. 23 and fig. 9], allude to his earthly environs. Sunny and gay, they hint of Los Angeles and its holiday mode of existence. Both are touched by a yellow glow, suggesting in one the warmth of the sun, in the other the glare of klieg lights. *Yellow Brown* calls to mind a day by the sea with sailboats aglide on Pacific tides. *Searchlights*, in contrast, betokens the city with Neutra and Schindler-type cubic buildings lined with strip windows and hit by lights such as those that announce motion picture premieres.

In 1947 Fischinger crafted his *Motion Painting #1* [see illus. 19], an inventive synthesis of easel art and film which traces the progress of an abstraction that the artist rendered on both sides of six plexiglass sheets. With a camera trained on his easel, Fischinger filmed each application of paint on a separate frame of the reel.[15] Because we never see the brush on screen, the painting seems to be self-generated. Magically, the forms build and transmute into changing designs, moving in rhythm, although not in synchrony, to Bach's *Brandenburg Concerto #3*. As the lens follows the work's maturation, tracking lines as they swell into planes, and planes as they build into complex structures, it gives filmic translation to Klee's famous adage of a dot developing into a line, a plane, and space over time.[16]

In his focus on the creative event, Fischinger compares with Knud Merrild and the New York Action Painters who were also then exploring the

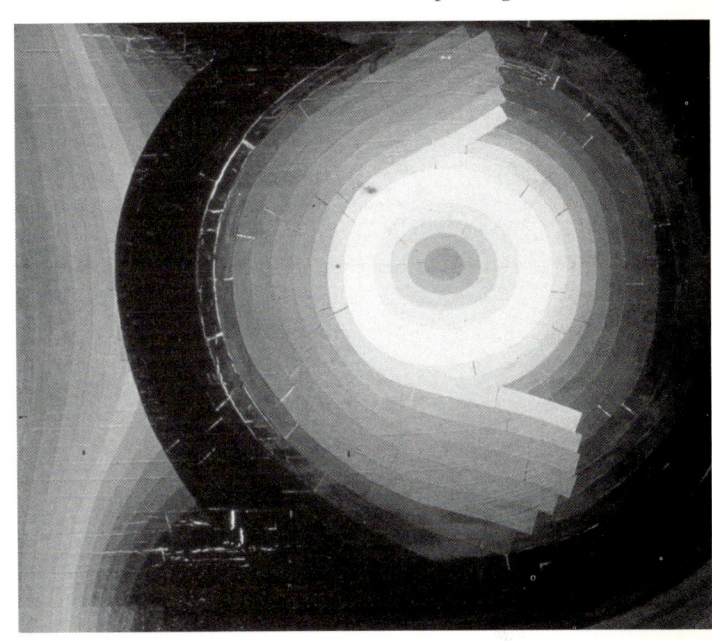

Illus. 19. OSKAR FISCHINGER, *Motion Painting No. 1*, 1947-1948, oil on plexiglas, 18 x 24". Collection of The Fischinger Archive. (not in exhibition)

terms of plastic invention. What they displayed on canvas he recorded on film, catching the performance as it evolved, in a testament to process. Fischinger felt that his filmic technique foretold a brave new world of invention:

> *"Motion paintings" give to the painter a new potentiality. He must develop and become something like a "visual-motionist," creating not only in space but also in time... he must create sentence after sentence of moving, developing visual images changing ... in continuously different ways.... Forms are basic, but changes develop from the orchestration of forms and lines and colors. This is a tremendous new world, a tremendous new tool—a challenge to creativeness comparable only to music.*[17]

Others shared his enthusiasm. Screened at the Art Center School by Lorser Feitelson in 1947, *Motion Painting #1* earned ovations from viewers who packed the auditorium.[18] Two years later, it won the *Grand Prix* at the International Film Festival in Brussels and currently stands as a masterpiece in the annals of film animation.

During the late 1940s, Fischinger turned his attention to stereoptics. While reflecting the vogue for 3-D movies, his Stereo paintings stand distinctive as early ventures in Optical art. Premiered in 1951 at the Frank Perls Gallery in Beverly Hills, they foreshadowed the later work of artists such as Victor Vasarely, Yacov Agam, and Bridget Riley.[19]

In order to finance his abstract movies and paintings and to support his family, which in the 1950s included five children, Fischinger created promotional films for television. Among these commercial projects were animated pitches for Muntz T.V. and special effects for *Captain Midnight*.[20]

Meanwhile, the artist sustained his pictorial focus on cosmic themes, as witnessed by *Yellow Moon*

Fig. 9. OSKAR FISCHINGER, *Yellow Brown,* 1944, oil on celotex, 32 x 38". Long Beach Museum of Art, Long Beach, California.

and *Tower* [color pl. 24 and 25]. Snowflake discs in the latter spin gracefully in their orbits, leaving webs of delicate trails in their wake. In contrast to this fluid gliding, elements in *Tower* race in sharp, staccato bursts. From a bright nucleic spark in a midnight void, filaments explode into crystalline stars.

Fischinger took heart in his work from the support of like-minded friends in the arts. Among those included in his social sphere were musicians Leopold Stokowski and Edgar Varese, photographer and film historian Lou Jacobs, Jr., experimental filmmakers James and John Whitney, film director William Dieterle, and talent agent Paul Kohner. While working at the Disney Studios, Fischinger befriended Ub Iwerks, Robert McIntosh and Jules Engel whose devotion to abstraction he shared and encouraged.[21]

The Fischingers were especially close to sculptor-designer Harry Bertoia and his wife Brigitta Valentiner (daughter of the director of the Los Angeles County Museum of Art) and with Blue Four dealer Galka Scheyer. A kindred spirit, Scheyer shared their commitment to abstraction and, further, bolstered them financially during difficult times. Like Karl Nierendorf, she afforded them access to her outstanding collection of modern art which she enriched with a few Fischinger pieces. Also figuring prominently in their orbit were Scheyer's lawyer Milton Wichner, whose holdings now can be seen at the Long Beach Museum of Art, U.C.L.A. librarian Kate Steinitz, art historian Alois Schardt, and artist Lorser Feitelson.[22] Appreciated by discerning patrons, Fischinger's paintings entered many public and private collections. They also were chosen for group exhibitions throughout the country, appearing at, among others, the Solomon R. Guggenheim Museum in New York (1942 and 1945), the Art Institute of Chicago in Illinois (1947), the San Francisco Museum of Art (1947), the Los Angeles County Museum of Art (1948, 1952, 1953), the Pasadena Art Museum (1959), the Long Beach Museum of Art (1963), the University of California at Los Angeles (1961), the Fisher Art Gallery of the University of Southern California (1963), the Long Beach Museum of Art (1964 and 1981), the San Francisco Museum of Modern Art (1976), the National Collection of Fine Arts in Washington, D.C. (1977), and the Laguna Art Museum (1982).

After his solo debut in New York in 1938, Fischinger was honored in a series of one-man shows, at the Stendahl Gallery in Los Angeles (1938), the American Contemporary Gallery in Hollywood (1947), the Art Center School in Los Angeles (1949), the Forsythe Gallery in Hollywood (1950), the Frank Perls Gallery in Beverly Hills (1951), the San Francisco Museum of Art (1953), the Pasadena Art Museum (1956), the Ernest Raboff Gallery in Los Angeles (1963 and 1964), the Long Beach Museum of Art (1970), the Goethe Center in San Francisco (1971), Occidental College (1973), and, most recently, at the Tobey C. Moss Gallery in Los Angeles

(1982 and 1988).[23]

During the 1950s Fischinger suffered a series of strokes which progressively drained his strength. Debilitated by these seizures, which were exacerbated by diabetes, he died of heart failure in Los Angeles on 31 January 1967.[24]

NOTES

1. Elfriede Fischinger, interview with author, 2 October 1977, and telephone conversation, 29 August 1984.

2. Dr. William Moritz, "The Films of Oskar Fischinger," *Film Culture*, Nos. 58-60 (New York, H. Gantt, 1974), 37-188. (These groundbreaking studies of Fischinger and his work provided valuable insights for this essay.)

3. Ibid., 57-60.

4. Joan M. Lukach, *Hilla Rebay: In Search of the Spirit in Art* (New York: George Braziller, 1983), 140-141.

5. Moritz, "The Films of Oskar Fischinger," 61.

6. Ibid., 61-64. For further discussion of Fischinger's relationship with the Disney Studios see Moritz's enlightening "Fischinger at Disney Or, Oskar in the Mousetrap," *Millimeter*, 5, No. 2 (February 1977), 25-30, and 65-67, and Moritz's "Oskar Fischinger: 'Fantasia's' Forerunner," *Coast F.M. and Fine Arts*, 11, No. 6 (June 1970), 44-45.

7. Moritz, "The Films of Oskar Fischinger," 66.

8. Ibid., 67, and Elfriede Fischinger, interview with author, 2 October 1977.

9. Elfriede Fischinger, interview with author, 2 October 1977.

10. Ibid. Mrs. Fischinger relates that her husband staunchly resisted ties with religious groups but briefly joined the Anthroposophic Society of Ding le Mei in the 1940s due to Hilla von Rebay's insistence.

11. Moritz, "The Importance of Being Fischinger," *International Animated Film Festival*, Ottawa, Canada, 1976, 2-6.

12. Elfriede Fischinger, telephone conversation with author, 29 August 1984.

13. Additionally, Fischinger shared with Kandinsky an interest in correspondences, or the coincident experience of different sense perceptions. Deriving from the preoccupations of the nineteenth-century Symbolists, synaesthesia was a subject of interest to many European abstractionists, particularly those with a mystical bent. Responsive to vanguard currents of thought, Fischinger and Kandinsky explored along parallel tracks the interactive effects of sight and sound. They may have been influenced further by Goethe and Rudolf Steiner, as well as by the Gestalt psychologists.

14. Long fascinated with the abstract play of pure colored lights, Fischinger, according to his wife and Dr. Moritz, had experimented in Europe with a color-projection machine. In 1950 he brought his experiments to fruition with his remarkable Lumigraph, an apparatus resembling a piano that cast colored beams of light on a large white screen. While akin to the color organ that engineer-artist Charles Dockum of Altadena had earlier invented, Fischinger's Lumigraph was simpler and more compact, free of the complicated instrumentation that Dockum's required. Although the two artists were aware of one another's work -- Hilla Rebay had at one time asked Dockum to spy on Fischinger -- they seemed, according to Mrs. Fischinger (interview with author, 29 August 1984), uninterested in comparing notes.

15. Moritz offers an illuminating discussion of this movie in "The Films of Oskar Fischinger," 71 and 159-161.

16. Paul Klee, "Creative Credo," 1920, originally published in *Schopferische Konfession*, ed. Kasimir Edschmid (Berlin: Eric Reiss, 1920, *Tribune der Kunst und Zeit*, No. 13). English translation by Norbert Guterman from *The Inward Vision: Watercolors, Drawings and Writings by Paul Klee* (New York: Harry N. Abrams, 1959), 5-10.

17. Statement by the artist in an exhibition flier, *Oskar Fischinger*, Pasadena Art Museum, Pasadena, California, December 1956.

18. Elfriede Fischinger, interviews with author, 2 October 1977 and 12 August 1985, and Moritz, "The Films of Oskar Fischinger," 73.

19. Typically diptychs, the Stereo paintings consisted of like but unidentical images that represented left and right visual data. When seen through a viewfinder, the two depictions would merge into a single figuration that advanced illusionistically toward the beholder. For detailed descriptions of these paintings see Moritz, "The Films of Oskar Fischinger," 72, and for reproductions of two pieces see *Bildmusik: The Art of Oskar Fischinger*, Long Beach Museum of Art, Long Beach, California, 1970.

20. Elfriede Fischinger, interview with author, 29 August 1984, and Moritz, "The Films of Oskar Fischinger," 71, and "Chronology," *Bildmusik: Art of Oskar Fischinger*.

21. Elfriede Fischinger, interview with author, 2 October 1977, and Moritz, "The Films of Oskar Fischinger," 68-69.

22. Ibid.

23. Tobey C. Moss supplied this chronology in her exhibition catalogue, *Oskar Fischinger: A Retrospective*, Tobey C. Moss Gallery, Los Angeles, 1988.

24. Moritz, "The Films of Oskar Fischinger," 78.

Frederick Hammersley

(b. 1919)

A preeminent hard-edge painter, Frederick Hammersley enriched the Los Angeles art scene during the fifties and sixties with his stately, geometric abstractions. Born and raised in Salt Lake City, Utah, Hammersley studied at the University of Idaho for two years before moving to Los Angeles in 1940. Enrolling at Chouinard Art Institute, he took courses from Rico Lebrun whose virtuosic art and instruction left him greatly impressed.[1] With the outbreak of the Second World War, he joined the Army and served in its Infantry and Signal Corps in England, France and Germany. Upon his return to civilian status, he resumed his studies at Chouinard, and then in 1947 transferred to the Jepson Art Institute to train again with Lebrun.

A gifted draftsman, Hammersley was soon teaching his own art classes at Jepson and earning high regard for his masterful contour drawing. The linear strength that he showed in these drawings transferred to his paintings, which display a similar fine-tuned control. In 1952 these paintings became abstract, conceived, the artist informs us, on a spontaneous "hunch."[2]

As one of these early intuitive pieces, *Upon* [color pl. 26] states its non-objective intentions with clarity and conviction. Forms, treated with utmost precision, disport themselves with ease and assurance on a neutral field. Carefully placed within the frame, they yield a work tightly balanced and classically wrought.

The artist, in fact, stresses this placement by his judiciously chosen title. Regarding his titles as "second frames," he applies them to works after completion and keys them to the imagery's affective thrust. Thus, with *Upon*, he makes the viewer acutely aware of how the shapes sit atop one another and how they relate to the ground at their base. Subtly, and with measured refinement, these figurations respond to the pull of their neighbors. The rhythmic dance that they perform on the surface lends the painting an organic air.

Central to Hammersley's oeuvre, these organic rhythms stave off stasis and keep his images blithely alive. Often, too, they reveal an aesthetic wit, one which counters conventions, as in *Upon*, by skewing geometries. Thus, circles are spliced or pinched into teardrops and triangles curve with stiletto points. Abetting these quirky twists of construction are festive hues that spice the field with a vibrancy.

By the late 1950s Hammersley's works had distilled to a few basic shapes which upheld the stringent planarity of *Upon*. At the same time, they expanded in size and brightened in hue so as to attain an optical brilliance. Their winning conjunction of taut figuration and bright coloration made an impact on critic Jules Langsner, who included them in the fabled *Four Abstract Classicists* show that he organized at the Los Angeles County Museum of Art in 1959. Like the elegant paintings of John McLaughlin, Lorser Feitelson, and Karl Benjamin with which they were grouped, Hammersley's works treated formalist issues of placement, edge, surface, and structure with thoughtful regard. Langsner, as earlier noted, linked the four artists by their calculated handling and by their fusion of space and form into a Yin-Yang embrace. He found Hammersley's shapes to be poetic, indicative of "growing things," and his hues to exude a "carnival air."[3]

While painting these engaging abstractions, Hammersley taught classes at the Jepson Art Institute from 1948 to 1951, at the Pasadena Art Museum from 1956 to 1961, and at Pomona College from

1953 to 1962. In 1964 he accepted a teaching post at Chouinard Art Institute and four years later joined the faculty of the University of New Mexico in Albuquerque where he still lives and creates geometric paintings of stately authority.

Hammersley's oeuvre was selected for such prestigious invitational shows as the Whitney Museum of American Art's *Geometric Abstraction in America* and *Fifty California Artists* (both in 1962), the Museum of Modern in Art's *The Responsive Eye* (1965), and the Los Angeles County Museum of Art's *California - Five Footnotes to Modern Art History* (1977). Additionally, his works were honored in a succession of one-man exhibitions at the Pasadena Art Museum (1961), the Heritage Gallery in Los Angeles (1961 and 1963), Occidental College (1962), the California Palace of the Legion of Honor in San Francisco (1962), the La Jolla Art Museum (1963), the Santa Barbara Museum of Art (1965), the Hollis Galleries in San Francisco (1966), the University of New Mexico in Albuquerque (1969 and 1975), and L.A. Louver Gallery in Venice, California (1978).[4] During the 1980s Hammersley was represented by the Hoshour Gallery in Albuquerque, New Mexico and by Modernism in San Francisco.

NOTES

1. Frederick Hammersley, interview with author, 14 and 19 July 1981. A biographical synopsis and an essay on the artist by Van Deren Coke, reprinted with permission from the catalogue *Frederick Hammersley: A Retrospective Exhibition*, University of New Mexico Art Museum, Albuquerque, New Mexico, 1975, appears in *Frederick Hammersley*, L. A. Louver Gallery, Venice, California, 1978.

2. Hammersley, "About My Painting," p. 2 of a speech delivered on 6 October 1961, and "My Geometrical Paintings," *Leonardo*, Vol.3, (Great Britain: Pergamon Press, 1970), 181-184.

3. Jules Langsner, *Four Abstract Classicists*, Los Angeles County Museum of Art, Los Angeles, California, 1959, unpaginated.

4. Data was provided by L.A. Louver Gallery, Venice, California.

Illus. 20. FREDERICK HAMMERSLEY, *Abstraction*, 1953, oil on cardboard, 15 x 16". The Oakland Museum, Oakland, California. (not in exhibition)

Peter Krasnow

(1887-1979)

Animated by a *joie de vivre*, Peter Krasnow approached his art during its sixty-year course with energy and verve. A definitive Romantic artist, he spurned the trappings of success, living with willful austerity in a three-room cabin built with his own hands and eschewing all diversions that might distract him from his craft.

Born in 1887 in Zawill, a small Ukranian village, Krasnow formed an attachment to craft early in life. As a child of six, he learned to grind and mix paint from his housepainter father, to whom he was apprenticed in his teens.[1] In the wake of the Russian pogroms Krasnow fled to the United States, settling in Chicago in 1908 to study at the Art Institute. After earning his diploma in 1915 and working briefly as a children's art instructor at the Hebrew Institute of Chicago, Krasnow married social worker Rose Bloom and moved with her to New York City in 1919. While his wife taught Hebrew classes, Krasnow labored at manual jobs and tried to establish himself in his profession. His efforts were rewarded in 1922 when the prestigious Whitney Studio Club mounted an exhibition in his honor. Yet despite the success of this debut, Krasnow felt dissatisfied with his work and with congested tenement life in Manhattan. Lured by gentle weather and open space, he ventured with his wife to Southern California.

After six months of travel, the couple reached Glendale in the fall of 1922. In December of that year Krasnow participated in a four-person exhibition at the Los Angeles County Museum of History, Science and Art. Two months later, in February 1923, he was invited by Stanton Macdonald Wright to join the seminal *Group of Independent Artists of Los Angeles Exhibition*. This, together with his appearance in Whitney Studio Club Annuals of 1925 and 1926 and in one-man shows at the Los Angeles County Museum in 1927, the Oakland Municipal Art Gallery in 1928, the Stendahl Art Galleries in 1930, and the California Palace of the Legion of Honor in 1931, stamped Krasnow as a leading California modernist.

During these years Krasnow enjoyed an active social life, carousing with a small but energetic avant-garde. Included within his social orbit were photography critic Sadikichi Hartmann, architects Rudolph Schindler, Richard Neutra, Kem Weber, and Gregory Ain, bookseller Jake Zeitlin, Blue Four agent and art educator Galka Scheyer, pioneer Synchromist Stanton Macdonald-Wright, painters Lorser Feitelson, Knud Merrild, Boris Deutsch, and Henrietta Shore, film directors Lewis Milestone and Josef von Sternberg, art critics Anthony Anderson and Arthur Millier, and photographer Edward Weston. From the Westons the Krasnows purchased a parcel of land on which Peter constructed a studio cottage in 1924.[2] Headquartered in this simple shelter, he painted, sculpted, and dwelled for the next fifty-five years, intermingling his life and his art in a grand but spartan way.

Following a three-year sojourn in France from 1931 to 1934, Krasnow focused intensely on wood sculpture. Motivated by the truth-to-materials principle, he sought to exploit wood's natural traits, as he discussed in a 1944 article in *Arts and Architecture* magazine:

> ...*wood follows its own indigenous command. Nature and function must be retained inviolate. In the series of ordered sequences of form, and the progressive variations from plane to plane that make up the body of a work, the character of the material and the*

dynamics of its own demands must sanction concept and treatment.... Where the purity of the wood forms are authentically projected their harmonizing relationships with the character of the medium proper will substantiate the quality of the work.[3]

Krasnow's way of working yielded sculptures of bold, uncompromising power with a raw, unfinished look. Retaining memories of their origins,

Fig. 10. PETER KRASNOW, *Mahogany*, 1933, wood, 40" tall. Judah L. Magnes Museum Collection, Berkeley, California.

these monumental tree forms, some more than nine feet high, loom over the viewer as commanding organic presences.

Less imposing are Krasnow's elegant statuettes [color pl. 27 and fig. 10], which reveal a debt to tribal art filtered through Brancusi. With their upright bodies organically swelling and crowned by ovoid heads, they evince a likeness to ancestor figures of African cults.

In the early forties, Krasnow invented what he termed *demountables*, or plugged-and-slotted sculptures composed of interlocked sections of wood [fig. 11 and color pl. 28]. Participatory in concept, they were meant to involve the beholder and thus could be dismantled and theoretically grouped at will. The ethos operative in these works is that of carpentered assemblage comprising a joining of separate parts rather than a carving away. The jerry-built piece in the Fox collection [color pl. 28], brings units together in ad-hoc formations that insist upon their status as art even as they hint of their prior worldly functions. Crafted from furniture odds and ends, it links blocks and dowels and bent arms of chairs in an assemblage as balanced as that of acrobats in a finale pose.

Often Krasnow's demountables bear anthropomorphic qualities akin to those of his carved statuettes. Echoing the stance of the human body and sporting planked or knobbed heads, these whimsical figures seem to aspire to the status of homo sapiens. The anorexic duo in the Skirball collection put one in mind of a genteel couple—he tall and thin with a bone in his head, she short and knobby, standing skirted on a slim wooden leg. By virtue of their staging and extreme attenuation, they call to mind Max Ernst's *Lunar Asparagus* of 1935, although Krasnow claims that at the time he was not familiar

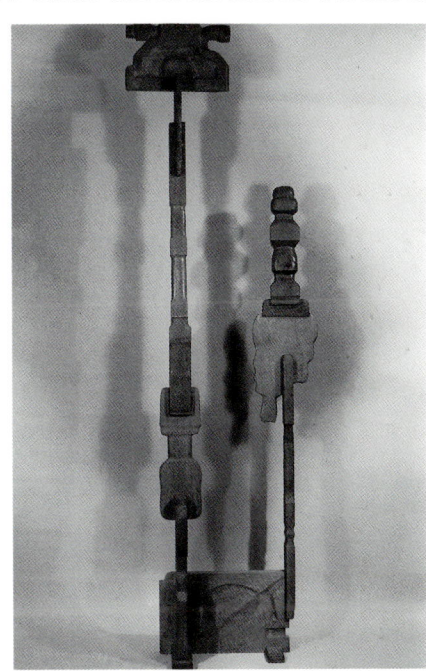

Fig. 11. PETER KRASNOW, *Demountable*, ca. 1935, mixed woods, 104 3/8 x 24 1/4 x 12 1/4". Skirball Museum of the Hebrew Union College, Los Angeles, California.

with this well-known Surrealist work.

Krasnow's demountables bear a resemblance to Isamu Noguchi's multipartite sculptures. In both artists' works, disparate pieces assembled together retain their particularity while acting in concert to yield an evocative whole. Krasnow's, however, rely exclusively on wood, thereby attaining an approachable warmth which differs from the chilly formality of Noguchi's stone. Compared to Noguchi's,

Fig. 12. PETER KRASNOW, *K-6*, 1942, oil on board, 24 x 28". The Oakland Museum, Oakland, California. Estate of the artist.

they are more homespun and humble, more ingenuous in address.[4] Informally gathered, they invite a hands-on response.

The playfulness of these objects contrasts starkly with the high sense of purpose that Krasnow's oil paintings of the early forties displayed. Born of an intense reaction to the Holocaust, they comprised an attempt to deal with the horrors of war through a pictorial language that would embody universal truths. Toward this end, Krasnow turned from his prior representational style to develop an art of purist geometry. Focusing on properties exclusive to easel painting, he exploited flatness and chroma, raising the key of his palette as he compacted space. "Color perspective instead of linear perspective," Krasnow resolved, later noting how "color came pure and unadulterated ... to play upon the surface in pools of light."[5]

Krasnow's efforts to purify the medium were not unlike those of New York artists Barnett Newman, Mark Rothko, and Adolph Gottlieb who were concurrently striving to refine their means through an emphasis on color and surface structure. Krasnow's aim to "eliminate all superfluous growth ... save the roots and let painting stand upon its own strengths,"[6] compares with Newman's intent to rid his work of "obsolete props...that evoke associations with outmoded images,"[7] and with Gottlieb's and Rothko's goal to destroy illusionism.[8] It is more than coincidental that these impulses surfaced at the same historical moment—during the early years of the war—when civilization seemed destined for imminent collapse. Feeling compelled to "save the medium" and, by extension, human culture from what they perceived as its effete condition, Krasnow and these New York artists embarked upon a purification drive.

The results of this reductive process reveal themselves in Krasnow's paintings of the war years, which are simply and non-referentially titled with his surname initial followed by a number and the year of execution. Taking his cue from Mondrian, whom he held in high regard,[9] Krasnow anchored primary shapes to flat, structural grids, believing that these elemental units would be widely understood. Los Angeles art critic and painter Grace Clements concurred with the artist in a 1946 review of his paintings in which she compared their form and intention to those of Mondrian. Like Krasnow, she interpreted them metaphorically, finding their sturdy construction and interlocked shapes to symbolize a new world order based upon the "equality, unity, and fraternity ... to which enlightened man aspires."[10]

In contrast, however, to Mondrian and his American legatees, Krasnow inflected his architectonic formats with hedonistic color. Significantly, the black lines, white blocks, and primary palette on which de Stijl was based absent themselves from his paintings, which develop exotic hues and raise them to a brilliant pitch.

Krasnow's flexible stance toward bilateral symmetry also sets him apart from the Neo-Plasticists who favored asymmetrical formats to achieve a balance of "unequal but equivalent oppositions." In fig. 13 and fig. 14, Krasnow brackets a central core with mirroring columns of interlocked bars that secure this axiality. The bright bricks of color stacked atop each other seem designed in their stepped ascension to stimulate feelings of hope.

It was, in fact, Krasnow's intention to inspire optimism, believing that a buoyant vision might countermand despair. Thus, he conceived his works as symbolic vessels, paradigms of universal peace:

Fig. 13. **PETER KRASNOW,** *K-1,* 1944, oil on board, 48 x 35⅞". San Francisco Museum of Modern Art. Gift of the artist.

I painted again as darker grew the nights and bleaker the days. Between alerts, blackouts, rationing, brighter grew my palette ... symmetry for order, color for light. Now, when tragedy was at the deepest point, my paintings breathed joy and light—color structure instead of battle scenes, symmetry to repair broken worlds.[11]

Perceived as anodynes for the global conflagration, Krasnow's paintings were meant to embody the rationality, beauty, and light then threatened with extinction. Like the Constructivists and other Utopians after the First World War, Krasnow trusted in art's redemptive power. As such, his stable grids and luminous hues were meant to stand as correlatives for a perfected state of peace.

Yet even as they entertain a lofty ideal, Krasnow's paintings implicate everyday life as they conjure up the modern cubic architecture of Los Angeles. Indeed, their T-square formations of right-angled blocks align them with post-and-lintel constructions, while their flat facades, relieved at measured intervals by horizontal bars, give the impression of fenestrated walls. In light of Krasnow's long-standing friendships with architects Schindler, Neutra, Weber, and Ain, the tectonic feel of his work comes as no surprise. Clearly, Krasnow was conversant with these noted designers' streamlined buildings which dotted the local cityscape and appeared in frequent reproduction in *Arts and Architecture* magazine, a journal which featured his own work as well.[12]

Krasnow's penchant for architectonic structure fused in the mid-forties with an interest in eccentric figuration. Attesting to this move toward formal invention is the untitled piece of color pl. 30 which combines irregular shapes and notational glyphs with notched planks reminiscent of the demountables. The work has a musical quality, conveyed by its rhythmic calibration and intimations of orchestral notes.

As evidenced in color pl. 30, 31 and 32, Krasnow also began in the late forties to fill his

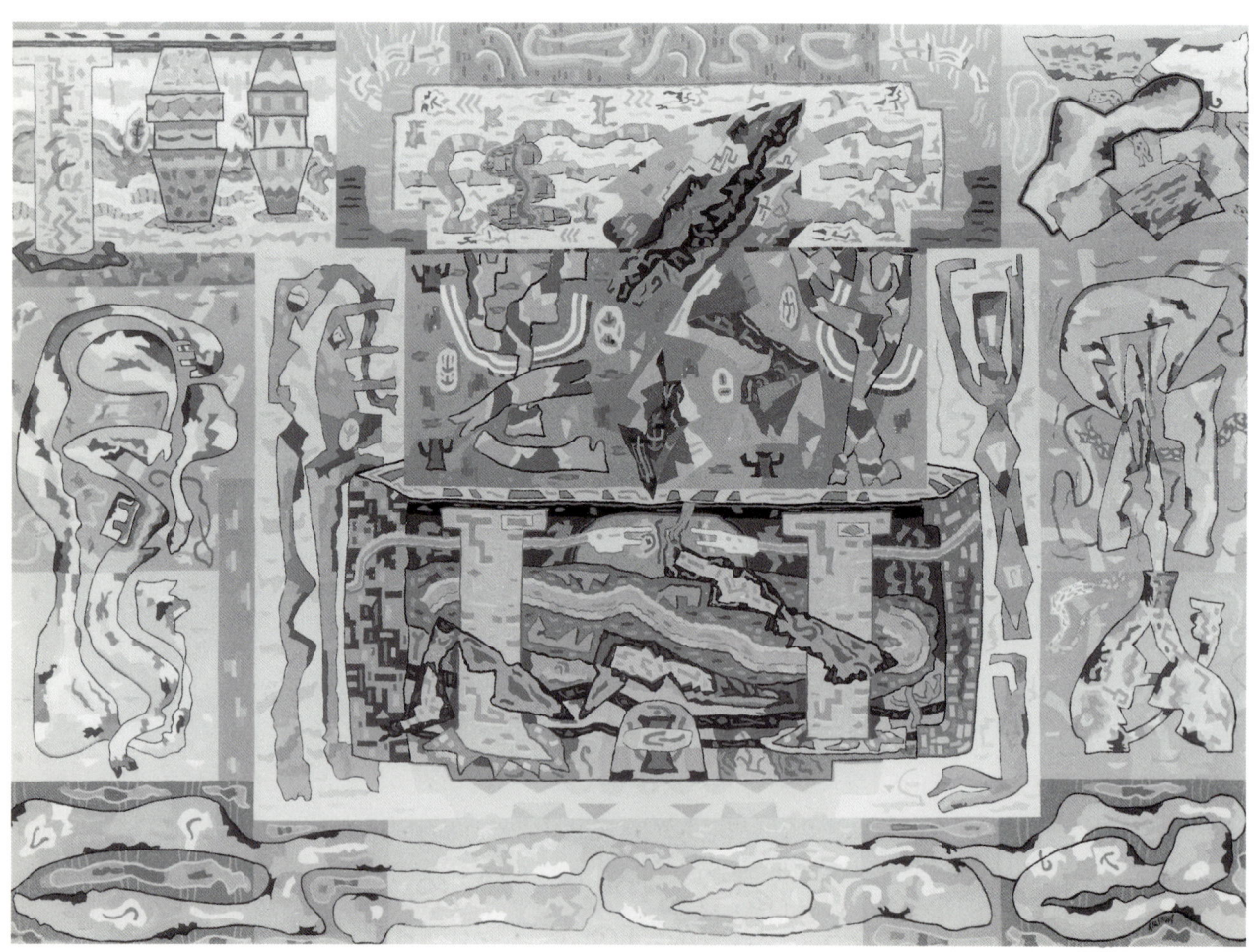

Fig. 14. PETER KRASNOW, *K-3*, 1953, oil on board, 47 3/4 x 67 1/8". San Francisco Museum of Modern Art. Gift of the artist.

Constructivist formats with pictographs and emblematic signs. In this he compares with New York artists Adolph Gottlieb and Joaquin Torres-Garcia who likewise placed ideographs and totems in sectioned compositions.

Krasnow, however, veers from these painters in his decorative élan and his more inventive palette, a quintessential product of Los Angeles. His juxtaposition of candied pinks and aquatic blues, henna mauves and grassy greens recalls the region's peculiar amalgam of the rustic with the plastic, the organic with the contrived. In his adroit handling of color, Krasnow rivaled Stanton Macdonald-Wright who also devised daringly luminous spectral hues around which he built his compositions. Importantly, though, he avoided the hazy, transparent effects which characterized Macdonald-Wright's Synchromist work.

If his radiant coloration approached that of Macdonald-Wright, Krasnow's biomorphic forms reveal an interest in primal sources which the Synchromist shunned. In keeping with archaizing trends of the 1940s, his pictographs and tapestried grounds invoke tribal and primitive models. Geometric patterns hint of Navajo blankets and Oriental rugs, while ciphers suggest Egyptian hieroglyphs and Phoenician script. Krasnow, however, denied these referents, claiming that his images sprang Athena-like from his head:

> *I was never at a loss, or in want of new form, material, content and subject matter.... [There was] an untapped source ever flowing more freely from my mind through my brushes. The knowing ones attached labels, Egyptian, Cambodian, Mayan, any ancient civilization meriting aesthetic recognition.*[13]

He did not, however, disclaim his allegiance to his environs or to his heritage. Thus, one often finds in his work stylized Hebrew letters, sometimes given positions of honor, sometimes placed on their sides. Intermingled with these ciphers are fanciful shapes and repetitive patterns that seem to imply elements of nature.

Sensed in this series of late forties paintings is an incipient spatial pull which tends to compromise the flatness of their fields. Although the figures are kept insistently flat, illusionism seeps into selected spots. In *K-6*, 1949 [color pl. 31], for example, tilting bars along the edges thrust toward an inner frame in which pleated panels push in and out like a folding screen. One gains a sensation of airborne perspective, an impression of sighting a "peaceable kingdom" from Olympian heights. This global view of the land, in turn, supports a cabalistic reading as humble and grand creatures take their place in an orderly cosmos conceived by omniscient plan. Vegetal and animal forms—snakes and amoebae, a man and a cow—fill the nooks of the composition like scrapbook mementos attesting to nature's abundance. Yet for all their allusions, these curious sprites refuse to disclose their identities. Even the artist found them to be enigmatic, confessing that they took him by surprise as they issued from his brush. Likening them to the unformed creatures of *Genesis*, he noted that they seemed to suggest a state of incipient being.[14]

Krasnow's sensitized relation to the ecosphere has a generous spirit that grants living beings, regardless of stature, an intrinsic worth. Seemingly, Martin Buber's "I-Thou" stance, with its neo-Hasidic embrace of the world, was one that Krasnow shared.[15] This acceptant embrace led him to notice what others might ignore and to celebrate the local terrain with unabashed delight. In *K-3* [fig. 14], for instance, he appears to boast of the nearby Mojave with snaking forms and with sizzling tints that conjure up the glare of a desert sun. Totemic figures with upraised arms enhance the desert aura as they recall votary objects of American Indian tribes.

The evocative character of Krasnow's forms encourages one to interpret them in Jungian terms as archetypes or "images of the human collective unconscious."[16] Krasnow, in fact, granted credence to these Jungian concepts which he echoed in a rationale for his imagery:

> *My paintings subscribe to no period or school. Their visual concept may ostensibly reveal characteristics of Time and Place, but the roots reach deep into ethnic strains of ancient culture through which the archetype*

emerges as indicator of the universal and eternal urge towards creation.[17]

Krasnow's belief in archetypes was not exclusive to him but was shared by many artists of the 1940s, including Jackson Pollock, whose *Guardians of the Secret* (1943, San Francisco Museum of Art) bears formal and conceptual affinities to *K-3*. Although different in palette, brushwork, and mood, both works deploy primitive totems, archaic script, and writhing organisms in stratified fields. Within each painting two sentries stand guard, securing boxes between them that harbor some arcane code. In addition to implicating archetypal forms, the two pieces wed impulses from Cubism and Surrealism as they conjoin strange biomorphs in layered, planar grids. Yet for all their similarities, they are ultimately distinctive; this would suggest that their points in common stem from like responses to strains of feeling and thought in the culture of their time.

And, for Krasnow, those strains included the special feel of Southern California, which he expressed through glowing coloration. It is here in his unusual palette that Krasnow's achievement resides, for his hues are at once *sui generis* and indicative of the stunning chromatics for which the region is known. Not only are his pigments distinctive, but they seem to emanate phosphorescent light. "California for color, American earth for form,"[18] exulted Krasnow as he explained his intent to reify the brilliant light and sturdy foundation of Los Angeles.

At the same time that he praised his adopted city, Krasnow interacted guardedly with its art community. On the one hand he enjoyed social intercourse, and on the other he cherished his solitude, deeming privacy essential to his creative growth. Thus, during the 1940s and 1950s he limited personal ties to a small coterie that included art critics Jules Langsner and Frode Dann, novelist Irving Stone, artists June Wayne, Grace Clements, and Hilaire Hiler, sculptor Harold Gebhardt, musicians Fred and Frieda Fox and engineer-light-artist Charles Dockum. Sequestering himself in his studio, he resisted subscriptions to magazines, rarely attended openings, and refused to join a gallery, believing that art was too sacrosanct to be subjected to the whims of the marketplace. Like Mark Rothko, he felt that art possessed a sanctity that demanded reverent care. Rather than compromise his values, he withdrew from commercial arenas, showing his works in his studio and placing them with collectors who had earned his trust.

With his anti-materialistic bias Krasnow would appear to have been a prescient neo-Marxist. Certainly, his assumption of control over the exhibition and distribution of his works foreshadowed the alternative space impulses of the present day. Notwithstanding his refusal to be co-opted by the system, Krasnow was too much the idealist, too little the collectivist to enlist in any creed's camp. His visionary faith in art and his dogged independence precluded his involvement with communal enterprise.

He did, nonetheless, wish his work to have an audience and thus participated in some group exhibitions and sanctioned several one-man shows at the California Palace of the Legion of Honor in 1931, the Fine Arts Gallery of San Diego in 1939, the University of California at Los Angeles in 1940, the Pasadena Art Institute in 1954, Scripps College in Claremont in 1964, and the Los Angeles Municipal Art Gallery in 1975. His last exhibition, co-sponsored by the Judah L. Magnes Museum in Berkeley and the Skirball Museum of the Hebrew Union College in Los Angeles, ran from 1977 to 1979. Ten months after this retrospective closed, in October 1979, Krasnow died in Los Angeles at the age of ninety-two.

In spite of their relatively limited exposure, Krasnow's sunny, assured expressions predicted certain aesthetic trends. His constructivist paintings of the 1940s, with their flat interlocked bricks of color, foretold the "hard-edge colorforms" which critic Jules Langsner lauded in the Abstract Classicists of the late fifties.[19] Recognizing this, artist-critic Fidel Danieli hailed them as "milestones in the development of American geometric painting."[20]

Krasnow's early celebration of the region's plastic glitz foreshadowed the "Finish Fetish" of the 1960s, also known as the "L.A. Look." By joining high-keyed chromas to quirky figuration, Krasnow also prophesied the spunky subjectivity of the 1980s. Moreover, his focus on ethnic content at a time when it was viewed as retrograde paved the way for artists such as Ruth Weisberg, Carlos Almarez and Frank Romero. In a similar way, his embrace of Hollywood's tinseled charm, which most artists chose to ignore, cleared a path that Billy Al Bengston, Ed Ruscha, Joe Fay, Peter Alexander, and David Hockney would later pursue.

Defying formal mandates and critical taboos, Krasnow marched to the rhythms of his self-directed tune. Crucially, in the process of heeding his inner voice, he invented correlatives for the city's natural splendor and synthetic sheen.

NOTES

1. Peter and Rose Krasnow, interviews with author, 23 January, 6 June, and 12 December 1978. Other sources of information for this essay were Nancy Berman and Joseph Hoffman's *Peter Krasnow: A Retrospective Exhibition of Paintings, Sculpture, and Graphics*, The Judah Magnes Museum, Berkeley, California, and the Skirball Museum of Union College, Los Angeles, California, 1977; Fidel Danieli, "Peter Krasnow: Pioneer Los Angeles Modernist," Artweek 6, No. 12 (22 March 1975), 5-6; and Dr. Aimée Brown Price, "The Work of Peter Krasnow," Humanities Working Paper, No. 26, California Institute of Technology, February, 1979.

2. Peter and Rose Krasnow, interview with author, 6 June 1978.

3. Krasnow, "An Honest Approach to Wood Sculpture," *Arts and Architecture*, 56, No. 1 (1944), 19.

4. Krasnow in an interview with the author on 23 January 1978 discounted Noguchi's influence on his work and claimed, to the contrary, that Noguchi had attended an exhibition of the demountables at the Beverly Fairfax Community Center in 1943. Krasnow's assertions, however, have not been verified.

5. Krasnow, "The Power of Art," *Los Angeles Institute of Contemporary Art Journal*, 8 (November/December 1975), 11-13.

6. Ibid., 11.

7. Barnett Newman, "The Sublime Is Now," excerpt from "The Ides of Art, Six Opinions on What is Sublime in Art?" *Tiger's Eye* (New York), No. 6 (15 December 1948), 52-53 as quoted in Herschel B. Chipp, Peter Selz, and Joshua C. Taylor, *Theories of Modern Art: A Source Book by Artists and Critics* (Berkeley: University of California Press, 1968), 553.

8. Adolph Gottlieb and Mark Rothko, "Statement," which appeared in Edward Alden Jewell's column in the *New York Times*, 13 June 1943 as quoted by Chipp, et. al, in *Theories of Modern Art*, 545.

9. Krasnow, interviews with the author, 23 January, 6 June, and 12 December 1978.

10. Grace Clements, "Peter Krasnow," *Arts and Architecture*, 43, No. 2 (February 1946), 32-34.

11. Krasnow, "The Power of Art," 12.

12. The magazine had devoted a page of its December 1931 issue to Krasnow's sculptures and bas reliefs. In January 1944 it published the artist's essay, "An Honest Approach to Wood Sculpture," accompanied by photographs of his works by Edward Weston and Frank Trieste. The February 1946 edition of this journal featured on its cover Krasnow's *K-1, Interlocking Forms* of 1944 (now in the San Francisco Museum of Modern Art) and carried Grace Clements' article on his paintings.

13. Krasnow, "The Power of Art," 12.

14. Krasnow, interview with author, 19 December 1978.

15. Krasnow had been acquainted with Hasidic groups in his native Zawill and was conversant with their philosophy. In discussions with the author he noted that often while painting he experienced moments of mystic illumination comparable to those described by neo-Hasidic scholar Abraham Joshua Heschel in *The Prophets* (New York: Harper Colophon Books, Harper & Row, Publishers, 1962).

16. C.G. Jung, *The Spirit in Man, Art, and Literature*, translated by R.F.C. Hull, Bollingen Series XX, 15 (Princeton, New Jersey: Princeton University Press, 1966), 80-91.

17. Krasnow, "A Statement," *The Work of Peter Krasnow*, Scripps College, Lang Galleries, Claremont, California, 1965, 9-10.

18. Krasnow, "The Power of Art," 12.

19. Jules Langsner, *Four Abstract Classicists*, Los Angeles County Museum of Art, Los Angeles, California, 1959.

20. Fidel Danieli, "Peter Krasnow: Pioneer Los Angeles Modernist," 5-6.

Rico Lebrun

(1900-1964)

I believe that if an authentic, unprecedented image of man is to appear, it will only be through a complete acceptance of that obligation to sponsor, reveal, and celebrate man's condition.[1]

Dedicating his art to the "human condition," Rico Lebrun probed problems of mortal existence with a mixture of terror and awe. If his vision was dark and insistently tragic, concerned with affliction and corrosive evil, it nonetheless sprang from an impassioned desire to supersede despair.[2]

Born in Naples, Italy on 10 December 1900, Lebrun earned a diploma from the National Technical Institute in Naples in 1917, after which he served in the Italian army. While completing his military duty, he began to study painting by taking evening courses at the Naples Academy of Fine Arts, copying Old Masters in museums, and assisting fresco painters. In 1924 he immigrated to the United States to design stained glass and oversee its production in a Springfield, Illinois factory. The following year he settled in New York City where he soon built a successful commercial art practice.

By 1930 Lebrun was prospering greatly in this career but feeling devoid of reward. He therefore abandoned his business and entered the field of fine arts. Trips to Italy to study fresco painting were followed by work in New York as a muralist on the Federal Art Project and as an instructor at the Art Students League. An impasse on the mural project and a stalemate in his marriage prompted Lebrun to move to Southern California in 1938.

Settling in Santa Barbara, he commuted to Los Angeles to conduct classes at the Chouinard Art Institute. Two years later he was teaching animators at the Disney Studios how to articulate the animal figure for the feature film *Bambi*.[3]

During the early forties Lebrun's oeuvre began to receive national attention. It was included, along with that of Knud Merrild and Helen Lundeberg, in the Museum of Modern Art's *Americans, 1942*, the inaugural exhibition of an annual series, and was selected by that same museum for its *Romantic Paintings in America* of 1944. Additionally, his work appeared in group exhibitions at New York's Whitney Museum of American Art and Metropolitan Museum and in a one-man show at the Julien Levy Gallery, also in Manhattan. With these honors, Lebrun was invited by Donald Bear, founding director of the newly opened Santa Barbara Museum of Art, to serve as artist-in-residence from 1945 to 1947.

Lebrun's work at the time featured representational figures lost in dreamy contemplation. Moodily Romantic, it typically focused upon picturesque tramps, musicians, and clowns remembered by the artist from his years in Naples. In addition to these reflective portraits, Lebrun experimented with Surrealist and Cubist modes of expression.

Pivotal in Lebrun's oeuvre are the semi-abstractions that he created of ranch equipment found on nature hikes and horseback rides in the pastoral valleys near his home. *Black Plow* [color pl. 33], one of the later works in this series, reflects his burgeoning interest in open structure and in everyday objects which he portrayed with forceful feelings. Painted in 1947, a year after Lebrun's second wife committed suicide, it seems to embody the emotional residue of the artist's bereavement. Clearly, it attains a fervor that far supersedes its identity as a prosaic tool. Interesting, too, is the way that it blends feelings of strength and aggression with those of pathos and yearning.

Invoking the pathetic fallacy, Lebrun invested this and other implements in the series with an anthropomorphic quality and, further, analogized them with the human body. In his notebooks he described them in anatomical terms, referring to the disk harrows as "vertebrate" and likening the seeding and planting devices to a locust and a mantis, which he characterized as "savage, alert, predatory."[4] This series proved to be crucial, marking Lebrun's turn from naturalism to semi-abstraction and from linear to painterly handling. Formally, it engaged figure and ground in an interactive dialogue and exploited the expressive potential of negative space. In his book *Drawings*, the artist described this critical change:

> ...*The discovery of agricultural implements was of immense help to my painting. Previously my work had been essentially linear, and I was now impatient with the isolation of objects and figures divorced from surrounding space.... Now the farm machinery had a quality of opened and colored structure, exactly what I had been looking for. Here I found expression in the new sense I needed. The expression was the structure: the interval, the span, was the physiognomy and the countenance.*[5]

His discoveries notwithstanding, Lebrun yearned for new challenges and thus accepted the post of master instructor at the recently opened Jepson Art Institute in Los Angeles near MacArthur Park. In 1947 he set up housekeeping in an apartment in the Baldwin Village complex designed by architect Reginald Johnson, whose spirited daughter Constance he would marry the following year.

A charismatic instructor with theatrical flair, Lebrun became known at Jepson for his dynamic teaching style. His drawing classes, attracting more pupils than one room could handle, filled three large studios, and his art history lectures, delivered weekly to staff and students, became standing-room-only events.[6]

Lebrun's popularity at the school was matched at the Los Angeles County Museum annuals where he frequently won top prizes. Highly regarded within the community, he rapidly earned a large following of patrons, disciples, and critics. His receipt of the coveted first prize in the Art Institute of Chicago's seminal *Abstract and Surrealist American Art* of 1947-1948 and of second place in the Metropolitan Museum of Art's *American Paintings Today* of 1951 enhanced his reputation nationwide as did reproductions of his works in *Life*, *Time*, and *Harper's Bazaar*.

From 1947 to 1950 Lebrun worked on his ambitious *Crucifixion* cycle. Heroic in conception and scope, the series comprised over two hundred drawings and paintings and a monumental triptych now in the Syracuse University collection [illus. 21]. In December 1950 the cycle was unveiled to capacity crowds at the Los Angeles County Museum of Art and then traveled early the following year to the M. H. de Young Museum in San Francisco.

Lebrun had intended to film the sequence and thus restricted his palette to black and white.

Illus. 21. RICO LEBRUN, *Crucifixion Triptych*, 1950, Syracuse University Art Collection. Gift of William C. Whitney Foundation.

His decision to limit his means also sprang from his belief, confirmed by Picasso's *Guernica*, that a monochromatic scheme would act as a "potent carrier of visual shock."[7]

In relating the series to film, Lebrun planned what he termed "tentative sequences," which were meant in the manner of avant-garde movies to evoke rather than to define. To this same end he overlapped shapes and repeated contours to conjure up cinematic motion. In attempting to forge a rapprochement between painting and film, Lebrun hoped to reach a broad audience:

In dealing with ideas, vision and techniques for the task of communicating to many, I hope for the day when a few of us, by using contemporary techniques (the camera, animation, the hand-made montage), will finally correlate some of the facts of contemporary vision, and ... collectively say what we feel about the world around us.[8]

Yet even as he addressed his era with filmic allusions, Lebrun looked retrospectively to a number of precedents. His large *Crucifixion Triptych* for instance, pays homage to Matthias Grunewald's *Isenheim Altarpiece*, to Il Rosso's *Deposition*, and, most importantly, to Picasso's magniloquent *Guernica* whose grisaille coloration and pained figuration it shares. For Lebrun, like Picasso, understood that in the barbaric clutches of evil, whether in Spain or in ancient Golgotha, hierarchic distinctions between man and beast evaporate.

Even inanimate objects, such as those in *The Wood of the Holy Cross* [fig. 16], attain an expressive dimension as their drooping forms and hovering shadows convey despondency. The dire declaration, charred with ashes and torn at its corner, and the crackling flames, smoldering fitfully over the surface, contribute their own disconsolate notes.

Comparing the cross to a decaying body, Lebrun rendered it, as he did other instruments of the Passion, as an apparitional wraith. In *Witness of the Resurrection* [color pl. 34], he cast the figures in shadow and flickered a light upon them to give them a spectral appearance. This veiling might be interpreted as a metaphor of perception, suggesting that one can only glimpse the past through the haze of historical memory.

Lebrun referred to the soldiers in this series as "nocturnal" creatures "armored against true compassion."[9] Because of their cruelty, he rendered them disfigured and disturbed. Indeed, the dreamers writhe and twist in spasmodic sleep, implying a controversion of rational norms in their entanglement. The way the one at right bares his teeth in a primal scream, his face submerged in the helmet he wears, makes him a distant cousin of the beast-headed tank in Hans Burkhardt's *War, Agony in Death* [p. 50]. Like Burkhardt's humanoid weaponry, this mutable, monstrous being exists as half sentient creature, half metal machine, deformed by iniquity.

Among the most powerful works in the series are *Woman of the Crucifixion* and *The Magdalene* [fig. 15 and color pl. 35] which incarnate agonic despair. In the former, line transmits the mourner's sobs with spasmodic jabs, while in the latter, pigment splashes down the surface to evoke her drenching in tears. A tangled skein in the one and an obdurate shell in the other imprison the penitent and imply her entrapment in unyielding grief.

Despite this dexterous handling, Lebrun did not intend to exult in his virtuosity. Rather, he sought to use his skills to assuage human affliction. Technique assumed importance to him only as a vehicle for his outrage and compassion:

So composition was born out of the shocked heart. First a man, second a draughtsman, I had to find out for myself that pain has a geometry of its own; and that my being, through a revulsion against all tolerable and

Fig. 15. RICO LEBRUN, *Woman of the Crucifixion (Mourning Woman)*, 1948, brown conte crayon and ink, 24 x 19". Collection of Mrs. Constance Lebrun Crown, Santa Barbara, California.

manageable skill, wanted to speak out in a single shout....Compassion and the resolute heart shall be the only guides, shall be, in fact, the technique.[10]

Like Burkhardt, Lebrun felt compelled to redress evil and had no qualms about dealing with the psychically ill and deformed. He conceived these Mourning Women, for example, as "bereaved mothers, empty houses pierced by screams," ravaged by remorse. Vessels of his pity and sorrow, they served him as conduits for cathartic release.

These figures invite comparison with Willem de Kooning's Women series of the early 1950s whose gestural handling and expressive distortions they share. Like de Kooning, Lebrun invoked the Existential theme of the "human predicament" by contrasting bold, athletic strokes with quivering contours that spoke of uncertainty. Moreover, Lebrun, like de Kooning, focused upon the human image which he perceived as both tragic and grand:

> *Man is the organic and spiritual marvel and the text for revelations. If I insist on themes with traditional dramatic content, on the recurring motif of the human figure disfigured by adversity, it is because I believe that painting can change what is disfigured into what is transfigured.*[11]

In 1952 Lebrun left the Jepson school and traveled to Mexico where he remained for a year and a half. While teaching at the Institute of San Miguel de Allende, he created a series of large collages which evinced an interest in formal abstraction. In *Mexican Street in the Rain*, jagged, irregular shapes spread across the planar support in a colorful patchwork montage. Denying distinctions of solid and void, they evoke the bustling congestion of village life. Cylindrical shafts with ribbed projections—abstractions of window shutters—hark back to the artist's *Black Plow* as they analogize with the human body to suggest vertebral columns.

Lebrun intended in this piece to capture the flux of insurgent life, "the illusiveness of... many forms in transit."[12] Thus, with jostling, fractional shapes he conveys the sensation of swift and disjointed sightings. These partially registered images—what

Fig. 16. RICO LEBRUN, *Wood of the Holy Cross*, 1948, oil and casein on canvas, 80 x 30". The Whitney Museum of American Art, New York.

Brian O'Doherty in reference to Robert Rauschenberg termed "the vernacular glance"[13]—vie for attention in the painting as they had in the Mexican streets.

Again, like Robert Rauschenberg, but without his Duchampian irony or youthful sense of rebellion, Lebrun maintained an approach-avoidance relationship with Abstract Expressionism. On the one hand, he shared its heroic ambition, its exultant passion, and its engagement with 'risk'—a term which he frequently used—but on the other hand, he decried its neglect of the human figure (which retrospectively proved only partially true), its improvisatory handling, and its devotion to the self-centered psyche. Although he talked about process and heeding the painting as it evolved,[14] he still presided authoritatively over aesthetic transactions. Moreover, while he saw abstraction as "intensely human"[15] and preemptively operative in his work, he refused to take it to its conclusion in non-objectivity.

Fig. 17. RICO LEBRUN, *Mexican Meat Stall*, 1954, collage, 97 x 49". Collection of Mrs. Constance Lebrun Crown, Santa Barbara, California.

Indeed, after his Mexican interlude, Lebrun resumed his prior direction, placing his art once again in the service of epic human affairs. Upon his return to Los Angeles in 1954 he began a series of drawings and paintings to memorialize the victims of the Holocaust. Knowing that moral accountability tends to wane over time, Lebrun understood what many fail to acknowledge today, that even right-minded women and men need to be reminded of humankind's bestial potential. Although emotionally drained by the Concentration Camp series, Lebrun found it to be a source of transcendence:

I wanted to remember that our image, even when disfigured by adversity, is grand in meaning; that no brutality will ever cancel that meaning: painting may increase it by changing what is disfigured into what is transfigured.[16]

Lebrun's grappling with human distress was resumed by a younger generation of Los Angeles Expressionists, among whom were Howard Warshaw, Arnold Mesches, Jan Stussy, and Edward Kienholz. That latter young master of mordant critique came to maturity in the late 1950s when Lebrun's authority was at its height. Thus, in all likelihood he would have seen Lebrun's attacks on moral depravity. Although he treated subjects closer to home with an eye to sexual politics, Kienholz yet showed a concern akin to Lebrun's with exposing corruption and degradation. Further, he did so with brutal imagery which, like Lebrun's, refused to grant an aesthetic veneer to the crimes that it reviled.

In 1958, a year after Kienholz co-founded the Ferus gallery with Walter Hopps, Lebrun left the region to teach at Yale and the next year served as an artist-in-residence at the American Academy in Rome. When he returned to Southern California, he began a monumental mural project at Pomona College in Claremont inspired by the biblical tale of Genesis. After completing the mural in 1961, Lebrun worked on a smaller, less exhaustive scale, rendering a suite of drawings and prints for Dante's *Inferno*. Stricken by cancer in 1963, Lebrun died on 9 May the following year at his home in Malibu.

Lebrun's legacy seems to be surfacing today in the dark visions of Los Angeles painter Jim Morphesis and of German Neo-Expressionist Anselm Kiefer. The former's interest in metaphors of the Passion, and the latter's concern with the moral repercussions of the Second World War, revive the Lebrun agenda. Clearly, these and other humanist painters in the resurgent Neo-Expressionist movement give Lebrun's oeuvre a new relevancy.

Devoted to issues of human existence and driven by high ambition, Lebrun aimed to reinvest art with ethical probity. If his religious subjects seem dated now, his commitment and power endure. At a distance of forty years, he still impresses us with his virtuosity and with his portraits of human strength in the grip of adversity.

NOTES

1. Rico Lebrun, statement in *New Images of Man*, The Museum of Modern Art, New York, 1959, 97.

2. Portions of this essay appeared in the author's "The Jepson Group: The School, Its Major Teachers and Their Drawings," in Nancy Dustin Wall Moure's *Drawings and Illustrations by Southern California Artists before 1950*, Laguna Beach Museum of Art, Laguna Beach, California, 1982, 44-55. A major source of information and insights for this essay were provided by Henry J. Seldis' "Beyond Virtuousity," *Rico Lebrun (1900-1964)*, Los Angeles County Museum of Art, Los Angeles, California, 1968, 11-35.

3. Frank Thomas and Ollie Johnston, *Disney Animation: the Illusion of Life* (New York: Abbeville Press, 1981), 339-342.

4. Rico Lebrun, "About Myself," *Rico Leburn, Drawings* (Berkeley: University of California Press, 1968), 10.

5. Ibid.

6. For an account of Lebrun's teaching at the school, see Ehrlich, "The Jepson Group," 45-46.

7. Lebrun, "Notes by the Artist on the Crucifixion Theme," *Rico Lebrun: Paintings and Drawings of the Crucifixion*, Los Angeles County Museum of Art, Los Angeles, California, 1950, 8.

8. Ibid.

9. Ibid.

10. Lebrun, *New Images of Man*, 97-99.

11. Lebrun, *Contemporary Religious Imagery in American Art*, Ringling Museum of Art, Sarasota, Florida, 1974, 4.

12. Lebrun, "Letter from Rico Lebrun," *Art Institute of Chicago Quarterly* I, No. 1 (1 February 1956), 18-19.

13. Brian O'Doherty, "Rauschenberg and the Vernacular Glance," *Art in America* 61 (September/October 1973), 82-87.

14. Lebrun in a letter to Donald Bear, director of the Santa Barbara Museum of Art, as quoted by Kenneth Ross, "Work of L.A. Artist Rico LeBrun[sic] Stirs Controversy," *Los Angeles Daily News*, 31 December 1949, 8.

15. Ibid.

16. Lebrun, "About Myself," 19.

Helen Lundeberg

(b. 1908)

My work has been concerned, in varying modes of pictorial structure and various degrees of representation and abstraction, with the effort to embody, and to evoke, states of mind, moods, and emotions.[1]

Seamlessly, Helen Lundeberg weds in her art a romantic penchant for fantasy with a classical sense of structure, a subjective approach to content with an objective treatment of form. In the ideal worlds that she conjures up, eternal issues of existence—birth, maturation, death, and remembrance—are borne by tranquil images that hover between reality and dream.

The calm that Lundeberg projects in her work may be traced to a peaceful childhood in rural Pasadena where she had moved with her family at the age of four from her native Chicago.[2] Intellectually gifted, Lundeberg pursued higher education at Pasadena City College, where she majored in English. After earning an Associated Arts degree in 1930, she took a drawing class from Lorser Feitelson at the Stickney Memorial School of Art in Pasadena and was so impressed with his instruction that she decided to become an artist.

By 1934 she had attained such maturity in her profession that she co-founded an art movement with Feitelson which they alternatively called "New Classicism" or "Post-Surrealism." Responsive to the example of Giorgio de Chirico, Rene Magritte, and the Italian Renaissance masters, they aimed to explore subjective content in works that were balanced and clearly wrought. "We were trying to do something with certain principles of Surrealism," she later explained, "but based on the normal functioning of the mind. There was nothing 'automatic' about our paintings; each composition was consciously planned."[3] In a catalogue essay, Lundeberg outlined the movement's parameters and its aesthetic goals:

In contrast to the surrealist program of intuitive expression and subconscious automatic recordings, Postsurrealism explores the field of psychological science to create a classic subjective expression. The pictorial elements are deliberately arranged to stimulate, in the mind of the spectator, an ordered, pleasurable, introspective activity, resulting in a configuration or subjective unity, which IS the esthetic order of the painting....[4]

This "subjective unity" well describes Lundeberg's *Double Portrait of the Artist in Time*, a stunning depiction of selfhood that has few peers [illus. 22]. Half a century after its creation, it still exerts a magnetic attraction, a power to beguile.

Musing on the issue of human maturation, the artist links her past and present selves through the device of the shadow, a reification of memory and time, projected on the wall. The equivocal relation between art and life, a theme which would long absorb her attention, plays itself out in the tension between the three-dimensional child—now but a phantom in the mind—and the flatly painted portrait of the real adult.[5]

A masterful image of psychic growth, the work personifies Jungian self-actualization via an intrasubjective *Gestalt*. Additionally, it gives a feminist reading to the oft-quoted maxim that the child is the father of the man. With characteristic clarity, the artist describes how this conception evolved:

...For the portrait of myself as a child I used a photograph ... the pose is pretty much exact. I also used the clock to show that it was a quarter past two which corresponds to the child's age. And instead of presenting myself as an adult before a painting of myself as a child ... I reversed this possibility where the child casts a shadow which is that of an adult who appears in the portrait on the wall.[6]

At once self-reflective and -referential, the painting deals with the mystery of existence, the fluidity of memory as it journeys through time, and the magic of representation as it extends the past's ephemeral holdings into the present and future. Its power resides in the eloquent voice that it gives to the interaction of art and life, yesterday's promise and today's realities.

This painting appeared with a number of other Lundeberg works in major Post-Surrealist shows at the San Francisco Museum of Art in December 1935 and at the Brooklyn Museum in New York the following spring through summer. In reviewing the latter exhibition, Edward Alden Jewell, art critic for the *New York Times*, reproduced *Double Portrait* in his newspaper column and commended Lundeberg and Feitelson as "California's universal thinkers... [who] know how to paint... and handle their brushes with cosmic authority."[7]

Shortly after this New York debut, Lundeberg, together with Feitelson and Merrild, was invited to participate in the Museum of Modern Art's epochal *Fantastic Art, Dada, and Surrealism* show of 1936. Six years later she and Merrild were again chosen by that museum for its *Americans 1942: 18 Artists from 9 States*, the first in a series that showcased native talent. With these exhibitions, augmented by the Art Institute of Chicago's *Abstract and Surrealist American Art* survey of 1947-1948, Lundeberg secured a national reputation.

Helping her earn this reputation were works such as *Microcosm and Macrocosm* [color pl. 37] which presents the theme of maturation in a cosmic paradigm. The artist, now enlarged and cropped by the framing edge, watches microbial creatures evolve from seabed to galaxy. Red-rimmed circles, signifying successive views through a looking glass, allow the viewer to witness developmental steps. Like the gray-colored images which they enclose, they function as abstractions separate from the "realistic" beings in the scene that they inhabit.

The Evanescent [color pl. 38], begun in 1941 and completed three years later, also investigates stages of life. Now, however, in seeming response to the war, it reflects a foreboding mood. Gone is the prior crystalline light and sense of new beginnings, replaced by a murky abyss, an overcast sky, and intimations of loss. At the far right a match briefly lights a dark chasm before its swift demise. Draped over a looming tombstone, two drawings align seasonal blossoms with rotations of the earth. Across the way a statuesque figure wistfully studies a flower whose transient beauty she correlates with her own. The past of this woman appears as a girl at play in the distance, while her future unfolds in the bent old crone who follows her trailing shadow to an open grave.

While retaining an interest in cyclical life, *Poetic Justice* replaces moody reverie with a wry, cerebral wit [fig. 18]. A gluttonous snail by a mountain road feasts on a leaf which it has almost devoured. Interrupting its meal, it notes a woman's hand with a disemboweled shell of one of its peers from which a plant sprouts. With a wink to ecology, the artist accords the herbivorous pest a fitting recompense.

Fig. 18. HELEN LUNDEBERG, *Poetic Justice*, 1945, oil on board, 13 x 17½". The Oakland Museum, Oakland, California. Museum Donors Acquisition Fund.

The fabulism entertained here partakes of the spirit of Lewis Carroll and tangentially of Walt Disney. While rejecting the filmmaker's cloying tone, Lundeberg displays a magical sense of fantasy, one which grants lowly creatures sentient features through the pathetic fallacy. Crucially, however, she raises her work to the level of art by spurning bathos and kitsch. Furthermore, she spins her tales with ironic detachment and with a self-conscious regard for the language in which they are told.

This self-reflection also emerges in *Spheres* [color pl. 39] which entertains a discourse between art and nature, illusion and fact. To this end, the titular globes, including the tack which pretends to float in the drawing it holds, echo one another in a hall-of-mirror game. Compounding illusions, the scene at right functions as both a painting and a window. Its reading depends on whether the bar at its base is seen as a sill or a strip of land. With these visual ploys that resist resolution, the artist poses on canvas what Fate does in life—options that stay open-ended.

The dialogue between light and shade that *Spheres* sustains led to the concept of day as a mantle behind which lay the night. In refining this notion, the artist created *The Wind that Blew the Sky Away #3* [color pl. 41], the last of three versions in which a cloud-dappled curtain languidly rises before a midnight void. The balmy heavens of California, observed with a perceptive eye, inspired this conception, as the artist relates in the passage below:

I was walking home from the market. The clouds and sun were so beautiful. I went home and made a little sketch. First it was greenish, with a blue sky. Then, I don't know how it happened, the idea of blowing the sky aside came to me.... I went on to conceive of the idea that the wind might even come blowing all the way from outer space and pull back the sky-illusion and show the darkness that lies behind.[8]

From the ordinary sights of everyday life, Lundeberg distills compelling imagery. The sensibility that she brings to bear in this scene shares something with the Abstract Imagists in New York and with mystic abstractionist Agnes Pelton in Cathedral City. Like these artists, she reveals her roots in nineteenth-century American landscape painting as she envisions a wondrous cosmos, inscrutable, lofty, and vast.

To emphasize this vastness, she stations a twig at the rim of night, thus pitting the finite against the infinite, the lowly against the grand. At the same time that she calls upon the Lilliputian tree to stress the immensity of the void, she lends the sky a Surrealistic edge by causing it to levitate eerily.

The issue of boundaries which this piece raises finds related treatment in the inside-outside exchange of *A Quiet Place* [color pl. 40].[9] An inner chamber, flanked by a dark hallway at left, meets a sandy expanse at the center capped by pale blue hills. This hard-edged construction of tinted panes resembles in two dimensions the modern cubic architecture of Los Angeles. Like the glass-paneled houses of Neutra, Schindler, Soriano, and Ain which graced the suburban terrain and appeared in reproduction in *Arts and Architecture* magazine [illus. 23], it boasts transparent walls that greet mountains and deserts and coax the outdoors into the room. Indeed, its architectonics suggest the free-standing scrims, modular units, and open-floor plans for which Southern California designers were known. At once expansive and enclosed, it offers shady shelter as it welcomes the countryside to its domain.

Allusions to California abide not only in its

Fig. 19. HELEN LUNDEBERG, *The Portrait*, 1953, oil on canvas, 30 x 36". Santa Barbara Museum of Art, Santa Barbara, California. Gift of Mr. and Mrs. Thomas C. McCray.

tectonic structure but in its sensation of viewing the world through layers of Southland smog. Its diaphanous planes test the spectator's optical powers by hovering on the edge of perception. The way that they float on visual borders, obliging sight to be vigilant, seems to foretell the investigations of light-and-space artists Robert Irwin, Larry Bell, Eric Orr and James Turrell.

Also dealing with perceptual thresholds, if less of the eye than of the mind, is Lundeberg's haunting *Portrait* [fig. 19], an image of her mother as a youth. Summarizing concerns of twenty years, it deals with the pull of the past on the present, as in *Double Portrait of the Artist in Time*, it ponders life's fragility, as in *The Evanescent*, and it explores the symbiotic relation of inside and outside, day and night, as in *The Wind that Blew the Sky Away*, *A Quiet Place*, and *Spheres*.[10]

Memory serves as the operative construct here. Interestingly, the artist's mother is shown, not as the adult that her daughter had known, but as a girl on the brink of maturity. Just as her three-year-old child had toyed with a sprig in *Double Portrait of the Artist in Time*, so does Lundeberg's mother clasp a delicate bud in her hand. Beneath her on the lip of the easel a three-dimensional flower calls attention to the reality that the simulacrum once possessed.

In its engagement with retrospection, the work has a Proustian air. Its thematic absorption in art and life, death and remembrance finds support in the vestibule. As the studio of the artist, the room refers to that magical zone where invention roams and can, if it wishes, recall the past through its charmed illusions. As a murky, inscrutable corridor it suggests the chambers of the mind in which bygone images dwell. In this regard, it also evokes the shrouded precinct of history and, by extension, eternity, to which the subject of the portrait has been consigned.

This piece and *A Quiet Place* signal Lundeberg's move toward reductive abstraction. During the course of the 1950s her oeuvre distilled to approach a state of purist refinement. By the 1960s it had become so laconic that, like the work of Lorser Feitelson and John McLaughlin, it verged on Minimalism. Yet however close it veered to the non-objective, it retained its ties to the external world, both real and reconfigured.

After achieving national stature in the 1930s, Lundeberg garnered countless invitations to group exhibitions; her credits include surveys at the Whitney

Illus. 22. HELEN LUNDEBERG, *Double Portrait of the Artist in Time*, 1935, oil on masonite. National Museum of American Art, Smithsonian Institution. Museum purchase. (not in exhibition)

Museum of American Art and the Metropolitan Museum of Art in New York, the University of Illinois in Urbana, the Carnegie Institute in Pittsburgh, Pennsylvania, the Los Angeles County Museum of Art, the Museu de Arte Moderna de Sao Paulo, Brazil, the Marion Koogler McNay Art Institute in San Antonio, Texas, and the National Museum of American Art in Washington, D.C.[11] In 1953 she merited a solo show at the Pasadena Art Institute and five years later was awarded a joint retrospective with Feitelson at Scripps College in Claremont, California. Her participation in the important *California Hard-Edge Painting*[12] exhibition of 1964 at the Pavilion Gallery in Balboa confirmed the key role that she played in defining the terms of pristine abstraction in Southern California.[13]

During the past two decades Lundeberg has been honored in a series of one-woman shows at the La Jolla Museum of Contemporary Art (1971), the Los Angeles Municipal Art Gallery (1979), the San Francisco Museum of Modern Art and the Frederick

S. Wight Gallery of the University of California in Los Angeles (in a duo retrospective with Feitelson from 1980-1981), the Palm Springs Desert Museum (1983), and the Laguna Art Museum (1987).

As the artist entered her eightieth year, she was feted by the American Art Council of the Los Angeles County Museum of Art in *A Birthday Salute*. The following year the Fresno Art Museum recognized her achievement with a major retrospective. These exhibitions, together with those that Tobey C. Moss has mounted annually at her Los Angeles gallery, celebrate an artist who has been enriching the Southern California community for more than fifty years.

NOTES

1. Statement by Helen Lundeberg for *Nine Senior Southern California Painters*, an exhibition organized by Fidel Danieli with a catalog printed in *The Los Angeles Institute of Contemporary Art Journal*, Number 3, December 1974, unpaginated.

2. Helen Lundeberg, interviews with author, 6 January 1981, 7 June 1984, 3 July 1984, 17 January 1985, and 2 April 1986. Major sources of information for this essay were Diane Degasis Moran's "Helen Lundeberg," *Lorser Feitelson and Helen Lundeberg: A Retrospective Exhibition*, San Francisco Museum of Modern Art, San Francisco, California, 1980; Joseph Young, "Helen Lundeberg: An American Independent," *Art International* 15, No. 6 (September 1971), 46-53; Henry Seldis, *Helen Lundeberg*, La Jolla Museum of Contemporary Art, La Jolla, California, 1971; and Eleanor Munro, "Helen Lundeberg," *Originals: American Women Artists* (New York: Simon and Schuster, 1979), 170-177.

3. Lundeberg, interview with author, 6 January 1981.

4. Statement by Lundeberg in *Americans 1942: 18 Artists from 9 States*, Museum of Modern Art, New York, 1942, 93.

5. This work was discussed in the author's paper, "Art in Los Angeles, 1920-1945," presented in the session *California Art and Culture, 1920-1945*, at the College Art Association's Annual Convention in Los Angeles, California on 14 February 1985.

6. Lundeberg as quoted by Young, "Helen Lundeberg: An American Independent," 46.

7. Edward Alden Jewell, "Brisk Pace in Museums," *The New York Times*, X, 17 May 1936, 10.

8. Lundeberg as quoted by Munro, "Helen Lundeberg," 177.

9. Moran discusses this exchange in depth and astutely relates it to Bachelard's poetics of space in "Helen Lundeberg," *Lorser Feitelson and Helen Lundeberg: A Retrospective Exhibition*, 26.

10. Ibid.

11. For a complete biography, chronology of exhibitions, and bibliography to 1980, see: *Lorser Feitelson and Helen Lundeberg: A Retrospective Exhibition*, 36-37, 74-76, and 79-80.

12. Organized by Jules Langsner, this exhibition joined Lundeberg and Feitelson with Southern California artists Florence Arnold, Karl Benjamin, John Barbour, Larry Bell, John Coplans, Frederick Hammersley, June Harwood, and Dorothy Waldman.

13. See Josine Ianco-Starrels, "Helen Lundeberg," in *Helen Lundeberg: Paintings 1960-1963*, Tobey C. Moss Gallery, Los Angeles, California, 1989.

Illus. 23. Case Study House, Southern California, 1950. Raphael Soriano, architect. *Arts and Architecture* 67, No. 12 (December 1950), 32.

Stanton Macdonald-Wright

(1890-1973)

I strive to divest my art of all anecdote and illustration and to purify it so that the emotions of the spectator can become entirely "aesthetic," as in listening to music.[1]

Creator of a modernist style based on pure, spectral color, Stanton Macdonald-Wright served as an early American pioneer of chromatic abstraction. Born in Charlottesville, Virginia on 8 July 1890, he developed an interest in art in his childhood when, after turning five, he took private painting instruction. In 1900 he moved with his family to Santa Monica, California, where he boasted dismissal from several schools. Courting adventure, he sailed the Pacific as a deck hand, stopping for a while on Maui to savor rustic existence.[2]

Back in Los Angeles in 1904, Macdonald-Wright took courses at the Art Students League in downtown Los Angeles with Warren T. Hedges, a one-time colleague of Ash Can painter Robert Henri.[3] Three years later, still itching with wanderlust and wishing to study abroad, he married and traveled with his bride to France. Settling in Paris, he took courses at the Sorbonne and sampled classes at the Academie Colorossi, the Academie Julien, and the Ecole des Beaux Arts.[4]

By 1910 his work had attained showcase stature and was accepted to the *Salon d'Automne*; two years later it gained entry to the prestigious *Salon des Independents*. Between these two shows, Macdonald-Wright befriended American artist Morgan Russell, with whom he developed a close working relationship. Together they investigated the serpentine rhythms of Michelangelo, the broken brushwork of the Impressionists, and the spatial plasticity of Cezanne.

At the same time they responded to Matisse and Picasso, whose works they encountered at Gertrude Stein's salon.[5] While absorbing the lessons of these masters they studied the color theories of Chevreul, Helmholtz, and Rood and took classes from the Canadian colorist Percyval Tudor-Hart. The latter formulated a scheme of chromatic triads by which works could be keyed to a dominant chord. Additionally, he compared painting with music, relating, for instance, luminosity, saturation, and hue to musical pitch, volume, and tone.[6]

Convinced of color's preemptive importance, Russell and Macdonald-Wright developed a movement predicated on hue. Naming it "Synchromism," meaning "with color," they introduced it in 1913 at Der Neue Kunstsalon in Munich and at the Galerie Bernheim-Jeune in Paris.[7]

Like the contemporary Orphist movement with which it has been compared, Synchromism joined the fragmented forms of the Cubists with the brilliant hues of the Fauves.[8] Importantly, however, it pushed the Fauve revolt further by liberating color from formal depiction. Freed from the burden of representation, color, in theory, could work independently as the prime agent of formal expression.

To justify an art of pure color divorced from depiction, Russell and Macdonald-Wright invoked the example of music. Like Tudor-Hart, the Orphists, and Vasily Kandinsky, they allied the two arts metaphorically, pointing to their shared expressive and formal traits. In the catalogue for their 1913 Munich show, they argued that painting equaled music in its sublimity:

Mankind has until now always tried to satisfy its need for the highest spiritual exaltation only in music. Only tones have been able to grip us and transport us to the highest realms. Whenever man had a desire for heavenly intoxication, he turned to music. Yet color is just as capable as music of providing us with the highest ecstasies and delights.[9]

These high ambitions inspired the artists to exhibit their works in London, Milan, and Warsaw in 1913 and in New York the following year. With the onset of the First World War, Macdonald-Wright fled to London where he roomed with his brother Willard Huntington Wright, an editor for *Smart Set* magazine, whom he assisted in writing books on art.[10] In 1916 he sailed to New York where he mingled in vanguard circles and participated in *The Forum Exhibition of Modern American Painters*.[11] Subsequent shows at progressive New York galleries, including Alfred Stieglitz's *291*, served to secure his East Coast reputation.[12]

Fig. 20. STANTON MACDONALD-WRIGHT, *Trumpet Flowers*, 1919, oil on canvas, 18⅛ x 13⅛". The Museum of Modern Art, New York. The Sidney and Harriet Janis Collection.

The artist, however, despite his success, felt uneasy with life in Manhattan. Thus, he left New York in 1918 and returned to Southern California. Inspired by the mountains and valleys surrounding his home, he trained his pictorial gaze on the verdant outdoors. In the process, he lightened his palette with streaks of white that invoked Santa Monica's damp coastal air.

In his California Synchromies, Macdonald-Wright brings his early discoveries to a state of perfection. Now, as before, color determines structure and obliges other elements to submit to its control. Operating as a spatial force, it grants forms plasticity. As the artist observed:

Form to me is color.... I conceive space itself as of a plastic significance that I express in color. Form not being simply the mass of each object seen separately, I organize my canvas as a solid block as much in depth as laterally.[13]

Clearly, color and form in these Synchromies function synergistically to yield an interwoven field in the mode of the late Cezanne. Luminous hues, harmonically grouped, give the impression of tiny, bright rainbows adrift in a moist atmosphere. In *Trumpet Flowers* [fig. 20], they lend the spiraling blossoms a balletic grace.

Like *Trumpet Flowers*, *California Landscape* and *Far Country Synchromy* [color pl. 42 and 43] sustain a light, impalpable air. Blithely, they accurately capture a sense of place—of gullies and bluffs sheathed in soft haze, of villas stacked on palisades overlooking cool bays. Gauzy white patches powder the field to evoke Santa Monica's ambient fog. The manner in which they blanket the forms recalls the Oriental landscape painting which the artist admired. The gaps that they create on the surface thus might be read, not as negative voids, but as resonant regions of light in accord with their Eastern models.

In the mid-twenties, Macdonald Wright codified his theories of color, prompted by his role as a teacher and director of the Los Angeles Art Students League. In his instructive *Treatise on Color*, published in 1924, he subjected chroma to in-depth analysis,

— 90 —

discussing it as pigment and light, physical substance and emotional force. He warned, however, that his findings only had meaning insofar as they yielded aesthetic harmony.[14] Toward this end he advised artists not to imitate nature but to translate its governing principles into a formal ideal:

> ...The serious painter must realize that his subject is merely an inspiration to the end of making a work of art...an ordered and harmonious canvas. To copy nature ... implies many kinds of ignorance. It shows that one considers nature and art to be the same thing; it exposes the greatest misunderstanding of the precepts of the masters .... The meaning of the masters is ... that the principles, or unalterable natural laws, which are nature, be studied; viz. balance, contrast, action, and re-action and the unification in multiplicity, etc., not the superficial aspects of nature.[15]

In line with these precepts, Macdonald-Wright's Synchromies stand as ideal paradigms that interpret the region as undefiled Eden. Their dreamy vistas of mountains and valleys, nestled in clouds of tropical color, convey a sense of tranquil well-being, of poised serenity.

In 1927 Macdonald-Wright organized a joint exhibition with Morgan Russell at the Los Angeles County Museum of Art where he showed again five years later. During the early thirties he exhibited his works at the Oakland Art Gallery (1930), the California Palace of the Legion of Honor in San Francisco (1931), Alfred Stieglitz's An American Place gallery in New York (1931), and the Stendahl Gallery in Los Angeles (1932).[16]

By this time, however, he had grown disenchanted with Synchromism, which he felt had become too scholastic. Turning to the Orient for inspiration, he delved into Asian calligraphy and studied the tenets of Tao and Zen.[17] His infatuation with the Far East reveals itself in a series of murals that he conceived for the Santa Monica Library (1933-1935) as well as in his private easel paintings which, more often than not, revolved around Buddhist myth.

From 1935 to 1942 Macdonald-Wright served as director of the Southern California division of the Federal Art Project under the Works Progress Administration. While performing his bureaucratic duties, he developed architectural murals in Southgate, Santa Monica, and Long Beach and perfected a mosaic compound that he termed Petrachrome.[18] When the Art Project disbanded in 1942, he joined the faculty of the University of California at Los Angeles where he taught classes in Eastern aesthetics and art history for the next twelve years. Meanwhile, he published articles on Oriental art and penned reviews for the Hollywood circular *Rob Wagner's Script*. Macdonald-Wright's works of the 1940s stand under the shadow of Georges Braque whose curvilinear Cubism they emulate. By the early fifties, however, they returned to key Synchromist tenets and recaptured some of their early panache.

During these and subsequent years the artist lived for extended periods in Hawaii, Italy, and Japan, where he spent months at a time in a monastery. Concurrently, he enjoyed several one-man shows at the Los Angeles County Museum of Art (1956), the Rose Fried Gallery in New York (1955, 1965), and the Esther Robles Gallery in Los Angeles (1963 and 1965). In 1967 his oeuvre was celebrated in a major retrospective at the National Collection of Fine Arts of the Smithsonian Institution in Washington, D.C., and three years later it was again so honored at the University of California at Los Angeles Art Galleries. Two major Synchromist shows in New York—the first organized by William C. Agee in 1965 for the Knoedler Gallery and the second by Gail Levin in 1978 for the Whitney Museum of American Art—acknowledged the artist's seminal role in American modernism.[19]

At his death in 1973, Macdonald-Wright stood as a major figure in American art history. Not only had he co-founded the avant-garde movement of Synchromism, but he had outlined a regional course of the future by celebrating the color and light of Southern California.

Illus. 24. STANTON MACDONALD-WRIGHT, *Cañon Synchromy*, 1919-1920, oil on canvas. Collection of the University of Minnesota. (not in exhibition)

NOTES

1. Macdonald-Wright in a statement for a 1916 exhibition of his work at Gallery 291 in New York in *The Art of Stanton Macdonald-Wright*, National Collection of Fine Arts, Smithsonian Institution, Washington, D.C., 1967. 12. [Several writers have cited 1917 as the date of the MacDonald-Wright show at Gallery 291.]

2. Biographical information for this section was obtained from the chronology that the artist prepared in *The Art of Stanton Macdonald-Wright*. 21-24.

3. Gail Levin, *Synchromism and American Color Abstraction 1910-1925* (New York: The Whitney Museum of American Art in association with George Braziller, 1978), 14.

4. Macdonald-Wright, *The Art of Stanton Macdonald-Wright*. 21-24.

5. Levin, 11-13.

6. Ibid., 14 and 26, and Ogden Rood, "Combination of Colours in Pairs and Triads," *Modern Chromatics*. 1879; reprint *Modern Chromatics by Ogden N. Rood (1831-1902)* (New York: Van Nostrand Reinhold Company, 1973), 242.

7. Levin, 20.

8. While Macdonald-Wright shared with the Orphists a penchant for swirling, fractured imagery and bright prismatic hues, he distinguished himself from his French counterparts by his indigenous subject matter and exotic palette. Compared to Leger, for example, he was more blue-stocking than blue collar, less the populist than the aesthete.

9. Macdonald-Wright and Morgan Russell, "In Explanation of Synchromism: Ausstellung Der Synchromisten Morgan Russell, S. Macdonald-Wright, Der Neue Kunstsalon, Munich June 1-30, 1913," in *Synchromism and American Color Abstraction 1910-1925*. 129.

10. Wright states that he worked with his brother Willard on *The Creative Will, The Future of Painting*, and *Modern Art, Its Tendency and Meaning*. The latter volume, published in Willard's name in 1915, traced the history of modernism, or "heretical" expression as it was termed, from Turner and Delacroix through the Impressionists and Post-Impressionists to the Fauves.

Cubists, and Futurists. While deeming Kandinsky a "lesser modern," it accorded the Synchromists pride of place, locating them at the climax of the avant-garde march.

11. The show was held at the Anderson Galleries on East 45th Street in New York in March 1916. Willard Wright sat on the advisory panel and published a catalogue essay that lauded the Synchromist enterprise. *The Forum Exhibition of Modern American Painters* [1916] (New York: Arno Press, 1968), 13-24. Also see Levin, 30.

12. As cited in his chronology, the artist had exhibited his work in New York at the Carroll Galleries in 1914 and at the Montross Gallery and the Daniel Gallery between 1916 and 1918.

13. Macdonald-Wright, "Introduction to the exhibition catalogue, Galerie Bernheim-Jeune, Paris, 1913" (translated from French by the artist) in *The Art of Stanton Macdonald-Wright*, 11.

14. Much like Kandinsky, Macdonald-Wright related painting to music, comparing chroma and sound, for example, in terms of interval, tone, vibration, and pitch. With regard to color's evocative meaning, he theorized that yellow was perfunctory, "frivolous" and "gay," while green, although feeble and "lackadaisical," conveyed tranquility. Blue connoted the "supramundane," while red exemplified passion. Violet he labeled "a cry de profundis" that conveyed sorrow, while orange, a "blatant braggart," bellowed loudly. *A Treatise on Color* (Los Angeles, California, c. 1924), 19-20, in *The Art of Stanton Macdonald-Wright*.

15. Ibid., 27-28.

16. Ibid.

17. Ibid., 13.

18. Ibid., 23. Macdonald-Wright describes his invention as follows: "In the Petrachrome process aggregates of colored stones and coloring matters are added to Medusa cement which is then cast on extruded metal lath in pictorial segments, polished, and set in the wall."

19. Ibid. Currently, the artist's work is shown at the Foster Harmon Gallery in Sarasota, Florida and at the Joseph Chowning Gallery in San Francisco, California.

John McLaughlin

(1898-1976)

My purpose is to achieve the totally abstract .... This I manage by the use of neutral forms.[1]

Committed to non-objective abstraction, John McLaughlin aimed for a purist art free from references to the mundane. Released from attachments to the world, this pristine structure, or "neutral form" as he termed it, would serve as a field for reflective thought. McLaughlin arrived at this abstract ideal during the 1950s by subjecting his restricted means—rectangular forms and an austere palette—to varied permutations.

Although he became a painter late in life, McLaughlin quickly achieved a taut body of work. Belonging to the first generation of Los Angeles pioneers, he held to its puritan values, living with humble simplicity and spurning materialism. For him, as for his Southland peers, art was a special enterprise that transcended secular cares.

Born in Sharon, Massachusetts on 21 May 1898 and raised in Boston, McLaughlin developed an early fondness for art, particularly that of the Orient which his parents collected. After completing his schooling at the Phillips Academy in Andover, Massachusetts and serving in the United States Navy during the First World War, he married and opened an art dealership that featured Japanese prints. Concurrently, he studied Oriental languages and in 1935 set sail with his wife for Japan where he remained for the next two years.[2]

As tensions between the United States and Japan began to mount, McLaughlin enlisted in the military as a translator. Commissioned as an officer, he trained in Honolulu, Hawaii and was there when Pearl Harbor was bombed. After completing his training, he served as a linguistic specialist in the Intelligence Corps on the Asian front.[3]

While in the service McLaughlin was assigned to different army bases in California so that he and his wife had a chance to enjoy the region's temperate climate. Charmed by the weather, they settled in the beachside town of Dana Point in 1946. On a lot purchased for three hundred dollars McLaughlin built a modest home and studio in which to commence his painting career. Supported by his wife, he devoted himself ambitiously to self-instruction.[4] Like Oskar Fischinger and Jules Engel, who were also self-taught, he skirted representation and proceeded directly into abstraction. "I wasn't going to make any pictures of trees or skies or anything like that," he noted. "Nothing the matter with them at all, but that wasn't for me. Time was wasting."[5]

It was thus with a sense of urgency and with a self-understanding born of maturity that McLaughlin began a serious study of the modernist masters. Delving initially into Cezanne, he progressed to Picasso and the Cubists, and then to Mondrian and Malevich. From the latter two he learned the formal potential of basic shapes and negative space.

McLaughlin, however, claimed to have found inspiration not so much in Malevich's art but in his title *White on White*. "I didn't have to see the painting ... at all," he later explained, "just those words. Tremendous."[6] In its blend of the simple and the profound, Malevich's title no doubt struck McLaughlin as consonant with the art of the Orient which he had long admired. Thus, through Malevich, McLaughlin could reconcile Eastern aesthetics with the Western abstract tradition.

The reductive lessons of Mondrian and Malevich seem to inform the untitled piece from the

Fig. 21. JOHN McLAUGHLIN, Untitled, 1951, oil on panel, 27⅞ x 23¾". Collection of Mr. David J. Supino, New York City.

Edward Albee collection [color pl. 44] which attains a state of succinct refinement. Shapes have been honed to rectangular planes, and hues have been trimmed to black, white, and green. Nesting within a large emerald field, a dark parallelogram faces the viewer with an impervious stare. A band of white at the left aligns with the vertical edge of the canvas to stress the support.

Stripped bare of detail, the painting exists as an iconic presence, impassive and austere. Clearly, it dares the viewer to come to terms with its ascetic facade. Confronted with this dearth of data, the eye scans the surface for stimulation, observing variations of placement, proportion, and scale. Ultimately, however, this survey involutes so that one becomes acutely aware of the process of perception. This, of course, is the key strategy of Minimal art and of McLaughlin's signature paintings, in which such highly reductive fields force the viewer into a state of heightened awareness. As such, this 1948 work marks McLaughlin as a prescient forerunner of Minimalism.

Also sparse in their handling are the untitled paintings of figs. 21 and 22. While akin to Josef Albers' designs on glass, fig. 21 has a faint flavor of Japan. Its rectilinear structure in black and white evokes the cream-colored walls trimmed with dark beams of modern Japanese buildings and shoji screens. Furthermore, its disc afloat on a pristine field bracketed by parallel bands vaguely recalls that nation's emblematic flag. Tectonic impulses also inform fig. 22, which likewise contains a series of bars painted in neutral tones. Now, however, these strips parade in a lateral line across a field which divides into white and black zones.

Although he removed hue from a number of pieces, McLaughlin did not yet want to ban it from his repertoire. While restricting his forms to the rectangle, he inflected his palette of black, white, and gray with accents of lemon, brown, green, or blue, sometimes an Indian red. In the untitled work of color pl. 45, the characteristic black and white planes are set off by a strip of pastel blue, while in the piece of color pl. 46, they are attended by two yellow bands. Due to its scarcity, color acquires importance, attracting the eye and influencing the way in which it proceeds. Applied in a single stripe, it rivets attention, but when doubled, as it is in color pl. 46, it sets up a tense confrontation between the gold slabs and the black and white brackets in which they sit. Granted equal importance, these islands of color, as in Lorser Feitelson's Magical Space Forms and Jasper Johns' targets with faces, visually compete. As a result, vision does not arrive at a point of rest as expected, but instead darts back and forth.

Art historian Susan Larsen called attention to this visual ploy early on, observing how McLaughlin

Fig. 22. JOHN McLAUGHLIN, Untitled, 1951-1952, oil on masonite, 24 x 28⅛". Collection of Mr. and Mrs. O. P. Reed, Jr., Malibu, California.

sets up tensions between his forms in a way that complies with Mannerist tactics rather than with Classical strategies.[7] Seeming at first to be classically balanced, his paintings reveal, with sustained inspection, a subtle equivocation that compromises stasis. Complexity thus operates in simplicity's guise and cues to movement lurk within deceptively staid facades. It is precisely because it confounds expectations, and does so with consummate subtlety, that McLaughlin's work intrigues.

The untitled piece of January, 1954 [color pl. 47], for example, sustains an optical shuffle within the classical form of a square. Matched inversely in structure but not in color, the lateral halves of the composition spar with one another. The white crosses abet this contest by appearing first to be positive shapes and then negative slits. Here, again, McLaughlin's work compares with that of Feitelson, which also prompts visual flux. His, however, avoids the existential anxiety that Feitelson's Magical Space

Forms exude.

As the years progressed, McLaughlin increasingly pared down his forms. "This position," he noted, "accommodated my conviction that the viewer become central to the neutrality of the non-expressive structure."[8] His intention was to generate works free of discrete entities, or "particulars." Starkly curbing pictorial data, he devised his mature aesthetic of rectangular planes in black, white, and gray, varied as figure and ground. In his exploitation of negative space, McLaughlin compared himself to the fifteenth-century Japanese painter Sesshu who encouraged entry into his works through a knowing use of voids:

> *Certain Japanese painters of centuries ago found the means to overcome the demands imposed by the object by the use of large areas of empty space. This space was described by Sesshu as the "Marvelous Void." Thus the viewer was induced to "enter" the painting unconscious of the dominance of the object. Consequently there was no compulsion to ponder the significance of the object as such. On the contrary, the condition of "Man versus Nature" was reversed to that of man at one with nature and enabled the viewer to seek his own identity free from the suffocating finality of the conclusive statement.[9]*

Resisting "conclusive statements," McLaughlin adopted open structures which he hoped would initiate a contemplative response. In this he resembles Helen Lundeberg, Agnes Pelton, Henrietta Shore, and Oskar Fischinger, whose art also served as subtle inducements to meditation.

McLaughlin clearly opposed the demonstrative ethos of Abstract Expressionism which in the 1950s still possessed critical clout. Instead of displaying emotion overtly as did the New York Action Painters and Los Angeles Expressionists Hans Burkhardt and Rico Lebrun, he rejected sentiment, opting for self-abnegation instead of confession. Above all else he sought simplicity, in his art as in his life:

> *My greatest emphasis is on simplicity...my own method...is to refrain from recording on the canvas my reactions to or understanding of some object or idea and instead I develop a composition which in theory at least contains those qualities which might enable the spectator to contemplate nature beyond the limitations of an image or symbolism.[10]*

In his drive to create a contemplative art devoid of traditional symbols, McLaughlin approached New York artist Barnett Newman whose call for imagery free of "impediments of memory... nostalgia, legend, myth,"[11] voices allied objectives. Closer yet did he come to New York painter Ad Reinhardt, with whom he shared an attachment to Oriental art and to reductive abstraction. From the start, he and Reinhardt used right-angled formats and showed an attraction to hue which they later rejected. Their puritanic eschewal of color was meant to permit their neutral forms to function preemptively. Within the bounds of their limited means—black squares with crosses for Reinhardt, black, gray, and white bars for McLaughlin—they sought to affect perceptual thresholds, prodding the spectator's vision beyond its normal range.

The brilliance of McLaughlin's achievement was recognized early on by the Los Angeles vanguard community. In 1951 curator James Byrnes included the artist in his *Contemporary Painting in the United States* survey at the Los Angeles County Museum of Art and two years later dealer Felix Landau gave him his first one-man show. In 1956 and 1958 respectively, the Pasadena Art Museum and the University of California at Riverside hosted McLaughlin retrospectives. Importantly, McLaughlin joined Karl Benjamin, Lorser Feitelson, and Frederick Hammersley in the *Four Abstract Classicists* exhibition at the Los Angeles County Museum of Art in 1959.

During the 1960s McLaughlin's reputation grew. His work appeared in numerous group exhibitions throughout the country, soloed regularly at the Felix Landau Gallery in Los Angeles, and was awarded retrospectives at the Pasadena Art Museum (1963), Occidental College (1968), and the Corcoran Gallery of Art in Washington, D.C. (1969). In the 1970s, his

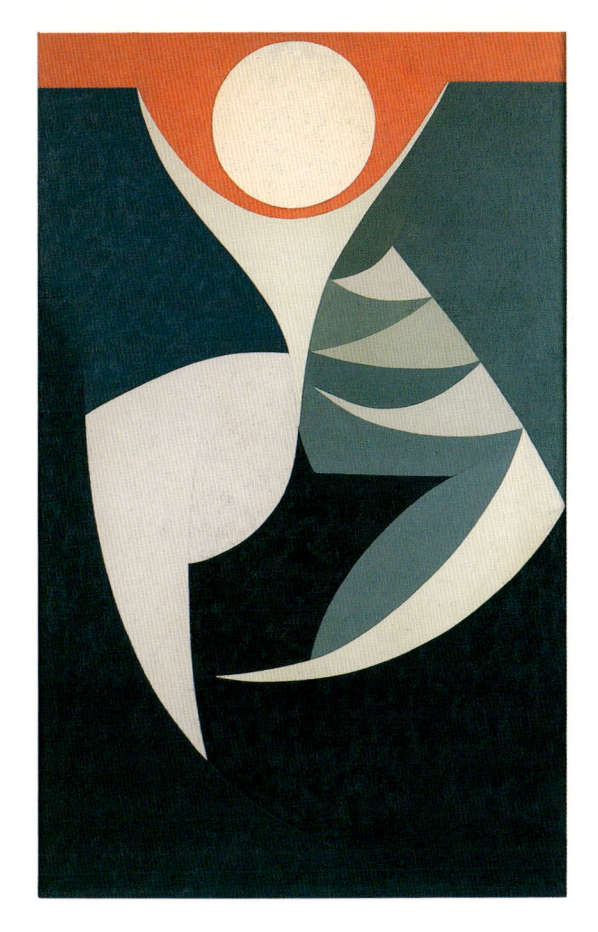

PLATE 1.
Karl Benjamin *White Figures on a Red Sky*, 1954, oil on canvas, 48 x 30⅛". Long Beach Museum of Art, Long Beach, California.

PLATE 2.
Karl Benjamin *Theme and Variation*, 1956, oil on canvas, 36 x 48". The Buck Collection, Laguna Niguel, California.

PLATE 3.

Ben Berlin *Surreal Portrait*, 1938, oil on canvas on board, 19½ x 14½". Collection of Fannie Hall and Alan Leslie, Palm Springs, California.

PLATE 4.
Ben Berlin *Duck, Cannon, Firecrackers*, 1937, oil and collage, 20 x 16". The Buck Collection, Laguna Niguel, California.

PLATE 5.
Ben Berlin *Woman with a Lute*, 1938, casein on firtex, 24 x 23½". Collection of the Nora Eccles Harrison Museum of Art, Utah State University. Gift of the Marie Eccles Caine Foundation.

PLATE 6.

William Brice *Land Fracture*, 1954-1955, oil and sand on board, 96 x 78". Collection of the Wight Art Gallery, University of California, Los Angeles. Gift of Mr. and Mrs. Ray Stark.

PLATE 7.
Hans Burkhardt *By the Sea (Dance)*, 1945, oil on canvas, 32 x 42". Jack Rutberg Gallery, Los Angeles, California.

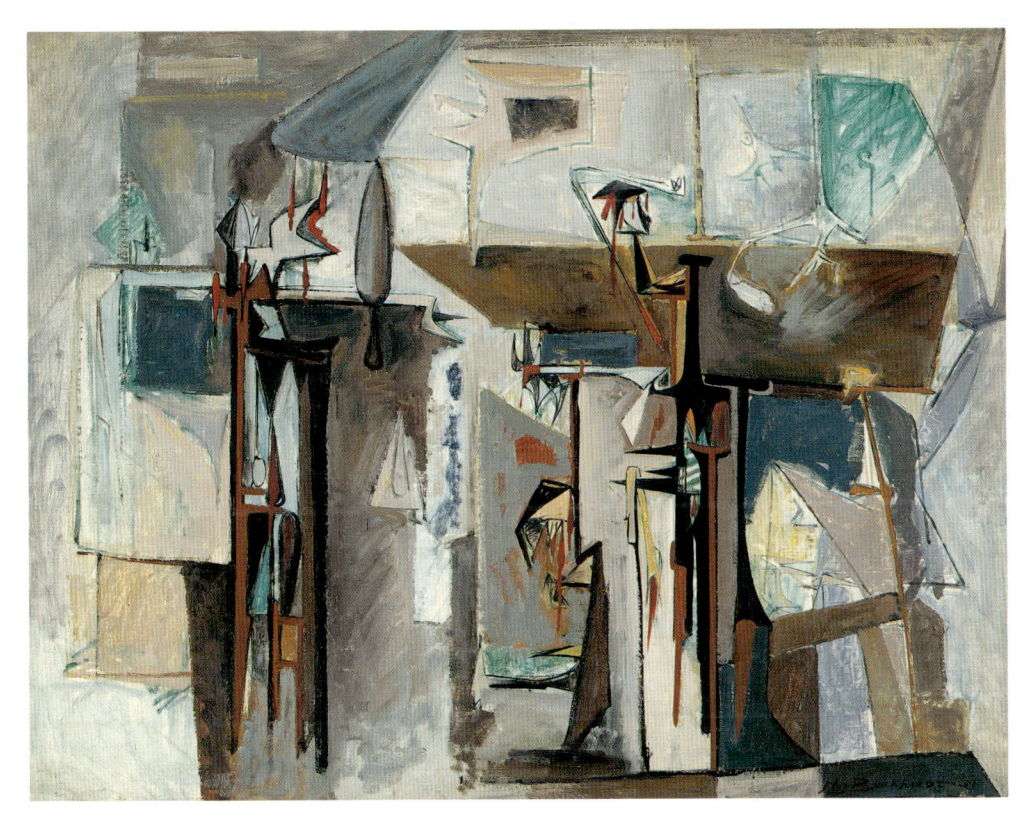

PLATE 8.
Hans Burkhardt *Studio of Gorky*, 1951, oil on canvas, 32 x 42". Sandy and Adrea Bettelman, Los Angeles, California.

PLATE 9.
Hans Burkhardt *Farewell to Mexico*, 1951-1952, oil on canvas, 32 x 40". Jack Rutberg Gallery, Los Angeles, California.

PLATE 10.
Hans Burkhardt *The Awakening*, 1953, oil on canvas, 53 x 36". Jack Rutberg Gallery, Los Angeles, California.

PLATE 11.
Hans Burkhardt *Song of the Universe*, 1953, oil on canvas, 53¼ x 38¼". Jack Rutberg Gallery, Los Angeles, California.

PLATE 12.

Grace Clements *Reconsideration of Time and Space*, 1935, oil on canvas, 42 x 34". The Oakland Museum, Oakland, California. Gift of the artist.

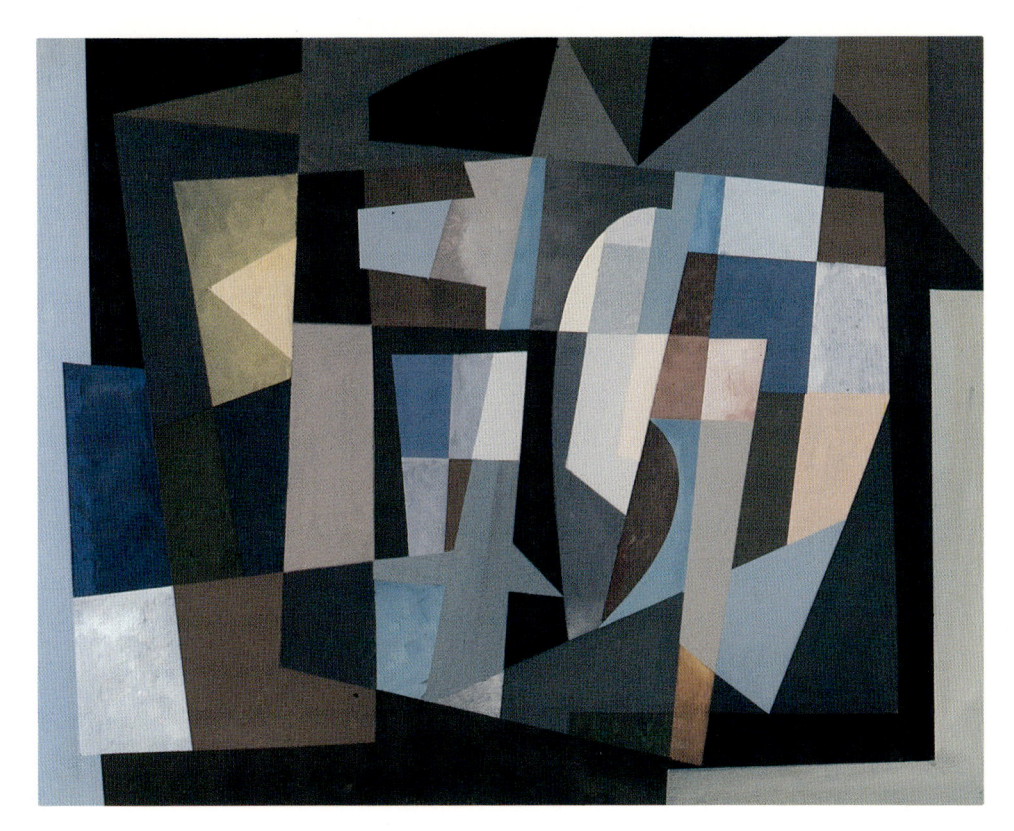

PLATE 13.
Jules Engel *Interior*, 1947, gouache on board, 24 x 20". Collection of the artist.

PLATE 14.
Jules Engel *Brilliant Moves*, 1946, gouache on paper, 19 x 25". Collection of Mr. and Mrs. Albert Kallis, Beverly Hills, California.

PLATE 15.

Lorser Feitelson *Magical Forms*, 1945, oil on canvas, 30 x 36". Lorser Feitelson and Helen Lundeberg Feitelson Arts Foundation. Courtesy of Tobey C. Moss Gallery, Los Angeles, California.

PLATE 16.

Lorser Feitelson *Magical Forms*, 1948-1950, oil on canvas, 45 x 40". Lorser Feitelson and Helen Lundeberg Feitelson Arts Foundation. Courtesy of Tobey C. Moss Gallery, Los Angeles, California.

PLATE 17.
Lorser Feitelson *Magical Space Forms*, 1951, oil on canvas, 57¾ x 81¾". The Whitney Museum of American Art, New York. Gift of the Los Angeles Art Association Galleries.

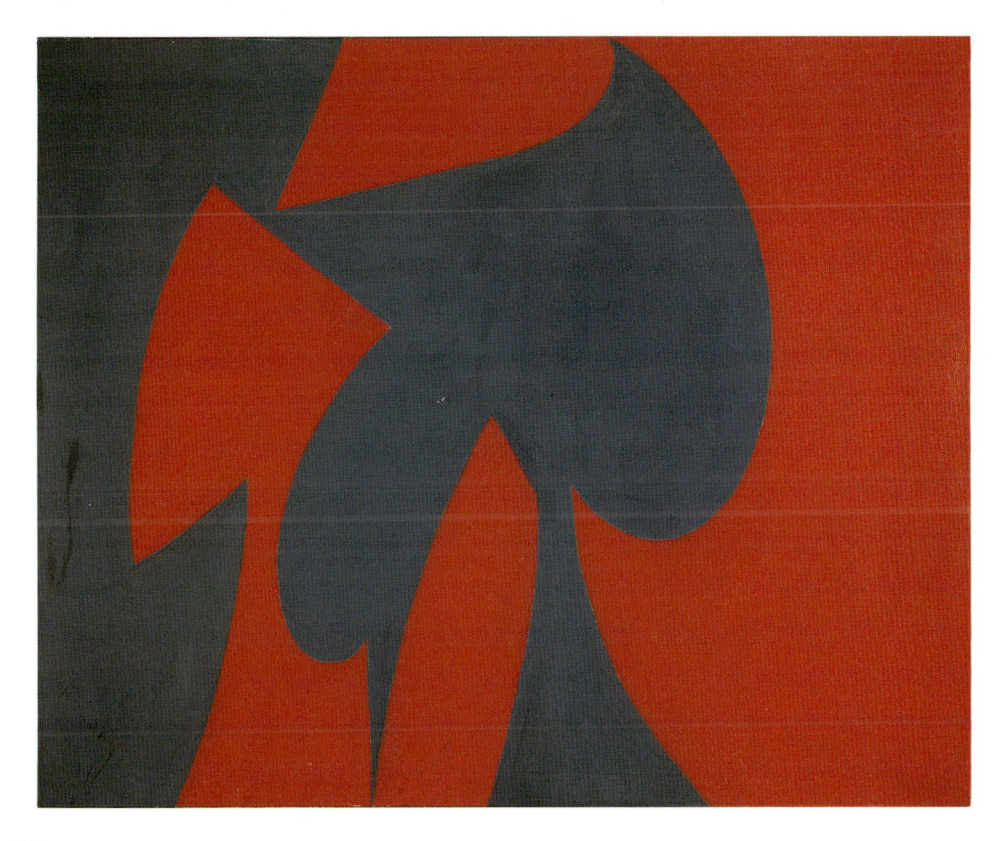

PLATE 18.
Lorser Feitelson *Magical Space Forms*, 1951, oil on canvas, 40 x 50". Private collection, Palos Verdes, California.

PLATE 19.

Lorser Feitelson *Magical Space Forms*, 1954, oil on canvas, 60 x 54". Lorser Feitelson and Helen Lundeberg Feitelson Arts Foundation. Courtesy of Tobey C. Moss Gallery, Los Angeles, California.

PLATE 20.
Oskar Fischinger *Experiment*, 1936, oil on canvas, 60 x 40". The Buck Collection, Laguna Niguel, California.

PLATE 21.
Oskar Fischinger *Circles, Triangles, and Squares*, 1938, oil on canvas, 48⅛ x 36". National Museum of American Art, Smithsonian Institution. Gift of Mrs. Oskar Fischinger.

PLATE 22.
Oskar Fischinger *Outward Movement*, 1948, oil on canvas, 48 x 26". Collection of The Fischinger Archive, Los Angeles, California.

PLATE 23.
Oskar Fischinger *Searchlights*, 1941, watercolor on paper, 18 x 14½". Collection of Mr. Charles J. Pollyea, Los Angeles, California.

PLATE 24.
Oskar Fischinger *Yellow Moon*, 1954, oil on canvas, 48 x 36". Collection of The Fischinger Archive, Los Angeles, California.

PLATE 25.
Oskar Fischinger *Tower*, 1954, oil on canvas, 37 x 49". Mr. Gordon Rosenblum, 609 Gallery, Denver, Colorado.

PLATE 26.

Frederick Hammersley *Upon*, 1955, oil on board, 13½ x 23½". Albuquerque Museum, Albuquerque, New Mexico.

PLATE 27.
Peter Krasnow *Sassafras*, ca. 1932, wood, 39". Skirball Museum of the Hebrew Union College, Los Angeles, California.

PLATE 28.
Peter Krasnow *Demountable*, 1946, mixed woods, 26½ x 14 x 6½". Collection of Fred and Frieda Fox, Los Angeles, California.

PLATE 29.
Peter Krasnow *K-5*, 1944, oil on paperboard, 35⅛ x 24". National Museum of American Art, Smithsonian Institution. Gift of the artist.

PLATE 30.
Peter Krasnow Untitled, 1946, oil on board, 48 x 23½". Private collection.

PLATE 31.
Peter Krasnow *K-6*, 1949, oil on board, 36 x 48". Collection of Fred and Frieda Fox, Los Angeles, California. Estate of Peter Krasnow.

PLATE 32.
Peter Krasnow *K-7*, 1949, oil on board, 33 x 47½". Private collection.

PLATE 33.
Rico Lebrun *Black Plow*, 1947, casein on masonite, 79 x 36". Collection of Dr. Lillian Carson and Sam Hurst, Santa Barbara, California.

PLATE 34.
Rico Lebrun *Witness of the Resurrection*, 1950-1951, Duco on Upson Board, 62 x 96". Courtesy of the Syracuse University Art Collections, Syracuse, New York. Gift of Mrs. Constance Lebrun Crown.

PLATE 35.

Rico Lebrun *The Magdalene*, 1950, tempera on masonite, 63 x 48". Santa Barbara Museum of Art, Santa Barbara, California. Gift of Wright S. Ludington.

PLATE 36.

Helen Lundeberg *Cosmicide*, 1935, oil on masonite, 40 x 24". Sheldon Memorial Art Gallery, University of Nebraska, Lincoln. Nebraska Art Association Collection. Gift of The Peter Kiewit Foundation.

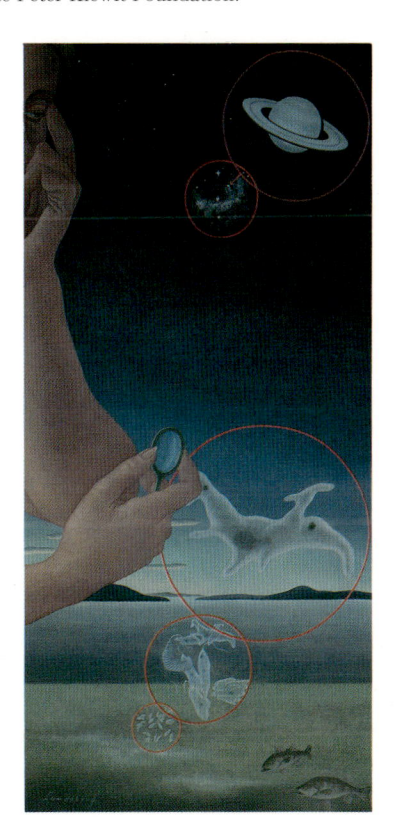

PLATE 37.

Helen Lundeberg *Microcosm and Macrocosm*, 1937, oil on masonite, 28½ x 14". Private collection. Courtesy of Tobey C. Moss Gallery, Los Angeles, California.

PLATE 38.

Helen Lundeberg *The Evanescent*, 1941-1944, oil on canvas, 38¾ x 60". Collection of Mr. and Mrs. Harry Carmean, Los Angeles, California.

PLATE 39.

Helen Lundeberg *Spheres*, 1945, oil on canvas, 22 x 19". Collection of Frank M. Finck, M.D., Los Angeles, California.

PLATE 40.
Helen Lundeberg *A Quiet Place*, 1950, oil on canvas, 16 x 20", Lorser Feitelson and Helen Lundeberg Feitelson Arts Foundation. Courtesy of Tobey C. Moss Gallery, Los Angeles, California.

PLATE 41.
Helen Lundeberg *The Wind that Blew the Sky Away #3*, 1951, oil on canvas, 36 x 51". The Buck Collection, Laguna Niguel, California.

PLATE 42.

Stanton Macdonald-Wright *California Landscape*, ca. 1919, oil on canvas, 30 x 22⅛". Columbus Museum of Art, Ohio. Gift of Ferdinand Howald.

PLATE 43.

Stanton Macdonald-Wright *Far Country Synchromy*, 1920, oil on canvas, 32 x 25¾". The Detroit Institute of Arts. Bequest of Vivian Stringfield.

PLATE 44.

John McLaughlin Untitled, 1948, oil on masonite, 27¾ x 24". Collection of Edward Albee and Jonathan Thomas, New York, New York.

PLATE 45.
John McLaughlin Untitled, 1953, oil on masonite, 38½ x 32½". Collection of Mrs. Joni Gordon, Los Angeles, California.

PLATE 46.

John McLaughlin Untitled, 1953, oil on board, 32 x 38". The Sadoff Collection, Beverly Hills, California.

PLATE 47.

John McLaughlin Untitled, 1954, oil on panel, 32 x 32". Collection of Mr. David J. Supino, New York, New York.

PLATE 48.

Knud Merrild *American Beauty, or the Movie Star*, 1928, oil and collage, 19 x 16". The Oakland Museum, Oakland, California. Gift of Else Merrild.

PLATE 49.

Knud Merrild *Perpetual Possibility*, 1942, enamel on composition board mounted on plywood, 20 x 16⅛". The Museum of Modern Art, New York. Gift of Mrs. Knud Merrild.

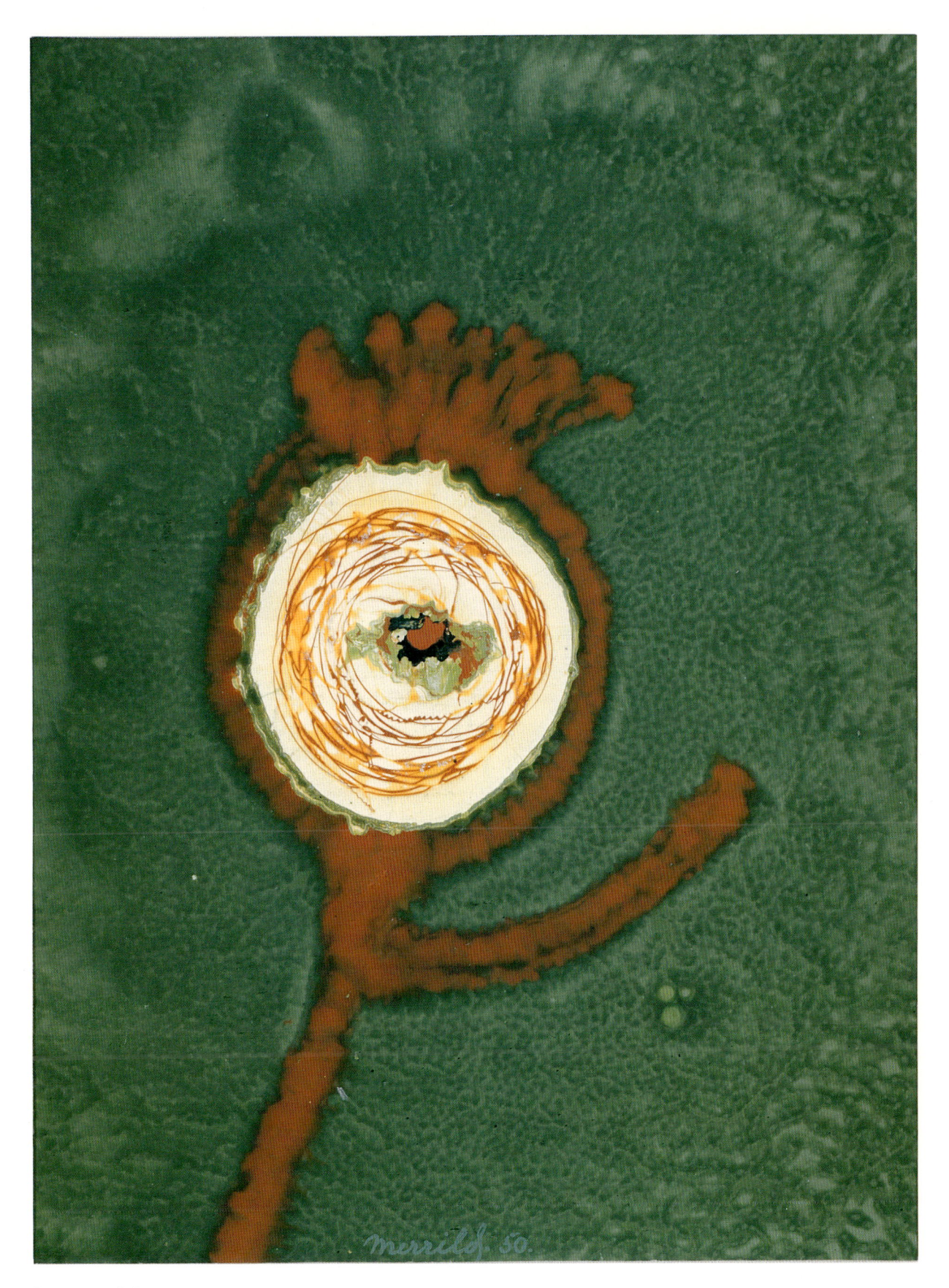

PLATE 50.
Knud Merrild *Flux Flower*, 1950, oil on canvas mounted on board, 16½ x 12". The Buck Collection, Laguna Niguel, California.

PLATE 51.
Lee Mullican *Peyote Candle*, 1951, oil on canvas, 50 x 35". Collection of the artist.

PLATE 52.

Lee Mullican *Measurement*, 1952, oil on canvas, 50 x 30". Newport Harbor Art Museum. Purchased with funds provided by the Acquisition Committee; partial donation of Herbert Palmer Gallery.

PLATE 53.

Agnes Pelton *Wells of Jade*, 1931, oil on canvas, 34 x 20". University Art Museum, University of New Mexico, Albuquerque. Jonson Gallery Collection.

PLATE 54.
Agnes Pelton *Orbits*, 1934, oil on canvas, 36¼ x 30". The Oakland Museum, Oakland, California. Gift of Concours D'Antiques, Art Guild, Oakland Museum Association.

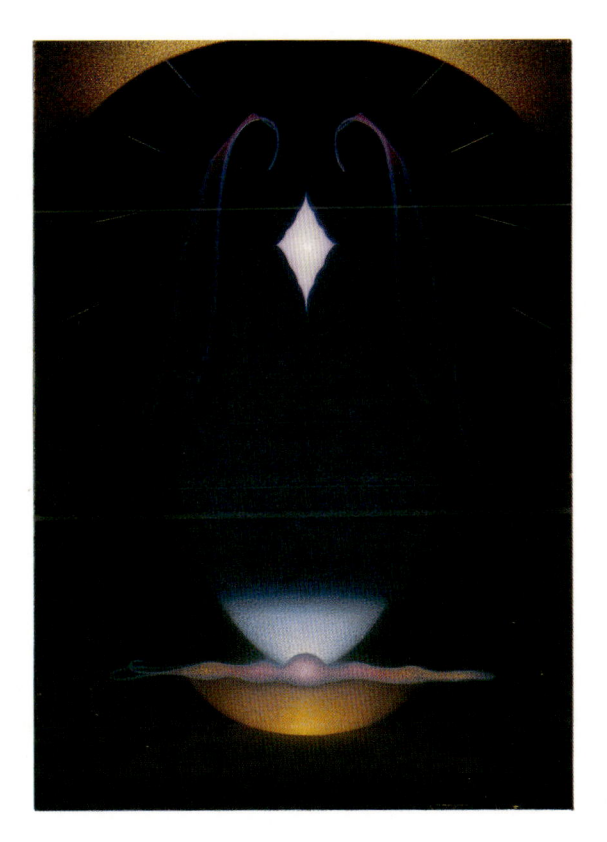

PLATE 55.
Agnes Pelton *Alchemy*, 1937, oil on canvas, 26¼ x 31⅜". The Buck Collection, Laguna Niguel, California.

PLATE 56.

Henrietta Shore *Two Worlds*, ca. 1921, oil on canvas, 30⅛ x 26⅛". Collection of the Nora Eccles Harrison Museum of Art, Utah State University. Gift of the Marie Eccles Caine Foundation.

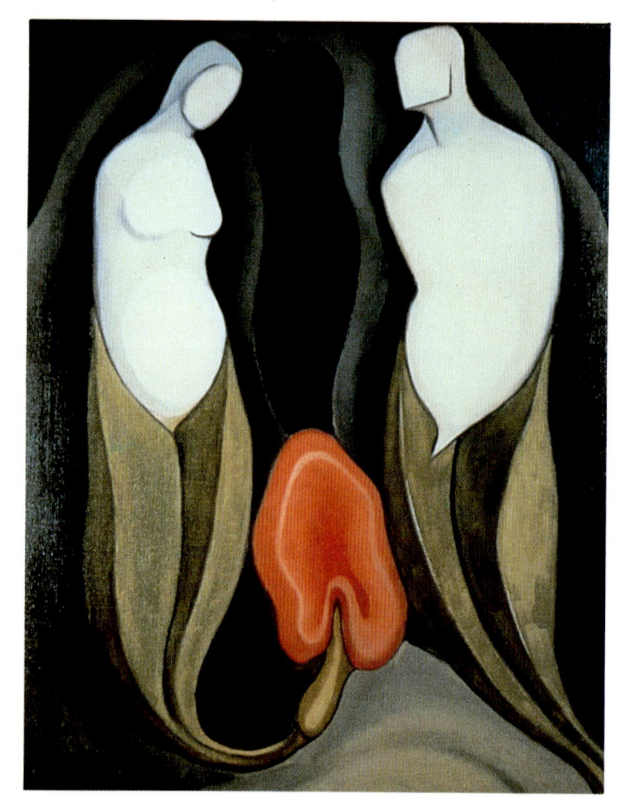

PLATE 57.

Henrietta Shore *Life*, ca. 1921, oil on canvas, 31½ x 26". Los Angeles County Museum of Art, Los Angeles, California. Gift of Linda and James Reis.

PLATE 58.

Howard Warshaw *The Spectator*, 1953-1955, oil on canvas, 70 x 72". Santa Barbara Museum of Art, Santa Barbara, California. Gift of the artist.

PLATE 59.

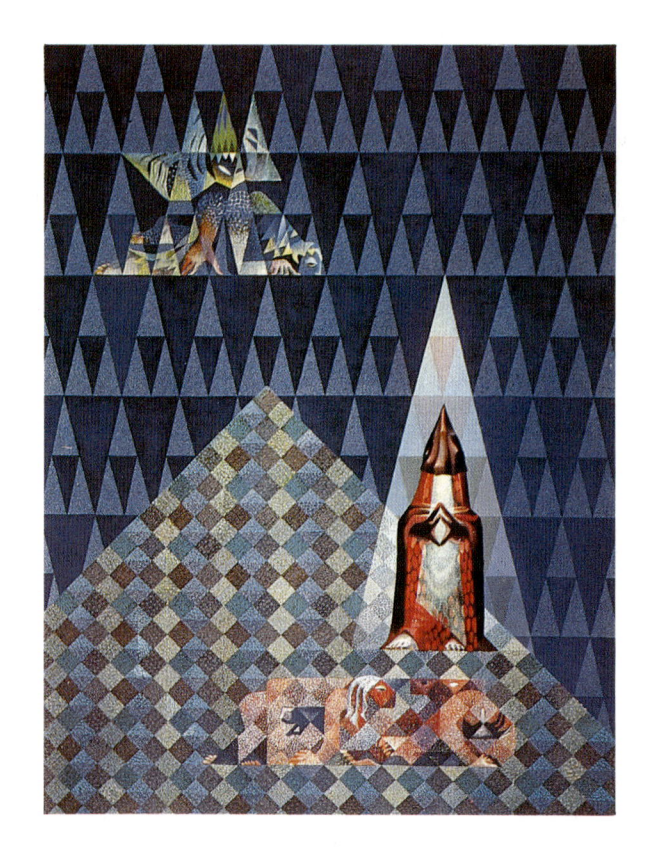

June Wayne *Cryptic Creatures*, 1948, oil on canvas, 36 x 30". Collection of the artist.

PLATE 60.

June Wayne *The Sanctified*, 1951, oil and wax on canvas, 40 x 30". Collection of the Palm Springs Desert Museum. Gift of Mr. and Mrs. Benjamin B. Smith.

work was showcased frequently at the Nicholas Wilder Gallery in Los Angeles and in one-man exhibitions at the University of California at Irvine (1971), the La Jolla Museum of Contemporary Art (1973), and the Whitney Museum of American Art and the André Emmerich Gallery in New York City (1974).

After his death at seventy-eight in 1976, McLaughlin was honored in a series of posthumous exhibitions at the Nicholas Wilder and Daniel Weinberg galleries in Los Angeles, at the André Emmerich Gallery in New York City, and at museums and commercial venues in London, Ulm (West Germany), and Tokyo.

In her study of the artist, Susan Larsen offers this lucid assessment of his oeuvre:

An evaluation of John McLaughlin's work is as difficult as he meant it to be. The almost impenetrable veneer of plainness holds; the painting is a meeting ground of mind and eye. It is also a place for testing. With an air of dignity and reticence he offers us a riddle.

Our ability to sense its depths and find an answer is a measure of McLaughlin's vision and our own.[12]

NOTES

1. John McLaughlin as quoted in *John McLaughlin, Paintings 1949-1975*, André Emmerich Gallery, New York, 1979, unpaginated.

2. Sheldon Figoten, "An Appreciation of John McLaughlin," *Archives of American Art Journal* 20, No. 4 (1980) (New York: Smithsonian Institution), 10-16.

3. Ibid., 11.

4. McLaughlin in interview with Fidel Danieli, *Los Angeles Art Community: Group Portrait*, Oral History Program, University of California, Los Angeles, 1974, 8 and 15-16.

5. Ibid., 8.

6. Ibid., 2.

7. Susan C. Larsen, "John McLaughlin," *Art International* 24 (January 1978), 8-13.

8. McLaughlin as quoted in *John McLaughlin, Paintings 1949-1975*.

9. McLaughlin, as quoted in *John McLaughlin, A Retrospective Exhibition*, Pasadena Art Museum, Pasadena, California, 1963, unpaginated.

10. McLaughlin as quoted in *John McLaughlin, Paintings 1949-1975*.

11. Barnett Newman, "The Sublime is Now," excerpt from "The Ides of Art, Six Opinions on What is Sublime in Art?", *Tiger's Eye* (New York), No. 6 (15 December 1948), 52-53.

12. Larsen, "John McLaughlin," 13.

Illus. 25. KNUD MERRILD, *NO-SO-2*, 1933, wood and metal assemblage, 12¼ x 9¼". The Oakland Museum, Oakland, California. (not in exhibition)

Knud Merrild

(1894-1954)

I may analogize but do not thereby seek reason or justification based on previous experiences for my work. Let it suffice for what it might be. It does not submit to reason for it is beyond the rational.[1]

Spurning constraints of convention and reason, Knud Merrild stood as an aesthetic free spirit who wished to blaze his own trails.[2] Born on the island of Jutland off the north shore of Denmark in 1894, Merrild decided in his youth to become an artist. At the age of fourteen he apprenticed himself to a housepainter, learning the skills of this trade while he studied art on his own.[3] In 1913 after seeing a Cubist exhibit in Copenhagen, he converted to modernism and became its proselytizer. When he found his views unwelcome at the art schools where he was studying, he formed the *Anvendt Kunst* society in 1917, a group dedicated to the merger of fine arts and crafts.[4]

In 1922 Merrild immigrated to America, believing that in this young, industrious nation, modernism would take root.[5] While in New York he established a friendship with Peter and Rose Krasnow and when they left for California later that year he followed suit. En route to the Pacific, he spent time as the guest of D. H. Lawrence and his wife Frida at their Taos, New Mexico ranch.

Merrild arrived in Los Angeles on 11 May 1923. A series of jobs as a painter and set decorator in the movie industry and as a designer in an architect's office ended in disappointment when Merrild refused to adapt to his employers' *retardataire* tastes.[6] Rather than compromise his values, he worked as a housepainter—by the 1940s he had his own business— and relied for the next thirty years on this trade as a means of support.

It was not long before Merrild became an integral part of the city's vanguard community. Between the 1920s and the 1950s his social orbit included artists Ejnar Hansen (a fellow Dane and partner in Merrild's painting business), Peter Krasnow, Lorser Feitelson, Grace Clements, and Man Ray, art critics Jules Langsner and Kenneth Ross, and collectors Ruth Maitland, Louis and Annette Kaufman, and Walter and Louise Arensberg, who acquired several works by Merrild and hired him to paint their house. Merrild's fondness for literature, reinforced by his correspondence with Lawrence, led him to bookish coteries where he established ties with rare book dealer Jake Zeitlin and writers Dudley Nichols, Clifford Odets, Irving Stone, Henry Miller, and Aldous Huxley (who authored the preface in Merrild's memoirs of D. H. Lawrence[7]). Progressive in politics as well as in art, Merrild co-founded the Los Angeles branch of the American Artists Congress in 1936. This circle of like-minded artists and writers no doubt provided Merrild with moral support for his aesthetic ventures.

Merrild's paintings of the 1920s, like those of Krasnow which they resemble, bear the imprint of Cubism inflected by Art Deco. His *American Beauty, or the Movie Star* [color pl. 48] employs a Cubist vocabulary with tubular figures and lines of force adopted from Fernand Leger and Juan Gris. Yet even as it borrows from the Cubist lexicon, the work asserts its own identity via its regional subject matter and tropical hues. Debunking Hollywood's plastic values (which Merrild's book also would do), it portrays a mannequin-starlet who, having heeded exhortations to banish wrinkles—headlined in the paper that she clutches to her breast—is now bereft of a face.[8]

Merrild continued in the thirties to work in a Cubist vein, augmenting his easel paintings with gesso-wax drawings on paper and assemblages such as *Volume and Space Organization* [fig. 23] and *No-*

Fig. 23. KNUD MERRILD, *Volume and Space Organization*, 1933, painted wood and metal, 13½ x 23¾ x 1". The Oakland Museum, Oakland, California. Gift of Mrs. Knud Merrild.

So-2 [illus. 25], both of 1933, and *Equilibrium* of 1938 [fig. 24]. Constructivist pieces in metal and wood, they engage in a dialectic of space with openings carved into the surface and attachments affixed to the base. Carefully crafted and knowingly ordered, they resemble the boxed constructions of Dadaist Kurt Schwitters and American abstractionist Vaclav Vytacil. Distinctive in *Volume and Space Organization*, and a feature which often identifies Merrild, is the appropriation of cast-offs from decorator stock—mesh wire screens and pieces of glass, patterned papers and dowel moldings that put one in mind of a paint applicator. In *Equilibrium*, totemic forms, vaguely recalling Hans Arp and Max Ernst, hint of Merrild's turn toward organic Surrealism. The term "equilibrium" thus might imply a formal and theoretical balance between Cubist and Surrealist proclivities.

This striving for balance was, in fact, central to the Post-Surrealist group which Merrild had joined in the mid-thirties. Co-founded by Lorser Feitelson and Helen Lundeberg in 1934, Post-Surrealism aimed to explore subjective content in tautly resolved structures. Holding likewise to this aim, Merrild exhibited with the Post-Surrealists at the Stanley Rose Gallery in Hollywood and the San Francisco Museum of Art in 1935, and at the Brooklyn Museum of Art in New York in the summer of 1936. The latter

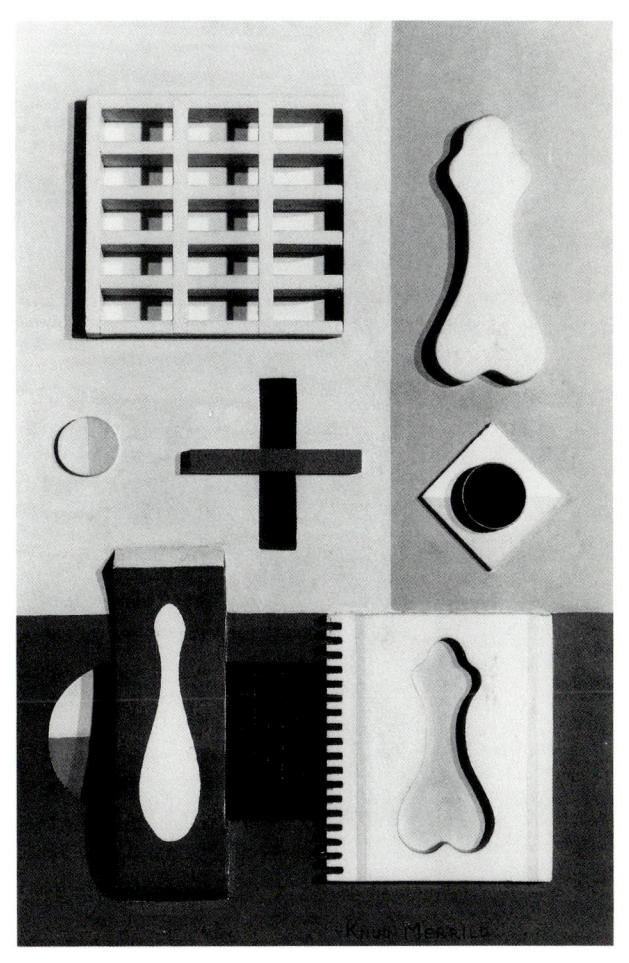

Fig. 24. KNUD MERRILD, *Equilibrium*, 1938, wood, metal, and paint, 21⅝ x 14⅞". The San Francisco Museum of Modern Art. Gift of Mr. and Mrs. Walter Arensberg.

exhibition brought him, together with Feitelson and Lundeberg, to the attention of Museum of Modern Art curator Alfred Barr, who included them in that museum's seminal show of 1936, *Fantastic Art, Dada, and Surrealism*.

Merrild's involvement with Post-Surrealism led in the early 1940s into the realm of automatism. While exploring the subconscious, Merrild arrived at a novel, free-form technique which he termed "flux."

As he described it, his flux technique consisted of pooling and dripping paint onto a wet surface and then angling the base board until the desired effects were achieved. Rejecting traditional palette knives and brushes, Merrild relied on the less conventional means of thrust and gravitational flow. With these tactics he brought into being what he poetically called his "automatic creation by natural law, a kinetic painting of the abstract."[9]

Merrild valued his method of painting by "remote control" because it signified untrammeled

Fig. 25. KNUD MERRILD, Untitled, 1942, oil flux on canvas on wood, 15 x 11⅞". The Oakland Museum, Oakland, California. Gift of Mrs. Else Merrild.

existence and enabled him to capitalize on intuition. In its responsiveness to chance, Merrild felt that his technique was paradigmatic of life. His courting of chance allies him with Dada as does his oath of allegiance to Nature's fortuitous ways:

> *Everything seems to depend on the whim or law of chance, accidental judgment by accidental authority and forced cause. And by chance and accident we live and die.*

> *To reflect this I attempt a personal intuitive expression.*[10]

The results of this flirtation with chance reveal themselves in *Perpetual Possibility* [color pl. 49] in which a network of lines sashay and glide in seemingly random abandon.

The strong resemblance of this piece to Jackson Pollock's fabled drip paintings of 1947-1950 throws Merrild's achievement into relief. It also raises questions about Pollock's possible awareness of Merrild's paintings which appeared in New York at the Pepsi Cola Company's *Paintings of the Year* in 1945 and at the Whitney Museum's Annual of 1946 as well as at the Art Institute of Chicago's *Abstract and Surrealist American Art* show of 1947 in which Pollock was represented.[11] Merrild foreshadowed Pollock's progression from archetypal imagery to free-form abstraction, as art historian Jeffery Wechsler has observed,[12] and also predicted his use of housepainter's tools and enamels.

Merrild's move into organic abstraction was conceivably reinforced by his contact with the Arensberg collection, which contained pieces by Klee, Kandinsky, Tanguy, Ernst, and Arp.[13] More crucial, however, to Merrild's venture into gestural art was his work as a housepainter. Daily, while performing his job-applying enamels to moldings and doors—he must have noticed, perhaps even studied, the random spatters of paint on his drop cloth and these in all likelihood served as the impetus for his novel technique.

In his embrace of uncertainty Merrild refused to commit himself to a single course and thus developed figuration. His reluctance to forge a signature style separates him from Pollock, as does his attachment to figurative imagery and easel scale. Furthermore, he seems to have worked at a slower, less hectic pace than that of his New York peer, but one that was in tune with the leisurely tempo of California living. As a result, his paintings resist both the urgent fervor and awesome sweep of their East Coast counterparts.

If he failed to match Pollock's grandiloquence, Merrild yet achieved success of another sort in works that spoke quietly in a humble voice. On fields of intimate size he conjured up nature's varied forms. Thus, in his *Insecurity of Values* [fig. 26], butterflies and an appliqué duck give an Edenic cast to the pool they inhabit. *Flux Flower* [color pl. 50] exudes a wistful poignancy as its titular figure, stranded upon a mottled blue field, addresses the void with an uplifted stem. Crowned with crimson plumes, it confronts the viewer with a Cyclopean stare. Clearly, the spirit of Redon, whose monocular spiders cast the same eerie spell, hovers over this strangely disquieting bud.

Merrild's engaging imagery flew in the face of critical dictates that censured extra-pictorial referents. Uninterested in dogma, Merrild concerned himself rather with art as a means for encouraging creative growth. Indeed, creativity served as his ultimate goal as he proclaimed, "It is not how we write or how we paint but how through art or otherwise we become artists in being."[14]

In his preference for process over product, Merrild drew philosophically close to New York critic Harold Rosenberg, who in December 1952 published his influential essay on Action Painting.[15] Rosenberg's notion of the canvas as an "arena" in which to perform a psychophysical "event" bears a relation to Merrild's conception of art which he aired in an exhibition catalogue nine months prior to Rosenberg's publication:

> *I am seeking art, perhaps, only to realize that it does not exist in itself. It exists only in the abstract, in different individuals' perceptions. Such perceptions must be deeply experienced and lived by, to keep it alive in its ever-changing flux, idea, belief, perception—all is flux ....*[16]

This passage once again recalls Jackson Pollock who, like Merrild, immersed himself physically and psychically in the act of painting. Pollock's oft-quoted remarks about "getting inside" the canvas merit comparison with Merrild's account of his transformation in the flux:

> Pollock: *When I am in my painting, I'm not aware of what I'm doing ... I have no fears about making changes ... because the painting has a life of its own. I try to let it come through.*[17]

> Merrild: *We can then start afresh to be transformed in the "flux" .... To place oneself in the realm of flux affords joy and liberation .... In the abstract we are of all things and of all mankind.*[18]

The way that these two artists savor the ego's release to the metamorphic will of the paint identifies their approach as Romantic, as does Merrild's reference to his work as a "venture into an uncharted realm."[19] In this he allies himself with a number of artists of the New York School and again with Harold Rosenberg, whose concept of artistic "risk" he obviously shared. Merrild, however, approached the unknown with enthusiasm and not, as in Rosenberg's model, with existential angst.

During his years in Los Angeles, Merrild earned a solid reputation. In addition to the earlier-mentioned exhibitions of the 1930s, he participated in the Museum of Modern Art's important *Americans, 1942: 18 Artists from 9 States*, the first of a spotlight series organized by Dorothy Miller. Between the mid-1940s and the early 1950s he enjoyed four major one-man shows: at the American Contemporary Gallery in Hollywood in 1944, at the Modern Institute of Art in Beverly Hills in 1948, and at the Pasadena Art Museum and the Bertha Schaefer Gallery in New York in 1952. Shortly after these last two exhibitions, Merrild suffered a heart attack and virtually ceased working. Unable to afford health care in the United States, he returned to Denmark where he died two years later. In 1965 the Los Angeles County Museum of Art honored Merrild with a posthumous retrospective. Subsequently his work was included in surveys at the San Francisco Museum of Modern Art (1976), The National Collection of Fine Arts in Washington, D.C. (1977), Rutgers University Art Gallery, New Brunswick, New Jersey (1977), The Fisher Gallery at the University of Southern California, Los Angeles (1983), and the Wight Art Gallery of the University of California, Los Angeles (1989).

NOTES

1. Knud Merrild. "A Statement on Flux Painting." *Contemporary American Painting*. University of Illinois. Urbana. Illinois. 1952. 214-215.

2. Portions of this essay appeared in the author's "Knud Merrild: To Be Transformed in the Flux," *Los Angeles Institute of Contemporary Art Journal*, No. 39 (September-October 1981), 22-25.

3. Biographical material for this section was obtained from Jules Langsner's *Knud Merrild: 1894-1954*, Los Angeles County Museum of Art, Los Angeles, California, 1965. Additional information was supplied by Else Merrild in Soborg, Denmark in a telephone conversation on 27 April 1979, and from the artist's nephew Mikael Merrild in Odense, Denmark in correspondence from 1984 to 1985.

4. Langsner, 5-6.

5. Ibid.

6. Merrild, *A Poet and Two Painters: A Memoir of D. H. Lawrence* (New York: The Viking Press, 1939). 291, 300, and 308.

7. Ibid., xv-xviii.

8. In 1923, the year of this portrait's execution, Merrild, as he later wrote in his book, visited a "coming up star" at a party in her home. "She was young and beautiful beyond words," he noted, "and as dumb." While initially impressed that she had read D. H. Lawrence's *Women in Love*, he soon discovered that she had merely "skimmed the surface" and thus had not absorbed the text's deep implications. Merrild was further disgusted by the starlet's delight in the fawning blandishments of her male guests. It is highly probable that this episode served as inspiration for the Oakland painting.

9. Merrild, "A Statement on Flux Painting," 214-215.

10. Ibid.

11. Citations were obtained from *Knud Merrild: Twenty-Five Year Retrospective*, The Modern Institute of Art, Rodeo Drive, Beverly Hills, California, 1948, and *Abstract and Surrealist American Art*, Art Institute of Chicago, 1947.

12. Wechsler refers to Merrild's work as an "interesting, if isolated, one-man prototype for the developmental years of the 'New York School,'" in *Surrealism and American Art, 1931-1947*, Rutgers University Art Gallery, New Brunswick, New Jersey, 57.

13. See *The Louise and Walter Arensberg Collection: Twentieth Century Section*, Philadelphia Museum of Art, Philadelphia, Pennsylvania, 1954.

14. Merrild in *Knud Merrild: Twenty-Five Year Retrospective*, unpaginated.

15. Harold Rosenberg, "Getting Inside the Canvas," excerpted from *Art News*, 51 (December 1952), 22-31.

16. Merrild, "A Statement on Flux Painting," 214-215.

17. Jackson Pollock, "My Painting," *Possibilities*, I (New York), Winter 1947/1948, 79, in Herschel B. Chipp's *Theories of Modern Art*, 546-548.

18. Merrild, "A Statement on Flux Painting," 214-215.

19. Ibid.

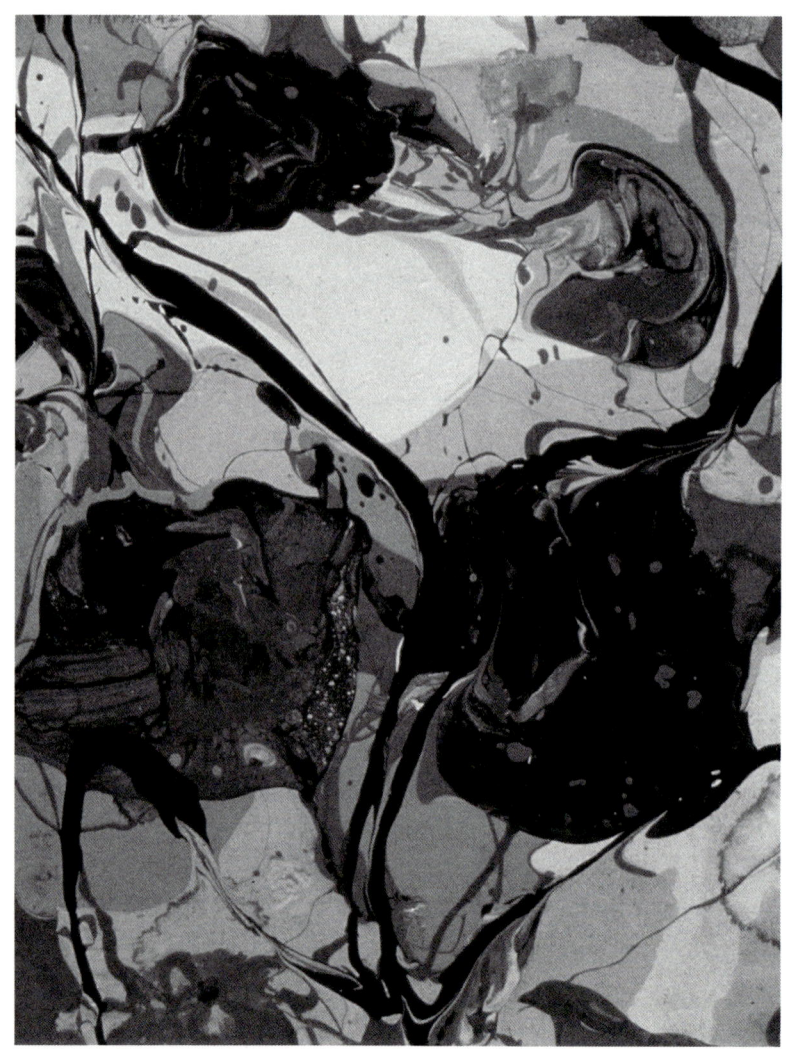

Fig. 26. KNUD MERRILD, *Insecurity of Values*, 1945, oil flux and collage, 17½ x 13⅜". The Oakland Museum, Oakland, California. Gift of Else Merrild.

Lee Mullican

(b. 1919)

There is a creative unconscious—an inscape—that defies the pictorial and the use of deep space. The subjective sense is in an objective frame.[1]

Responsive to inner wellsprings of thought, Lee Mullican has pursued the Romantic ideal, announced by the Symbolists and advanced by the Surrealists, of objectifying the subjective.

Born in Chickasha, Oklahoma on 2 December 1919, Mullican developed an interest in art in his teens which he nurtured with coursework at universities in Texas and Oklahoma. Subsequently, he trained for a year at the Kansas City Art Institute and earned his diploma in 1942.[2] Later that year he entered the Army Corps of Engineers. Serving as a topographic draftsman in the California desert, the South Pacific, and Japan, he constructed maps and photomosaics from aerial photographs. This training, he later reflected, made him acutely aware of abstract designs in the earth's topography.[3] His heightened awareness, in turn, affected his art, which often gives the impression of sighting the earth from an aerial vantage point.

After the war Mullican spent time in the Southwest and in 1947 settled in San Francisco. There he established friendships with Surrealists Gordon Onslow-Ford and Wolfgang Paalen and their wives Jacqueline Johnson and Luchita Hurtado. "It was a time of discovery, of freedom," Mullican later recalled, "a time in which creativity flourished."[4] From this creative ferment, the Dynaton ethos was born. Derived from the Greek word *dyn*, meaning "possible," and inspired by the Surrealist journal *Dyn* which Paalen had earlier published,[5] Dynaton implied "a limitless continuum in which all forms of reality are potentially implicit."[6] In their emphasis on potentiality and openness to non-Western sources the Dynaton artists showed similarities to the Abstract Imagists of the East Coast. Clearly, the name that they chose for their group was the same in translation as *Possibilities*, the title of the 1947 publication of Harold Rosenberg and Robert Motherwell which articulated key concepts of the New York School.[7] Like their counterparts in New York, they prized the art-making process, conceiving it as a magical journey that might lead to mythical realms. Sharing interests in primitive art and Surrealist automatism, they sought, like the Indian sand-painting shamans and the abstract Surrealists, to touch their subconscious spirits.

In contrast, however, to the Abstract Expressionists—in New York as well as in San Francisco—the Dynaton painters approached their work in a quietist way, replacing heroic gestures with pacific restraint. Conceived as objects of meditation, their paintings attained a self-possessed calm, a spiritual aura that obviated grandiloquence or angst. In her analysis of these artists, Whitney Museum curator Susan Larsen observed how they, as distinct from their East Coast peers, skirted the active control of the ego. Perceptively, she describes their stance:

It was a program which took them beyond European Surrealist sources toward an art which assumed a transcendental and abstracted point of view outside the self-expressive ethos of the emergent New York School. In retrospect, Dynaton offered a holistic vision, meditative rather than self-assertive. The artists often used the word "awareness" to describe a state of oneness

Fig. 27. LEE MULLICAN, *Mask (Head)*, 1954, painted wood construction, 28½ x 13¾ x 8". Herbert Palmer Gallery, Los Angeles, California.

with nature and with their plastic material and means.[8]

Dynaton was officially launched in 1951 at the San Francisco Museum of Art,[9] which two years before had hosted Mullican's one-man debut. Soon after its premier the group disbanded, and Mullican, explaining that Dynaton was never intended to be an "ism" or a school,[10] settled in Los Angeles the following year.

In his works of the early fifties, such as *Peyote Candle* and *Measurement* [color pl. 51 and 52], Mullican laces the field with short threads of paint which many have likened to stitchery. Applied with a knife, these tiny, ridged lines lend the surface an intricate texture. In the former they shoot from a circular core, while in the latter they travel predom-inantly in parallel tiers. Painted in yellows, ochres, and golds, these shimmering sparks evoke the rays of the sun. With their ritualistic, repetitive marks and allusions to earth, sunshine, and water, these works call to mind Indian sand painting, with which the artist, who lived for periods in the Southwest, was familiar. Further references to Indian customs arise in *Peyote Candle* which implicates the stimulant used in shamanic rites. While he did not experiment with the drug, Mullican found its ritual use fascinating and began to collect peyote fans in the early 1950s.[11] In his stream-of-consciousness musings below, which share the automatist flavor of his paintings, he seems to reflect a psychic bonding with American Indian culture.

> *On tour I walked, stopped, visited at Ninnekah, Anadarko, Pawnee, Shawnee before the Yellow Mesas appeared where colors ran together as mountains ran together I met the Corn Fathers, Blue Corn People, Yellow Corn People, Corn of all Colors People. I carried a slat of wood and a meal bag, a crooked stick and straight quills....*[12]

While often inspired by tribal models, Mullican yet derived his images from his imagination. It was his intent to project in his works "a personal vision...a new kind of world...based upon the one we all know,... but [with] a degree... of irreality."[13] "*Peyote Candle*", he remarked, "has to do with cosmic space, with the creation of new planets."[14] This he suggests with radiant forms in a luminous atmosphere. Against a warm, ambient field threaded with motes of light, the candle meets a looming disc cropped by the framing edge. Outlined by an aureole and leaving a striated stream in its wake, it conjures up a comet ablaze in a mythical universe. With its simplified forms and shimmering skin, the work attains a reductive concision, iconic in its power.

Although pure invention, *Measurement* seems to relate to the artist's work in the army engineer corps. Evocatively, it brings to mind an abstract topography seen from the air. Its free-form patterns recall geological stratifications, while its linear curves remind one of protractor pencil lines. Certainly, its title infers the calculations involved in constructing maps.

At the same time that he painted abstractions, Mullican crafted assemblages such as his impressive *Mask* [fig. 27]. An heir of his early *Tactile Ecstatics*, environmental objects in wood which were introduced in the Dynaton show, the piece transforms a cast-off box into an abstract presence. Stunningly, it configures a face which resembles masks of American Indians and the Dogon people of African Mali. Like the latter, its cuboid head is crowned with horns and garnished with beads and grains that allude to bounteous crops. As a spiritual kin to these ritual masks, the piece partakes of their totemic magic and also speaks of our primal roots in and dependence upon the soil.

Mullican's aesthetic involvements extended beyond the visual arts to include acting and writing. In 1954 he joined Rachel Rosenthal's Instant Theater which, as its name denotes, relied on improvisation. Devising extemporaneous sketches for an audience seated on the floor, he transferred his automatist penchant from the easel to the stage. Later, in an interview, he reflected how he and his colleagues in Instant Theater felt that they were mining new ground, new aesthetic territory. Their devotion to impromptu events shared in the spirit of Happenings[15] and foreshadowed Performance art, a field in which Rosenthal currently reigns as a recognized leader.

After his foray into theatre, Mullican returned to painting and object-making for which he won praise early on. During the course of the 1950s his work was showcased in Southern California at the Paul Kantor Gallery and entered numerous group exhibitions throughout the country. It appeared at, among others, the Los Angeles County Museum of Art (1951), the Chicago Art Institute (1951), the Metropolitan Museum of Art (1951) and the Whitney Museum of American Art (1953 and 1961) in New York City, the Detroit Museum (1953), and the University of Illinois in Urbana (1953). In 1955 it was included in Brazil's *The Third Biennial of Sao Paulo*, which traveled to major cities in the United States.

A Guggenheim Fellowship in 1960 enabled the artist to stay in Rome (where he established a friendship with Rico Lebrun), after which he sampled living in upstate New York. By 1961 he was back in Los Angeles, conducting summer school classes at the University of Southern California, enjoying a retrospective at the Pasadena Art Museum, and joining the faculty of the University of California at Los Angeles where he currently teaches.

In subsequent years Mullican's exhibition schedule remained highly active, and included solo shows at the Rose Rabow Gallery in San Francisco (1963, 1965, 1970, 1974), Mount St. Mary's College in Los Angeles (1964), the San Francisco Museum of Art (1965), the Sylvan Simone Gallery in Los Angeles (1965, 1967), the Esther Bear Gallery in Santa Barbara (1966, 1971), the Willard Gallery in New York (1967), the Museo Nacional de Bellas Artes in Santiago, Chile (1968), the Art Galleries of the University of California at Los Angeles (1969), the Jodi Scully Gallery in Los Angeles (1971), and the Santa Barbara Museum of Art (1973, 1976). In 1980 Mullican was awarded a thirty-year retrospective at the Los Angeles Municipal Gallery in Barnsdall Park, and eight years later enjoyed a two-man show with his son Matt at the Jonson Gallery at the University of New Mexico.[16] At the close of the 1980s, he was honored with a retrospective at the Heritage Museum in Santa Monica and an exhibition of recent work at the Herbert Palmer Gallery in Los Angeles.

NOTES

1. Lee Mullican, "An Artist's Perspective." *Visions of Inner Space: Gestural Painting in Modern American Art*, Wight Art Gallery, University of California, Los Angeles, California, 1987, 9.

2. Biographical data for this essay was derived from the artist's interview with Joann Phillips for *Los Angeles Art Community: Group Portrait*, Oral History Program, University of California at Los Angeles, 1977 and from *Lee Mullican, Selected Works, 1948-1980* (Basel and New York: Galerie Schreiner, Publishers, 1980, and from Lee Mullican, interview with author, 2 October 1989.

3. Mullican in interview with Joann Phillips, 38-39.

4. Mullican, "Thoughts on the Dynaton," *DYNATON Re-Viewed*, Gallery Paule Anglim, San Francisco, California, 1977, unpaginated.

5. Published by Paalen earlier in the 1940s while he was living in Mexico, *Dyn* made a great impact on Mullican, who read it with avid interest during his years in the army.

6. Wolfgang Paalen, "Theory of the Dynaton," *Dynaton*, San Francisco Museum of Art, San Francisco, California, 1951, 22.

7. Robert Motherwell, Harold Rosenberg, Pierre Chareau, John Cage, *Possibilities 1*, Winter 1947/1948 (New York: Wittenborn, Schultz, Inc., Publishers, 1947).

8. Susan C. Larsen, "Lee Mullican," *Moderns in Mind: Gerome Kamrowski, Lee Mullican, Gordon Onslow-Ford*, The Mark Rothko Foundation, Artists Space, New York, 1986, 14.

9. The catalogue for the Dynaton exhibition contained reproductions of works by Mullican, Onslow-Ford, and Paalen and essays by Paalen ("Metaplastic") and Jacqueline Johnson ("Taking a Sight 1951").

10. Mullican, "Thoughts on the Dynaton."

11. Mullican, interview with author, 2 October 1989.

12. Mullican, *Lee Mullican, Selected Works, 1948-1980*, rear cover.

13. Mullican, interview with Joann Phillips, 119.

14. Mullican, interview with author, 2 October 1989.

15. Mullican, interview with Joann Phillips, 135.

16. For a chronology, exhibition history, and selected bibliography, see *Lee Mullican, Selected Works, 1948-1980* and *Mullican & Mullican*, Jonson Gallery, University Art Museum, University of New Mexico, Albuquerque, New Mexico, 1989, 22-23.

Agnes Pelton

(1881-1961)

There is a spirit in nature as in everything else. I don't try to express myself, I try to capture that spirit in nature.[1]

Sensitized to her environment, Agnes Pelton sought to encode the mysteries of nature in her organic abstractions. Born to American parents in Stuttgart, Germany on 22 August 1881, Pelton spent her childhood in Switzerland, France, and New York, where she was educated at home in the fine arts. Her father died when she was nine years old, leaving her in the care of her mother, an accomplished pianist and granddaughter of the Brooklyn abolitionist editor, Theodore Tilton. As a young woman Pelton studied at the Pratt Institute in Brooklyn, from which she earned a certificate in 1900, and then trained with Arthur Wesley Dow, W. L. Lathrop, and Hamilton F. Field. By 1913 she had become so accomplished that two of her oil paintings were accepted in the landmark Armory Show.[2]

A loner who cherished her solitude, Pelton left the East Coast in 1931 to settle in Cathedral ity, a desert outpost near Palm Springs. Like Peter Krasnow, she opted for a spartan existence, dwelling in a simple studio-cabin whose construction she supervised, and subsisting without amenities such as a typewriter and a car.[3] To support herself she painted portraits and studies of the desert's palm and date trees.

Pelton's aesthetic favored reductive, organic forms that reflected a reverence for nature.[4] In *Wells of Jade* [color pl. 53] smoothly-surfaced bulbous forms, emanating a pale green glow, rise from a stratum of stony matter like eerie spectral ghosts. Dense with referential meaning, the cavernous space which they inhabit suggests things elemental, serving in myth as the site of such rites as birth, death, and transfiguration.

Likewise absorbed with the elemental is *Primal Wing* [fig. 28] whose titular subject glides magically over a twilit desert, replete with a lake mirage. In its buoyant ascent, the wing conveys aspiration as it soars in ethereal flight. Gleaming with a pale pink light, it looms like an angelic apparition.

This radiant light, a signature feature of Pelton's oeuvre, was regarded by the artist as crucial. "Light is the keynote," she observed, "not as it plays on objects in the natural world, but through space and forms, seen on the inner field of vision."[5] Such is the case of *Orbits* [color pl. 54] in which scalloped clouds, viewed at dusk or awakening day, attain an incandescence.

Captivated by the desert, its magical light and majestic sky, Pelton conveyed in words as well as in paint her feelings of wonderment:

The vibration of this light, the spaciousness of these skies enthralled me. I knew there was a spirit in nature as in everything else, but here in the desert it was an especially bright spirit. I became particularly interested in skies. I found wonders there.[6]

In her spiritualized response to nature Pelton appears to be a soul-sister to Henrietta Shore. Her *Wells of Jade*, for example, has points in common with Shore's *Waterfall* [fig. 29] just as her *Orbits* recalls Shore's *Two Worlds* [color pl. 56].[7] Clearly, these two Southern California artists shared a devotion to nature whose mysteries they conjured up in their works with evocative forms. In abstracting from the physical world and from their inner visions, they followed the modernist impulse to pare figurations down to essentials and hold them on the frontal plane for close inspection. Pelton's urge to encode the mysteries of nature was also reflected in her active, if geographically distant, membership in the Transcendental Group, based in New Mexico. In her correspondence with fellow Transcendentalist Raymond Jonson[8] and in her published writings, Pelton voiced a conception of art that held much in common with the nineteenth-century Symbolists and with their legatee Vasily Kandinsky. Art, in her view as in theirs, served not as a record of surface appearance but as a conduit to mystical truths. Like Kandinsky and Oskar Fischinger, too, she valued her gift of inner sight through which she sought to correlate vibrations of color and sound:

The aim of these abstract paintings...has been to give life and vitality to the visual images which have appeared to me from time to time in receptive moments as symbols of fleeting but beautiful experiences. The forms and activities expressed are no doubt related to experience but only as distillations and seen on that plane that is neither past nor future ... where shadow may become as

Fig. 28. AGNES PELTON, *Primal Wing*, 1933, oil on canvas, 24 x 25". San Diego Museum of Art. Gift of the artist.

sound, and color enhance to power or light to radiation.

...In abstract expression this choice [of color] is simplified to intensity so that its higher vibratory voice can speak directly, as does sound in music.[9]

Pelton's ultimate aspiration, consistent with that of Kandinsky and of Los Angeles modernists Krasnow, Shore, Merrild, Mullican, Fischinger, and McLaughlin, was to heighten perception through abstract art. And sensitized sight, she felt in turn, could lead to spirituality. Convinced of art's illuminative power, she believed, as did her Southern California peers, that painting could expand and intensify the faculties of vision, and in so doing could enhance existence itself:

...Art...can contribute to the apprehension of spiritual life and the expansion of a deeper vision. Of all the arts, painting is the foremost in the use of color, having within its scope the possibility of the direct communication of its vibratory life, an essential element in light.[10]

Although Pelton remained isolated in the desert, her work appeared regularly in group and one-person shows, primarily in California, but also in other parts of the country. Her paintings soloed biennially at the Desert Art Galleries in Palm Springs from 1932 to 1940 and could be seen in one-woman exhibits at the Grace Nicholson Galleries in Pasadena in 1929, the Argent Galleries in New York in 1931, the San Francisco and the San Diego museums in 1943, the E.B. Crocker Art Gallery in Sacramento in 1944 and 1947, Pomona College in 1947, the University of Redlands in 1951, and the Desert Art Center in Cathedral City in 1951 and 1955. Additionally, they were included in several group shows at the Pennsylvania Academy of Fine Arts in Philadelphia in 1932, the California Pacific International Exposition in San Diego in 1935, the Golden Gate International Exposition in San Francisco in 1939, and in recent years, at the San Francisco Museum of Modern Art in 1979, the Helen Euphrat Gallery, De Anza College in Cupertino, California in 1981, and at the Fisher Gallery, University of Southern California in 1984. In the fall of 1989, her works earned a retrospective exhibition organized by Margaret Stainer at the Ohlone College Art Gallery in Fremont, California.

NOTES

1. Agnes Pelton as quoted by Ed Ainsworth, "Agnes Pelton, the Woman Who Found Wonders in the Sky," *Palm Springs Villager*, Summer Edition, June-July 1957, unpaginated.

2. Penny Perlmutter of Perlmutter Fine Arts in San Francisco; Margaret Stainer, curator of the Art Gallery of Ohlone College in Fremont, California; Jan Rindfleisch, director of the Helen Euphrat Gallery at De Anza College in Cupertino, California; and Tiska Blankenship, assistant curator of the Jonson Gallery of the University of New Mexico, Albuquerque, New Mexico provided information for this section.

3. Margaret Stainer, "Agnes Pelton," *Staying Visible: The Importance of Archives*, Helen Euphrat Gallery, De Anza College, Cupertino, California, 1981.

4. In all likelihood Pelton was influenced by her studies with Arthur Wesley Dow who stressed the distillation of nature's forms in order to grasp their essentials. Additionally, she seems to have gained from Dow, via the Japanese prints he admired, a respect for flat, curving design.

5. Pelton in notes from the Jonson Archives, Jonson Gallery, University of New Mexico, Albuquerque, New Mexico.

6. Pelton as quoted by Ed Ainsworth, "Agnes Pelton, the Woman Who Found Wonders in the Sky."

7. Distressingly it has not to date been determined whether these two painters knew about one another's work. Pelton could have seen Shore's paintings in New York in 1923 when they were shown at the Erich Gallery, although by that date she may have already established her artistic direction. During the three years that Shore lived in New York, from 1920 to 1923, Pelton's paintings were not exhibited. Before 1930 few works of either artist were reproduced in journals and those that appeared in print tended to be naturalistic.

8. These letters are preserved in the Jonson Archives at the Jonson Gallery.

9. Pelton as quoted by Raymond F. Piper and Lila K. Piper in *Cosmic Art* (New York: Hawthorn Books, Inc., 1975), 27.

10. Ibid.

Henrietta Shore

(1880-1963)

Shore ... realizes a fusion of her own ego with a deep universality.... When she paints a flower she IS that flower, when she draws a rock she IS that rock.[1]

As her friend Edward Weston observed in 1933, Henrietta Shore identified empathically with her subject matter. Like Weston, whose modern ideals she shared, Shore explored natural forms in her art with patient, close-focused lucidity.

The youngest of seven children, Shore was born in Toronto, Canada on 22 January 1880. In her early teens she decided to become an artist when in a prophetic moment she perceived herself and nature to be intimately wed:[2]

> *I was on my way home from school and saw myself reflected in a puddle. It was the first time I had seen my image completely surrounded by nature, and I suddenly had an overwhelming sense of belonging to it—of actually being part of every tree and flower. I was filled with a desire to tell what I felt through painting.*[3]

After this revelation, Shore embarked upon a concerted study of painting, training first with Toronto artist Laura Muntz and then with William Merritt Chase and Robert Henri in New York City. Henri's vitalist views, which regarded art as a spiritual force, no doubt reinforced Shore's beliefs in the intimate ties between art and life. Moreover, his aesthetic credo to stress essentials and disregard incidentals served as the operative principle of Shore's own creations.[4]

In 1913, beguiled by travels along the Pacific Coast, Shore immigrated to Los Angeles. By the following year she had established herself within the art community and was earning commendations from *Los Angeles Times* critic Anthony Anderson.[5] This recognition, buttressed by silver medals in 1914 and 1915 at the Panama-California Exposition in San Diego, encouraged her to join with her friend Helena Dunlap and a few other artists in founding the Los Angeles Modern Art Society in 1916. The group, although small, hoped to promote awareness in the region of contemporary art.[6]

At that time and throughout the teens, Shore worked in a painterly Realist mode indebted to Henri.[7] When, however, she returned to New York in 1920 for a three-year sojourn, she developed a semi-abstract style given to nature symbolism. In accord with current modernist trends, she pared forms down to essentials and flattened them on the picture plane. Typically, as in *Two Worlds* and *Waterfall* [color pl. 56 and fig. 29] large, planar figurations flow or pulse on the surface in ways that suggest elemental forces.

While synopsizing the forces of nature, these pulsant forms also serve as vessels of thought and desire. As such, they convey feelings of wonder, awe for the vast expanse of the cosmos, esteem for the swelling power of water. A jagged peak in *Two Worlds*, for example, imparts a sensation of transcendent yearning as it rises towards a moon in a whorling sky. Relatedly, the surging white form in *Waterfall*, shaped like a petal and painted as densely as the mountain, implies the oneness of plants, water, and earth. Indeed, the artist conceived nature's forms, and thus her abstractions of them, as interdependent and unified:

To be true to nature one must abstract.

Fig. 29. HENRIETTA SHORE, *Waterfall*, ca. 1922, oil on canvas, 26 x 26". Collection of Richard Lorenz, San Francisco, California.

Nature does not waste her forms. If you would know the clouds—then study the rocks. Flowers, shells, rocks, trees, mountains, hills—all have the same forms within themselves used with endless variety.[8]

In her aim to express universals in nature, Shore reveals her Symbolist roots. As such, she shows an accord with Symbolist heirs Paul Klee and Vasily Kandinsky[9] as well as with the American modernists Arthur Dove and Georgia O'Keeffe. Like Dove and O'Keeffe, Shore felt an intuitive bond with nature, whose vitalism she aimed to evoke in synoptic pictorial form. Clearly, the way that she treats her subjects, abridging their forms and holding them, magnified, on the foremost plane, bears a relation to the approach of these two East Coast painters whose oeuvre Shore may well have known.[10]

It also relates to the ethos of Agnes Pelton and Edward Weston who harbored similar aspirations and paralleled Shore in interesting ways.[11] While Shore's knowledge of Pelton remains conjectural, her attachment to Weston, whom she met and befriended in 1927, has been firmly established. Allies in spirit, Shore and Weston shared a purist aesthetic that sought to portray quintessentials in nature. Focusing on organic matter, she with her brush, he with his lens, they treated it with circumspect care and monumentalized it in their visual frames. In the process they lent nature's forms a pristine concision and iconic grandeur.

In *Life* [color pl. 57] Shore joins abstractions of nature with figurative imagery. Calling upon evocative forms that imply germinal growth, she creates a symbolic paradigm for human procreation. Male and female personifications rise at the right and left sides of the field to frame between them a dark, phallic shadow and a red, ovular shape. Touched by a native puritanism, they sublimate erotic desire as they stand apart and transmute at their groins into vegetal stems.

Formally, these statuesque figures, with their sharply hewed contours and marble-toned skin, appear as if chiseled from stone. This blend of sculptural form and primordial theme puts one in mind of Constantin Brancusi, whom Shore greatly admired.[12] Like Brancusi, Shore distills images to their gist and lends them a primal signification. As Brancusi did with his marble *Bird*—which her figures vaguely recall—she grants her subject a universality by reducing it to a pithy core. This tactic enables her to look at once to the past and the future, thus conjuring up, in the mode of Brancusi, both pristine existence and streamlined modernity.

Back in Southern California in 1923, Shore operated a diner, the Studio Inn, where she displayed her works. At the same time, she participated in group exhibitions throughout the United States as well as in England and France. In 1927, she was awarded one-woman shows at the Los Angeles County Museum of Art and at the Fine Arts Gallery of San Diego. The next year brought solo exhibitions at the Brick Row Gallery and Jake Zeitlin's Bookstore in Los Angeles, and at the California Palace of the Legion of Honor in San Francisco, which held a retrospective of her work in 1931.[13] By that time, Shore, following Weston's example, had moved from Los Angeles to the Northern California coastal town of Carmel.

Although she continued to paint in Carmel, Shore concentrated on teaching and rarely exhibited. After a major retrospective at the M. H. De Young Museum in San Francisco in 1933, her career declined. Work in the mid-1930s on murals in Santa Cruz and Monterey for the Treasury Relief Arts Project,[14] was succeeded by poverty and diminished production. Toward the end of the 1950s, Shore was institutionalized in San Jose, where she died in 1963 at the age of eighty-three.

NOTES

1. Edward Weston in Merle Armitage. *Henrietta Shore* (New York: E. Weyhe. 1933). 11 as quoted by Roger Aikin in "Henrietta Shore: A Retrospective. 1900-1963." *Henrietta Shore: A Retrospective, 1900-1963*. Monterey Peninsula Museum of Art. Monterey. California. 1986. 21.

2. Aikin. 12. Aikin's ground-breaking monograph provided valuable data and insights for this essay. as did Penny Perlmutter of Perlmutter Fine Arts. San Francisco.

3. Henrietta Shore as quoted by Aikin. 12.

4. Aikin. 13: Robert Henri as quoted in Barbara Rose. *Readings in American Art, 1900-1975* (New York: Praeger Publishers. 1975). 37-40.

5. Ibid.. 15.

6. Nancy Dustin Wall Mouré, *Artists' Clubs and Exhibitions in Los Angeles before 1930* (Glendale. California: Dustin Publications. 1975). unpaginated.

7. Aikin. 13.

8. Shore as quoted by Aikin. 31-32.

9. By 1927. when she loaned Weston a book on Kandinsky. Shore was conversant with Kandinsky's writings. See *California*. vol. 2 of *The Daybooks of Edward Weston*. edited by Nancy Newhall (New York: Aperture. Inc.. 1961). 34.

10. Aikin. 16-17. Aikin relates that Shore might have seen O'Keeffe's work in 1923 when they both exhibited their paintings in New York City.

11. According to Penny Perlmutter's unpublished chronology of the artist. Pelton did not exhibit her abstractions until 1929. well after Shore had evolved her mature aesthetic.

12. Aikin. 17.

13. A chronology and citation of exhibitions appear in *Henrietta Shore, A Retrospective Exhibition*. 70-71.

14. For an excellent account of these works. see Richard Lorenz. "Henrietta Shore: The Mural Paintings." *Henrietta Shore, A Retrospective*. 39-43.

Howard Warshaw

(1920-1977)

Howard Warshaw belongs to a young generation of Los Angeles modernists who came to artistic maturity in the postwar years. As an influential instructor at the Jepson Art Institute, where he taught with Rico Lebrun and William Brice,[1] and as a frequent exhibitor and prize-winner at the Los Angeles County Museum of Art, he assumed a position of prominence in the art community during the late 1940s and early 1950s.

Born in New York on 14 August 1920, Warshaw excelled in art as a youth and served as a cartoonist for his high school newspaper.[2] At the age of fourteen, he began to take courses at the Pratt Art Institute, which he followed with studies at the Art Students League. There he trained with Homer Boss, a former pupil of Robert Henri, and with Howard Trafton, whom he credits with awakening him to what he termed "the history of graphic ideas."

With the outbreak of the Second World War, Warshaw tried to enlist in the armed forces but was disqualified from service by a problematic knee. Moving to Los Angeles where his parents had relocated, he supported himself as an animator at the Walt Disney Studio and painted in his spare time.[3] A display of his work at the James Vigeveno Gallery in Westwood brought him to the attention of actor-collector Vincent Price who purchased a number of pieces. Emboldened by this sale, Warshaw resigned from Disney and returned to New York to focus exclusively on his painting.[4] While there he impressed art dealer Julien Levy who later would showcase his work in New York in 1946 and 1948.[5]

Back in Los Angeles at mid-decade, Warshaw obtained a job as an animator at the Warner Brothers Studio where he drew Bugs Bunny cartoons.[6] His tenure at Warner's, however, was brief, as he had the good fortune to win again the support of Vincent Price. Not only did he live and work for a while at Price's Benedict Canyon estate, but in 1944 he enjoyed a one-man debut at the Little Gallery in Beverly Hills which Price ran with fellow actor George Macready.[7] Located next to Del Haven's Bar on Santa Monica Boulevard, Price's showroom, as described by Warshaw, attracted a lively crowd of celebrities. Among those who came there to chat and view art were actors John Decker and John Barrymore, stripper Gypsy Rose Lee, and comedienne Fanny Brice, with whose son William Brice, Warshaw established a close working relationship. Also included in this social circle were Aldous Huxley, Christopher Isherwood, Igor Stravinsky, and Eugene Berman, who became Warshaw's mentor in the 1940s.[8]

From this cosmopolitan group Warshaw found his devotion to Western art culture reinforced. Later, in an interview he remarked that while New York artists were attempting to sever their ties with Europe, he and his coterie in Los Angeles were, contrarily, reaffirming those bonds.[9]

This desire to honor Western conventions prompted Warshaw by way of Berman to follow Renaissance norms. In accord with Berman's neo-Romantic aesthetic, he rendered forms illusionistically and focused on dolorous subject matter marked by the ravages of time. Images of abandoned buildings, animal skulls, and pallid figures expressed, as did Berman's disconsolate waifs, the war era's despondency. Because he gave forceful voice to the postwar depression, Warshaw earned numerous honors. In 1948 he won second place in the *Artists of Los Angeles and Vicinity* show at the Los Angeles County Museum of Art and the following year captured two first prizes at that museum's comprehensive *California*

Centennials Exhibition. Thrust into the limelight by these awards, he received national coverage in 1950 issues of *Time* and *Life* magazine. In the latter he was heralded as one of the most promising young artists in the United States.[10]

Helping Warshaw earn this acclaim was his prize-winning gouache in the *Centennials* show, *Wrecked Automobiles* [fig. 30]. A seminal piece in the

Fig. 30. HOWARD WARSHAW, *Wrecked Automobiles*, 1949, gouache on canvas, 23½ x 46". Los Angeles County Museum of Art, Los Angeles, California.

artist's oeuvre, it signals his movement away from the neo-Romantic ethos of Berman toward the Cubo-Expressionist style of Lebrun. Overlapped and fragmented shapes, a moody palette of somber hues peppered with sharp tonal contrasts, and a post-Cubist structure of shifting planes reflect his debt to Lebrun. Warshaw, however, replaces Lebrun's theological icons with modern-day subject matter, as he depicts the industrial waste of twentieth-century mass production. From a tangled heap of detritus—inspired by a junk yard near Pomona—a phantom cab emerges, riding the pile of fenders and hoods like a metallic ghost. As a latter-day Vanitas piece, the work points to the frailty of human existence. Importantly, though, it skirts the morose by wedding mellow hues and rhythmic curves into a pleasing structure.

With its focus on the automobile, the painting betokens Los Angeles living, legendary then as now for its private transportation. It belongs, in fact, to a series in which the artist explored the parameters of the region's vehicular culture. Related depictions of traffic signals and roadway disasters, some blurred as if seen from a passing car, were meant to invoke automotive travel and the signage on which it relies. Reviewing these works in a 1950 show at the Frank Perls Gallery in Beverly Hills, art critic Jules Langsner discussed the sources from which they derived:

Strongly influenced by the semantics of Alfred Korzybski, Warshaw is interested in the visual symbols which play such an important part in our life. In this vast and sprawling city, where one lives on wheels, driving constantly during the normal day, highway markings, traffic lights, wig-wags and striped curbs are silent guardians of our survival.[11]

Additionally, Langsner reports, Warshaw was swayed by John Dewey, whose view of reality as an ongoing process he tried to convey in this series. While Warshaw's absorption with process seems to relate to Action Painting, it springs from different intentions. For Warshaw, process entailed a description of the external world rather than an athletic display or a cathartic release of emotion. Intellectual in his approach, he sought complete formal control and therefore rejected spontaneous handling and its courting of chance. Thus, while flux was central to his conceptions, it expressed itself not through free-wheeling gestures but by overlays and dissolves that held points in common with motion pictures. In this regard, Warshaw seems to have drawn from his experience in film animation. Here again he compares with Rico Lebrun as well as with Oskar Fischinger and Jules Engel, whose involve-ments with film likewise transferred to their easel paintings and drawings.

A filmic quality comes to the fore in Warshaw's *The Spectator*[12] [color pl. 58], which amplifies the spatial shifts of *Wrecked Automobiles*. Clearly, its overlays of substance and shadow maintain cinematic analogies, as does its sequenced imagery, or what the artist termed "transactional figuration." Interesting, too, is the way that the figure's arm points outside the canvas, almost as if it were calling forth a subsequent frame in a reel. The filmic traits that this painting displays stem, of course, from a Cubo-Futurist stance; as Warshaw observed:

If one is thinking of observing the world in time, then those intervals [of space] change; they're not consistent.... cubism ... says, "I'm examining this by turning it over and looking at both sides of it, and the space goes with it." ...If the vision of the observer is shifting, then everything shifts, not just some object in an otherwise static world.[13]

In *The Spectator*, Warshaw portrays on canvas the shadowed projections of his subjective truths. Moreover, by holding mutable figures in a spatial grid, he invoked at once the flux of the world and his aesthetic constraints upon it. Concerned with signification, he intended his extra-pictorial referents to stimulate memory:

...There's a relationship between the fact of the painting and the references the painting makes to the experience out of which it grew that's not unlike memory....The memory is an overtone, a referential something that isn't here but which one must think about. And one thinks about it relative to the present moment.... It is the present moment of the past.[14]

In his tethering of the past to the present, Warshaw refused to conform to the modernist mandate of novelty. Newness, as such, was less crucial to him than bonding with history:

[The history of graphic ideas] isn't chronological in the sense that one idea leads to another in the way it does in fields of technology, in which one thing makes another obsolete. You get a faster fighter plane, and you don't continue to make the old ones. But T. S. Eliot doesn't obviate John Donne because he's more modern, any more than Picasso makes El Greco obsolete. Quite the contrary: he confirms El Greco's presence by finding him germinal, alive again in his own work. So this history is, as I say, not chronological: it's a set of graphic ideas that can constantly be interchanged, moved in their relative positions. It's a lacework, a network.[15]

It was thus through this chain of graphic ideas, which he learned from Trafton and found confirmed by Lebrun, that Warshaw avowed and updated his ties with the past. While affirming his Cubist legacy with fragmented imagery, he linked it to current issues and themes. His cinematic treatment of form, his exposition of signification, his existential incertitude, and his recognition that much of modern-day life is conditioned by the automobile, attest to the contemporaneity of his vision.

Warshaw's aesthetic blend of the present and past, fact and allusion yielded an art that attracted a wide audience. From the late 1940s through the 1950s his works appeared throughout the United States in numerous group exhibitions. Significantly, they entered major shows at the Whitney Museum of American Art (1945, 1947, 1948, 1949, 1950, 1953, 1958, and 1959), the Metropolitan Museum of Art (1952) and the Solomon R. Guggenheim Museum (1954) in New York City, the Santa Barbara Museum of Art (1953, 1955, and 1957), the California Palace of the Legion of Honor (1951, 1952, and 1955) and the M. H. de Young Museum (1953 and 1957) in San Francisco, the Carnegie Institute in Pittsburgh (1946, 1947, and 1955), the Pennsylvania Academy of Fine Arts in Philadelphia (1945, 1949, and 1957), the Art Institute of Chicago (1949 and 1952), and the University of Illinois at Urbana (1951 and 1959). The Los Angeles County Museum of Art celebrated Warshaw, together with Lebrun and Brice, in a three-man exhibition in 1949 and granted his works top prizes in its *Artists of Los Angeles and Vicinity* shows of 1948, 1949, 1953 and 1956.

After his one-man debut at Price's Little Gallery, Warshaw received solo shows at the Frank Perls Gallery in Beverly Hills in 1950, 1952, and 1953, and at the Felix Landau Gallery in Los Angeles in 1959 and 1963. By then, his reputation had been well-established by a 1955 retrospective of his oeuvre at the Pasadena Art Museum. Shortly after this exhibition, Warshaw accepted a teaching position at the newly-established University of California in Santa Barbara where he settled permanently in 1956.

Meanwhile, he continued to paint and exhibit his work, participating in group shows at the University of California at Berkeley, Davis, Los Angeles, Riverside, San Diego, and Santa Barbara (1963-1964) and at the Corcoran Gallery of Art in

Washington, D.C. (1961). Additionally, he illustrated covers for *Center Magazine*, a publication of the Center for the Study of Democratic Institutions, and for *Psychology Today*. The Santa Barbara Museum of Art, the University of California at Santa Barbara, and the Vincent Price Gallery at East Los Angeles City College serve as major repositories of Warshaw's oeuvre.

During the early fifties Warshaw became involved with mural painting, an art form which accorded well with his heroic imagery. In line with traits announced in *The Spectator*, he developed his style of shifting, transparent forms on a monumental scale. After completing his first commission in 1953 for the Wyle Laboratories in El Segundo, California, he executed murals for University of California campuses at Santa Barbara, San Diego, Los Angeles, and Riverside as well as for the Santa Barbara Public Library, the Golden West Savings and Loan in Redwood City, California, and Bowdoin College in Brunswick, Maine. His achievements in this field were celebrated in *Warshaw, A Decade of Murals*, an exhibition co-sponsored by the Bowdoin College Museum of Art and the Santa Barbara Museum of Art from 1972 to 1973.

Four years after this retrospective, Warshaw's career was cut short by cancer, to which he succumbed in August 1977, a few days shy of his fifty-seventh birthday. In a posthumously published book on his drawings, Warshaw provides a fitting epitaph to his distinguished career, matching the majesty of his paintings with his eloquent prose:

> *Faith, belief, religion ... exist for me in the life of painting without conflicting with my sense of reason ... life is an animating spirit requiring material substance as a vehicle of its expression. I believe this same spirit of human life can animate such inert things as colored earth ground in linseed oil. I believe further that such animation may achieve a state of grace.*[16]

NOTES

1. For a discussion of this coterie see the author's "The Jepson Group: The School, Its Major Teachers and Their Drawings," in Nancy Dustin Wall Mouré's *Drawings and Illustrations by Southern California Artists before 1950*, Laguna Beach Museum of Art, Laguna Beach, California, 1982, 44-55.

2. Information for this section was derived from Howard Warshaw in an interview with Susan Einstein for *Los Angeles Art Community: Group Portrait*, with an introduction by Lawrence Weschler, Oral History Program, University of California at Los Angeles, California, in 1977.

3. Warshaw, interview in *Los Angeles Art Community: Group Portrait*, 13.

4. Ibid., 15-16.

5. Julien Levy, *Memoir of an Art Gallery* (New York: G. P. Putnam's Sons, 1977), 310-312.

6. Ibid., 35 and 150.

7. Ibid., 50. Price's patronage resulted in an impressive collection of Warshaw's oeuvre which is now housed in the Vincent Price Gallery at East Los Angeles College in Monterey Park, California.

8. Ibid., 17 and 22.

9. Ibid., 23.

10. "Abstract Traffic," *Time* 56, No. 6 (7 August 1950), 56; "Nineteen Young American Artists," *Life* 28, No. 12 (20 March 1950), 84 and 93.

11. Jules Langsner, "Scheduled for Los Angeles," *Art News* 49, No. 4 (June 1950), 35 and 63-64.

12. *The Spectator* was included in *Four Americans*, a show of Warshaw, William Brice, Robert Chuey, and Channing Peake at the Frank Perls Gallery in Beverly Hills in 1952. Jules Langsner observed that in this work "decision, economy and controlled light add up to a restrained intensity that seems about to edge over into frenzy" in "Art News from Los Angeles," *Art News* 51, No. 8 (December 1952), 41.

13. Warshaw, interview in *Los Angeles Art Community: Group Portrait*, 73-74.

14. Ibid., 77-78.

15. Ibid., 58. For an expansion of these ideas, see pp. 59-65, and also Warshaw's posthumously published book, *Drawings on Drawing: A Graphic Reflexion on the Language of Drawing* (Santa Barbara, California: Ross-Erikson Publications, 1981).

16. Warshaw, "Postscript," *Drawings on Drawing: A Graphic Reflexion on the Language of Drawing*, 77.

June Wayne

(b. 1918)

It is inevitable that painting, having exhaustively explored the problems of structure, will turn increasingly to images, symbols, and allegory to express our human needs. The work of June Wayne is a step in this direction because it synthesizes the cerebral with the intuitive, the plastic with the scientific, the symbol with an attitude.[1]

As a young artist in the 1940s and 1950s, June Wayne became intrigued with signification. With skill and inventive wit, she devised allegories in paintings and prints that evoked humanity's plights. Conceived by a sprightly imagination, her pictorial tropes gave whimsical voice to modern-day foibles, frustrations, and fears.

Raised in Chicago by her single, working mother and her grandmother, Wayne displayed as a child precocious talents in art and a passionate love of learning. With characteristic self-reliance, she taught herself to paint and in 1935 made her artistic debut at Chicago's Boulevard Gallery. Two years later, at nineteen, she was managing Marshall Field's art galleries, and by 1938 was working as an easel painter on the Federal Art Project.[2]

In 1939 Wayne moved to New York City, lured by a post in the fashion industry as a jewelry designer. After the outbreak of World War II, she travelled to Southern California where she studied technical drawing at the California Institute of Technology in Pasadena. This training, which led to a certificate in production illustration, sparked her interest in optics which she explored in her paintings and prints of the postwar years.[3]

After her California sojourn Wayne worked as a writer for a radio station in Chicago and then returned to Los Angeles in 1946. She soon became a prominent figure within the art community. Gravitating toward the circle of artists, writers, and designers around *Arts and Architecture* magazine, she counted among her friends Charles and Ray Eames, John Entenza, Rico Lebrun, Jules Engel, Peter Krasnow, Lorser Feitelson, and Jules Langsner. A kindred spirit to the latter, she shared Langsner's passion for science, literature, and art.[4]

In 1947 Wayne delved into the field of lithography, a medium in which she would rapidly earn international fame. Collaborating with printmaker Lynton Kistler, she produced a distinguished body of work that won honors in numerous exhibitions throughout the country and overseas.

Often Wayne would treat a subject in both lithographs and oils. *Cryptic Creatures* [color pl. 59], which served as a prototype for a print, draws on her studies of optics, anatomy, and literature.[5] Hybrid figures derived from this research mix references to brain cells and optical fibers with a trumpet, a fortress, a mole, and a scale of justice inspired by Franz Kafka's books.[6] Strung next to one another, they form a serpentine chain of allusions. In obliging the eye to follow their sinuous trail, they challenge the mind to decipher the meaning of their arcane codes.

In *The Quiet One* [illus. 26], painted the following year, Wayne pursues her interest in optics and cryptic figuration.[7] Playing with shifting perspectives, she varies the structure's orthogonal lines to confound recessional cues. Like Feitelson, Engel, and Fischinger, who shared her concern with perceptual flux, she tilts planes to destabilize space and generate visual tensions. Then, to abet these tensions, she invents a strange creature whose awkward contortions convey disquietude. Seemingly trying to hide from the viewer, the ungainly being, with scales on its thighs and spines on its feet, covers its face and twists its rubbery limbs. The floral object that blooms near its chest and the ringlets that crown its head suggest that this biomorph is female. If such is the case, then the figure's containment within a tight frame can be read as a metaphor for the social constriction of women. Much like *noir* films of the 1940s and the Kafka novels which Wayne admired, the piece bespeaks existential restraints in a puzzling universe.

The Dark One [fig. 31] also alludes to the "human predicament" via its titular figure which personifies the atom bomb.[8] Incarnating the new technology, the Dark One stands half human being, half steely machine. According to the artist, it was derived from photographs in *Life* magazine; its head was inspired by a cluster of neutrons while its collar and cap (the serrated hemisphere overhead) were based on a mass of plutonium.[9] With deft economy Wayne here suggests both the detonation of the bomb and the entombment of beings it leaves in its wake.

While related to Wayne's work in lithography, the painting's monochromatic scheme also belongs to a postwar moment when artists such as Jackson Pollock, Willem de Kooning, and Franz Kline in New York and Lorser Feitelson and Rico Lebrun in Los Angeles were severely restricting their palettes. Leached of color suggestive of life, their tenebrous paintings, like gloomy images in *noir* movies, give an impression of darkness and evil, often of forces surpassing control. This, of course, is the case of the Dark One whose cataclysmic powers imperil the human race. Concerned with more than mere issues of form, Wayne sought to stimulate thought with provocative imagery:

> *In addition to communicating a rewarding pattern or configuration, I am trying to involve the spectator more deeply, and on other levels. We live in a confused age without a widespread heritage or meaningful symbols. Yet, sometimes the artist helps to crystallize and create symbols, as well as utilizing those already available. For me these may be found somewhat readily in the predicament of our times... at any rate, allegory once again seems a real possibility to me.*"[10]

In accord with these allegorical aims, *The Sanctified* [color pl. 60] parodies human pretensions. Wittily, through a series of puns, it plays with cherished shibboleths concerning the holy and the profane. Commanding a spotlight, the titular red-robed star dominates the scene. Piously, he faces the viewer,

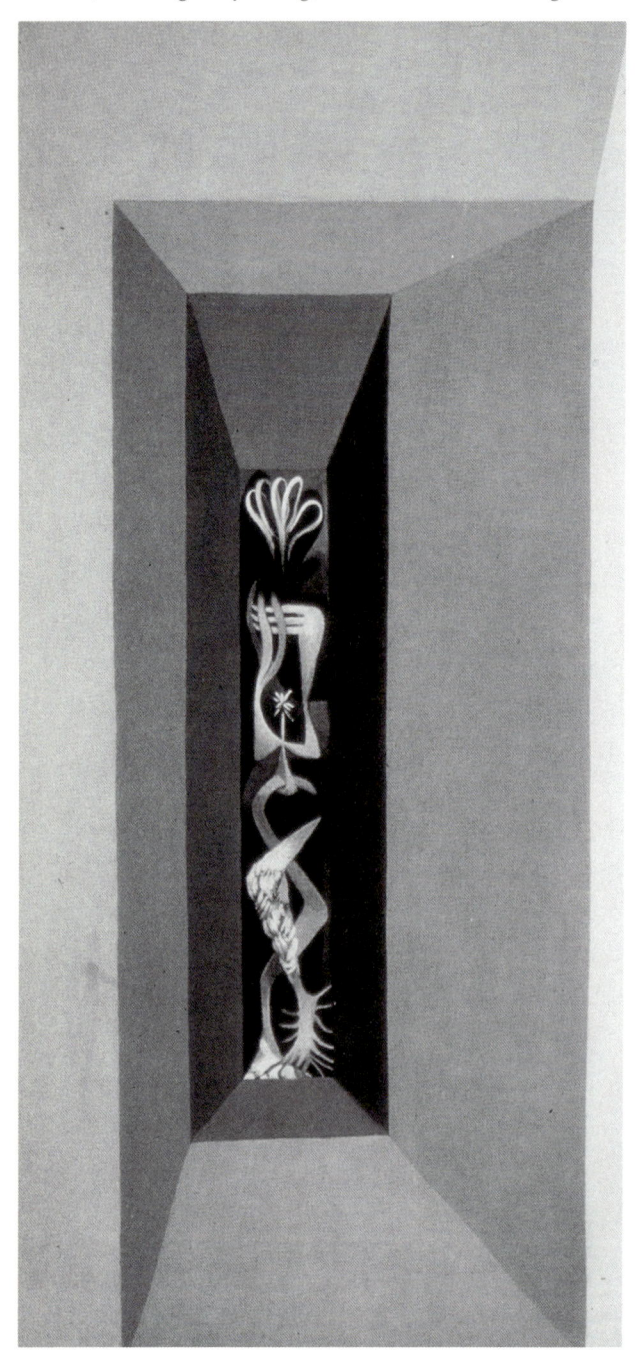

Illus. 26. JUNE WAYNE, *The Quiet One*, 1950, oil on canvas. Private collection. (not in exhibition)

Fig. 31. JUNE WAYNE, *The Dark One*, 1950, oil on canvas, 58 x 27½". Collection of the artist.

proving his sanctity by his garb and his rever-ential pose. With this whimsical figure the artist critiques the affectations of righteous reformers who, like today's televangelists, assume devout postures as they promote their personal agendas. Tangentially, too, she pokes fun at Rico Lebrun's *Woman of the Crucifixion* [fig. 15] whose stance the preacher mimics.[11]

Because she tapped the social psyche so deftly, evoking its strains with intriguing symbols, Wayne earned numerous honors. In 1950 she was accorded one-person shows at the San Francisco Museum of Art and the Santa Barbara Museum of Art and two years later received a "Woman of the Year Award" from the *Los Angeles Times*. A banner decade for Wayne, the 1950s saw her exhibiting in solo shows at the Pasadena Art Museum and the Art Institute of Chicago (1952), the Santa Barbara Museum of Art (1953 and 1958), the Art Center of La Jolla (1954), the M. H. de Young Museum of Art in San Francisco (1956), the Palace of the Legion of Honor in San Francisco (1958), the Los Angeles County Museum of Art (1959), and the Long Beach Museum of Art (1959).

The sixties opened with Wayne winning a Ford Foundation grant and becoming the founding director of the Tamarind Lithography Workshop. Legendary in its own time, Tamarind garnered world renown for its superb craftsmanship. At the end of the decade the Cincinnati Art Museum mounted a retrospective of Wayne's work.

In 1970 Wayne formed the Tamarind Institute at the University of New Mexico, in Albuquerque. Freed from the demands of directing the workshop, she extended her creative energy into varied aesthetic domains, designing tapestries (the *Burning Helix* and *Tidal Waves* series of the early seventies), writing and hosting a television show (1972), and producing the acclaimed film *Four Stones for Kanemitsu*, which was nominated for an Academy Award. Meanwhile, she contributed to group exhibitions as well as to numerous one-person shows at, among others, the Grunwald Center for the Graphic Arts of the Wight Art Gallery at the University of California at Los Angeles (1971), the Los Angeles Municipal Art Gallery in Barnsdall Park (1973), the Van Doren Gallery in San Francisco (1974 and 1976), the Musée Municipal in Brest, France (1977), the Lang Art Gallery of the Claremont Colleges (1978), the Museum of Chartres and the Museum of Art in Lyon, France (1979), the San Diego Museum of Art (1981), the Jewish Museum in New York (1982), the Crocker Museum in Sacramento (1982), the San Jose Institute of Contemporary Art (1983), the Tobey C. Moss Gallery in Los Angeles (1983 and 1985), the Associated American Artists Gallery in New York (1985 and 1988), and the Fresno Art Museum (1988).

Despite the demands of this ambitious schedule, Wayne has played a prominent role in the art community. Beginning in 1951, when she appeared at City Hall to oppose the Red-baiting of artists shown in the All-City Municipal Festival in Griffith Park,[12] she has actively championed artists' rights. In addition to publishing numerous articles, she has served on many committees and boards of directors, and participated in the creation of television programs and films. Lauded as the "conscience of the art world,"[13] she stands as a leading arts advocate, as witnessed by her current work to raise the status of women artists and to improve conditions within her profession.

NOTES

1. Jules Langsner, "Creative Pursuit -- June Wayne," *Arts and Architecture* 67, No. 3 (March 1950), 30.

2. June Wayne, in chronology given to author. A primary source of information for this essay was Mary W. Baskett's *The Art of June Wayne* (New York: Harry N. Abrams, 1969).

3. Wayne, interview with author, 23 February 1988.

4. Ibid.

5. Dated December 1948, this painting relates to Wayne's lithograph *Kafka Symbols, Second Version* of February 1949.

6. Wayne, interview with author. The symbols were inspired by Kafka's *Amerika, Burrow, Castle,* and *Penal Colony*.

7. *The Quiet One* won first purchase prize at the Los Angeles County Fair in 1950.

8. *The Dark One* was included in the ambitious survey organized by James Byrnes, *Contemporary Painting in the United States*, at the Los Angeles County Museum of Art, California, 2 June - 22 July 1951.

9. Wayne, interview with author.

10. Wayne, *Contemporary American Painting* (University of Illinois, Urbana, Illinois, 1951), 222-223.

11. Wayne, telephone conversation with author, 27 September 1989.

12. Arthur Millier, "Reaction and Censorship in Los Angeles," *Art Digest* 26, No. 4 (15 November 1951), 9.

13. Suzanne Muchnic, "College Arts Meeting Signals New Awareness," *Los Angeles Times*, 9 February 1990, F1.

Checklist

KARL BENJAMIN

White Figures on a Red Sky, 1954, oil on canvas, 48 x 30⅛". Long Beach Museum of Art, Long Beach, California.

Theme and Variation, 1956, oil on canvas, 36 x 48". The Buck Collection, Laguna Niguel, California.

BEN BERLIN

Woman with a Lute, 1938, casein on firtex, 24 x 23½". Collection of the Nora Eccles Harrison Museum of Art, Utah State University. Gift of the Marie Eccles Caine Foundation.

Duck, Cannon, Firecrackers, 1937, oil and collage, 20 x 16". The Buck Collection, Laguna Niguel, California.

Surreal Portrait, 1938, oil on canvas on board, 19½ x 14½". Collection of Fannie Hall and Alan Leslie, Palm Springs, California.

WILLIAM BRICE

Parched Land, 1954, oil and sand on board, 40 x 60". Private collection, Beverly Hills, California.

Land Fracture, 1954-1955, oil and sand on board, 96 x 78". Collection of the Wight Art Gallery, University of California, Los Angeles. Gift of Mr. and Mrs. Ray Stark.

HANS BURKHARDT

By the Sea (Dance), 1945, oil on canvas, 32 x 42". Jack Rutberg Gallery, Los Angeles, California.

Woman With a Wine Glass, 1947, oil on canvas, 37 x 46". Jack Rutberg Gallery, Los Angeles, California.

Studio of Gorky, 1951, oil on canvas, 32 x 42". Sandy and Adrea Bettelman, Los Angeles, California.

Farewell to Mexico, 1951-1952, oil on canvas, 32 x 40". Jack Rutberg Gallery, Los Angeles, California.

The Awakening, 1953, oil on canvas, 53 x 36". Jack Rutberg Gallery, Los Angeles, California.

Song of the Universe, 1953, oil on canvas, 53¼ x 38¼". Jack Rutberg Gallery, Los Angeles, California.

GRACE CLEMENTS

Reconsideration of Time and Space, 1935, oil on canvas, 42 x 34". The Oakland Museum, Oakland, California. Gift of the artist.

JULES ENGEL

Outdoor Sculpture, 1945, gouache on board, 20½ x 14". Collection of the artist.

Interior, 1947, gouache on board, 20 x 24". Collection of the artist.

Untitled, ca. 1947, gouache on paper, 10¼ x 13". Collection of the artist.

Brilliant Moves, 1946, gouache on paper, 19 x 25". Collection of Mr. and Mrs. Albert Kallis, Beverly Hills, California.

LORSER FEITELSON

Genesis, First Version, 1934, oil on celotex, 24 x 30". San Francisco Museum of Modern Art. Gift of Helen Klokke.

Magical Forms, 1945, oil on canvas, 30 x 36". Lorser Feitelson and Helen Lundeberg Feitelson Arts Foundation. Courtesy of Tobey C. Moss Gallery, Los Angeles, California.

Magical Forms, 1948, oil on canvas, 36 x 30". San Francisco Museum of Modern Art. Gift of the Lorser Feitelson and Helen Lundeberg Feitelson Arts Foundation, Los Angeles, California.

Magical Forms, 1948-1950, oil on canvas, 45 x 40". Lorser Feitelson and Helen Lundeberg Feitelson Arts Foundation. Courtesy of Tobey C. Moss Gallery, Los Angeles, California.

Geomorphic Metaphor, 1950-1951, oil on canvas, 58 x 82". Los Angeles County Museum of Art. Gift of Mr. and Mrs. Thomas C. McCray.

Magical Space Forms, 1951, oil on canvas, 57¾ x 81¾". The Whitney Museum of American Art, New York. Gift of the Los Angeles Art Association Galleries.

Magical Space Forms, 1951, oil on canvas, 40 x 50". Private collection, Palos Verdes, California.

Magical Space Forms, 1954, oil on canvas, 60 x 54". Lorser Feitelson and Helen Lundeberg Feitelson Arts Foundation. Courtesy of Tobey C. Moss Gallery, Los Angeles, California.

OSKAR FISCHINGER

Experiment, 1936, oil on canvas, 60 x 40". The Buck Collection, Laguna Niguel, California.

Circles, Triangles, and Squares, 1938, oil on canvas, 48⅛ x 36". National Museum of American Art, Smithsonian Institution. Gift of Mrs. Oskar Fischinger.

Searchlights, 1941, watercolor on paper, 18 x 14½". Collection of Mr. Charles J. Pollyea, Los Angeles, California.

Untitled, 1942, oil on canvas, 13¾ x 16¾". The Solomon R. Guggenheim Museum, New York. Hilla von Rebay Collection.

Yellow Brown, 1944, oil on celotex, 32 x 38". Long Beach Museum of Art, Long Beach, California.

Outward Movement, 1948, oil on canvas, 48 x 26". Collection of The Fischinger Archive, Los Angeles, California.

Yellow Moon, 1954, oil on canvas, 48 x 36". Collection of The Fischinger Archive, Los Angeles, California.

Tower, 1954, oil on canvas, 37 x 49". Mr. Gordon Rosenblum, 609 Gallery, Denver, Colorado.

FREDERICK HAMMERSLEY

Upon, 1955, oil on board, 13½ x 23½". Albuquerque Museum, Albuquerque, New Mexico.

PETER KRASNOW

Sassafras, ca. 1932, wood, 39". Skirball Museum of the Hebrew Union College, Los Angeles, California.

Mahogany, 1933, wood, 40" tall. Judah L. Magnes Museum Collection, Berkeley, California.

Demountable, ca. 1935, mixed woods, 104⅜ x 24¼ x 12¼". Skirball Museum of the Hebrew Union College, Los Angeles, California.

Demountable, 1946, mixed woods, 26½ x 14 x 6½". Collection of Fred and Frieda Fox, Los Angeles, California.

K-6, 1942, oil on board, 24 x 28". The Oakland Museum, Oakland, California. Estate of the artist.

K-5, 1944, oil on paperboard, 35⅛ x 24". National Museum of American Art, Smithsonian Institution. Gift of the artist.

K-1, 1944, oil on board, 48 x 35⅞". San Francisco Museum of Modern Art. Gift of the artist.

Untitled, 1946, oil on board, 48 x 23½". Private collection.

K-6, 1949, oil on board, 36 x 48". Collection of Fred and Frieda Fox, Los Angeles, California. Estate of the artist.

K-7, 1949, oil on board, 33 x 47½". Private collection.

K-3, 1953, oil on board, 47¾ x 67⅛". San Francisco Museum of Modern Art. Gift of the artist.

RICO LEBRUN

Black Plow, 1947, casein on masonite, 79 x 36". Collection of Dr. Lillian Carson and Sam Hurst, Santa Barbara, California.

Woman of the Crucifixion (Mourning Woman), 1948, brown conte crayon and ink, 24 x 19". Collection of Mrs. Constance Lebrun Crown, Santa Barbara, California.

Wood of the Holy Cross, 1948, oil and casein on canvas, 80 x 30". The Whitney Museum of American Art, New York. Museum purchase.

Witness of the Resurrection, 1950-1951, Duco on Upson Board, 62 x 96". Courtesy of the Syracuse University Art Collections, Syracuse, New York. Gift of Mrs. Constance Lebrun Crown.

The Magdalene, 1950, tempera on masonite, 63 x 48". Santa Barbara Museum of Art, Santa Barbara, California. Gift of Wright S. Ludington.

Mexican Meat Stall, 1954, collage, 97 x 49". Collection of Mrs. Constance Lebrun Crown, Santa Barbara, California.

HELEN LUNDEBERG

Cosmicide, 1935, oil on masonite, 40 x 24". Sheldon Memorial Art Gallery, University of Nebraska, Lincoln. Nebraska Art Association Collection. Gift of The Peter Kiewit Foundation.

Microcosm and Macrocosm, 1937, oil on masonite, 28½ x 14". Private collection. Courtesy of Tobey C. Moss Gallery, Los Angeles, California.

The Evanescent, 1941-1944, oil on canvas, 38¾ x 60". Collection of Mr. and Mrs. Harry Carmean, Los Angeles, California.

Poetic Justice, 1945, oil on board, 13 x 17½". The Oakland Museum, Oakland, California. Museum Donors Acquisition Fund.

Spheres, 1945, oil on canvas, 22 x 19". Collection of Frank M. Finck, M.D., Los Angeles, California.

A Quiet Place, 1950, oil on canvas, 16 x 20", Lorser Feitelson and Helen Lundeberg Feitelson Arts Foundation. Courtesy of Tobey C. Moss Gallery, Los Angeles, California.

The Wind that Blew the Sky Away #3, 1951, oil on canvas, 36 x 51". The Buck Collection, Laguna Niguel, California.

The Portrait, 1953, oil on canvas, 30 x 36". Santa Barbara Museum of Art, Santa Barbara, California. Gift of Mr. and Mrs. Thomas C. McCray.

STANTON MACDONALD-WRIGHT

California Landscape, ca. 1919, oil on canvas, 30 x 22⅛". Columbus Museum of Art, Ohio. Gift of Ferdinand Howald.

Trumpet Flowers, 1919, oil on canvas, 18⅛ x 13⅛". The Museum of Modern Art, New York. The Sidney and Harriet Janis Collection.

Far Country Synchromy, 1920, oil on canvas, 32 x 25¾". The Detroit Institute of Arts. Bequest of Vivian Stringfield.

JOHN MCLAUGHLIN

Untitled, 1948, oil on masonite, 27¾ x 24". Collection of Edward Albee and Jonathan Thomas, New York, New York.

Untitled, 1951, oil on panel, 27⅞ x 23¾". Collection of Mr. David J. Supino, New York, New York.

Untitled, 1951-1952, oil on masonite, 24 x 28⅛". Collection of Mr. and Mrs. O. P. Reed, Jr., Malibu, California.

Untitled, 1953, oil on masonite, 38½ x 32½". Collection of Mrs. Joni Gordon, Los Angeles, California.

Untitled, 1953, oil on board, 32 x 38". The Sadoff Collection, Beverly Hills, California.

Untitled, 1954, oil on panel, 32 x 32". Collection of Mr. David J. Supino, New York, New York.

KNUD MERRILD

American Beauty, or the Movie Star, 1928, oil and collage, 19 x 16". The Oakland Museum, Oakland, California. Gift of Else Merrild.

Volume and Space Organization, 1933, painted wood and metal, 13½ x 23¾ x 1". The Oakland Museum, Oakland, California. Gift of Mrs. Knud Merrild.

Equilibrium, 1938, wood, metal, and paint, 21⅝ x 14⅞ x 1¾". The San Francisco Museum of Modern Art. Gift of Mr. and Mrs. Walter C. Arensberg.

Perpetual Possibility, 1942, enamel on composition board mounted on plywood, 20 x 16⅛". The Museum of Modern Art, New York. Gift of Mrs. Knud Merrild.

Untitled, 1942, oil flux on canvas on wood, 15 x 11⅞". The Oakland Museum, Oakland, California. Gift of Else Merrild.

Insecurity of Values, 1945, oil flux collage, 17½ x 13½". The Oakland Museum, Oakland, California. Gift of Else Merrild.

Flux Flower, 1950, oil on canvas mounted on board, 16½ x 12". The Buck Collection, Laguna Niguel, California.

LEE MULLICAN

Peyote Candle, 1951, oil on canvas, 50 x 35". Collection of the artist.

Measurement, 1952, oil on canvas, 50 x 30". Newport Harbor Art Museum. Purchased with funds provided by the Acquisition Committee; partial donation of Herbert Palmer Gallery.

Mask (Head), 1954, painted wood construction, 28½ x 13¾ x 8". Herbert Palmer Gallery, Los Angeles, California.

AGNES PELTON

Wells of Jade, 1931, oil on canvas, 34 x 20". University Art Museum, University of New Mexico, Albuquerque. Jonson Gallery Collection.

Primal Wing, 1933, oil on canvas, 24 x 25". San Diego Museum of Art. Gift of the artist.

Orbits, 1934, oil on canvas, 36¼ x 30". The Oakland Museum, Oakland, California. Gift of Concours D'Antiques, Art Guild, Oakland Museum Association.

Alchemy, 1937, oil on canvas, 26¼ x 31⅛". The Buck Collection, Laguna Niguel, California.

HENRIETTA SHORE

Two Worlds, ca. 1921, oil on canvas, 30⅛ x 26⅛". Collection of the Nora Eccles Harrison Museum of Art, Utah State University. Gift of the Marie Eccles Caine Foundation.

Waterfall, ca. 1922, oil on canvas, 26 x 26". Collection of Richard Lorenz, San Francisco, California.

Life, ca. 1921, oil on canvas, 31½ x 26". Los Angeles County Museum of Art. Gift of Linda and James Reis.

HOWARD WARSHAW

Wrecked Automobiles, 1949, gouache on canvas, 23½ x 46". Los Angeles County Museum of Art, Los Angeles, California.

The Spectator, 1953-1955, oil on canvas, 70 x 72". Santa Barbara Museum of Art, Santa Barbara, California. Gift of the artist.

JUNE WAYNE

Cryptic Creatures, 1948, oil on canvas, 36 x 30". Collection of the artist.

The Dark One, 1950, oil on canvas, 58 x 27½". Collection of the artist.

The Sanctified, 1951, oil and wax on canvas, 40 x 30". Collection of the Palm Springs Desert Museum. Gift of Mr. and Mrs. Benjamin B. Smith.

Bibliography

Journals, Magazines, Periodicals, and Archival Materials

Ball, Maudette. "Los Angeles and the Modern Era." *Artweek* 11, No. 3 (8 November 1980): 5.

Danieli, Fidel. "Nine Senior Southern California Painters." *Los Angeles Institute of Contemporary Art Journal* 2 (October 1974): 32-33.

Ehrlich, Susan. "Los Angeles Painters of the 1940s." *Los Angeles Institute of Contemporary Art Journal* 28 (September-October 1980): 59-69.

Harwood, June. "Four Abstract Classicists." *Los Angeles Institute of Contemporary Art Journal* 5 (April/May 1975): 13-19.

Karlstrom, Paul J. "Los Angeles in the 1940s: Post-Modernism and the Visual Arts." *Southern California Quarterly* 69, no. 4 (Winter 1987): 301-328.

Los Angeles Art Community: Group Portrait. Edited by Lawrence Weschler. Interviews by Susan Einstein, George M. Goodwin, Merle Schipper, Fidel Danieli, Joann Phillips, Kathryn Smith. Oral History Program, University of California, Los Angeles, 1974-1977.

Moran, Diane Degasis. "Five 'Footnotes' to California History." *Artweek* 8, No. 13 (26 March 1977): 1, 16.

Plagens, Peter. "The Soft Touch of Hard Edge." *Los Angeles Institute of Contemporary Art Journal* 5 (April/May 1975): 16-19.

Seldis, Henry J. "Artists of the West Coast." *Art in America* 44, No. 3 (Fall 1956): 37-40, 60-61.

_____. "Art Trends of the West Coast." *Art in America* 42, No. 4 (December 1954): 297-301.

Wight, Frederick. "Coast to Coast." *Art Digest* 28, No. 5 (1 December 1953): 18.

Wortz, Melinda. "Nine Senior Los Angeles Artists." *Artweek* 5, No. 3 (14 December 1974): 16.

Exhibition Catalogues and Brochures

Amon Carter Museum of Western Art, Fort Worth, Texas. *The Artists' Environment: West Coast*. 1962.

Art Institute of Chicago, Chicago, Illinois. *Abstract and Surrealist American Art: Fifty-Eighth Annual Exhibition of American Painting and Sculpture*. 1947.

Brooklyn Museum, New York. *Oil Paintings and Watercolors by California Moderns: The Post Surrealists*. 1936.

Laguna Beach Museum of Art, Laguna Beach, California. *Drawings and Illustrations by Southern California Artists before 1950*. 1982.

_____. *Southern California Artists: 1940-1980*. 1981.

Long Beach Museum of Art, Long Beach, California. *Arts of Southern California—XIV: Early Moderns*. 1964.

_____. *Early Modern Paintings by California Artists*. 1964.

Los Angeles County Museum of Art, Los Angeles, California. *Annual Exhibition of Artists of Los Angeles and Vicinity*. 1941 through 1951.

_____. *California Centennials Exhibition of Art: Section II: Artists of California*, 1949.

_____. *California: 5 Footnotes to Modern Art History*. 1977.

_____. *Four Abstract Classicists*. 1959.

_____. *Los Angeles Prints, 1883-1980*. 1980.

_____. *Painting and Sculpture in Los Angeles, 1900-1945*. 1980.

Museum of Modern Art, New York. *Americans, 1942: 18 Artists from 9 States*. 1942.

_____. *Fantastic Art, Dada and Surrealism*. 1936.

Oakland Museum, Oakland, California. *The Art of California: Selected Works from the Collection of the Oakland Museum*. 1984.

Pasadena Art Institute, Pasadena, California. *1949/1959: A Decade in the Contemporary Galleries*. 1969.

Pomona College Gallery, Montgomery Art Center, Claremont, California. *Painters of the Nineteen-Twenties*. 1972.

Rutgers University Art Gallery, New Brunswick, New Jersey. *Realism and Other Realities: The Other Side of American Painting 1940-1960*. 1982.

_____. *Surrealism and American Art: 1931-1947*. 1977.

_____. *Vanguard American Sculpture: 1913-1939*. 1979.

San Francisco Museum of Modern Art, San Francisco, California and National Collection of Fine Arts, Smithsonian Institution, Washington, D.C. *Painting and Sculpture in California: The Modern Era*. 1976.

Tobey C. Moss Gallery, Los Angeles. *California: 1920-1945*. 1985.

_____. *Four Abstract Classicists*. 1982.

_____. *Los Angeles 1920s-1960s*. 1981.

University of California at Los Angeles, California. *Fifty Paintings by Thirty-Seven Painters of the Los Angeles Area*. 1961.

University of Southern California, Los Angeles, California. *Ceci n'est pas le surrealisme: California: Idioms of Surrealism*. 1983.

Whitney Museum of American Art, New York. *Fifty California Artists*. 1962.

Books

Ayres, Ann. *Los Angeles Modernism and the Assemblage Tradition*. Ph.D dissertation. University of Southern California, Los Angeles, California. 1983.

Banham, Reyner. *Los Angeles: The Architecture of the Four Ecologies*. New York: Penguin Books, 1978.

Ehrlich, Susan. "Five Los Angeles Pioneer Modernists." Ph.D. dissertation. University of Southern California, Los Angeles, California. 1985.

McWilliams, Carey. *Southern California: An Island on the Land*. Santa Barbara, California: Peregrine Smith, Inc., 1973.

Mouré, Nancy Dustin Wall. *Artists' Clubs and Exhibitions in Los Angeles before 1930.* Publications in Southern California Art, No. 2. Glendale, California: Dustin Publications, 1975.

_____. *Dictionary of Art and Artists in Southern California Before 1930.* Publications in Southern California Art, No. 3. Glendale, California: Dustin Publications, 1975.

Perine, Robert. *Chouinard: An Art Vision Betrayed.* Encinitas, California: Artra Publishing, Inc., 1985.

Plagens, Peter. *Sunshine Muse: Contemporary Art on the West Coast.* New York: Praeger Publishers, Inc., 1975.

Taylor, John Russell. *Strangers in Paradise: The Hollywood Emigrés 1933-1950.* New York: Holt, Rinehart, & Winston, 1983.

SELECTED BIBLIOGRAPHIES

KARL BENJAMIN

Benjamin, Karl. Interview conducted by William L. Weiss, 10 September 1981. Archives of American Art, Smithsonian Institution.

Karl Benjamin Papers, microfilm 2786. Archives of American Art, Smithsonian Institution.

Pepperdine University, Art Gallery, Malibu, California. *Karl Benjamin: Paintings from the Fifties.* 1981.

Schipper, Merle. "Karl Benjamin." *Karl Benjamin: Selected Works 1979-1986.* Los Angeles Municipal Art Gallery, Barnsdall Park, Los Angeles, California, 1986.

_____. "Karl Benjamin." *Karl Benjamin: A Retrospective 1955-1987.* Redding Museum and Art Center, Shasta College Art Gallery, Redding, California, 1989.

WILLIAM BRICE

Kessler, Jascha. "William Brice: An Interview." *Art International* 23, Nos. 5-6 (September 1979): 89.

Museum of Contemporary Art, Los Angeles, California. *William Brice: A Selection of Painting and Drawing 1947-1986.* 1986.

Santa Barbara Museum of Art, Santa Barbara, California. *William Brice: Paintings, Watercolors, Drawings 1946-1958.* 1958.

HANS BURKHARDT

Burkhardt, Hans. Interview conducted by Susan Einstein, 1976. Oral History Program, University of California, Los Angeles, California.

Burkhardt, Hans. Interview conducted by Paul Karlstrom, 25 November 1974. Archives of American Art, Smithsonian Institution.

California State University, Northridge, California. *Hans Burkhardt: Inaugural Exhibition of Works Donated by Hans and Thordis Burkhardt.* 1975.

Gardner, Colin. "An Interview with Hans Burkhardt." *Arts* 59, No. 6 (February 1985): 104-111.

Jack Rutberg Gallery, Los Angeles, California. *Hans Burkhardt: Basel.* 1983.

_____. *Hans Burkhardt: Pastels.* 1984.

_____. *Hans Burkhardt: The War Paintings, A Catalogue Raisonné.* 1984.

Hans and Thordis Burkhardt Papers, unfilmed. Archives of American Art, Smithsonian Institution.

Long Beach Museum of Art, Long Beach, California. *Hans Burkhardt: Retrospective Exhibition 1950-1972.* 1972.

San Diego Art Institute, San Diego, California. *Hans Burkhardt: Paintings, Drawings, Studies.* 1966.

Santa Barbara Museum of Art, Santa Barbara, California. *Hans Burkhardt: Retrospective Exhibition 1931-1961.* 1961.

GRACE CLEMENTS

Armitage, Merle. *An Exhibition of Modern Paintings by Grace Clements.* Los Angeles County Museum of History, Science and Art, Los Angeles, California, 1931.

Peter Krasnow Papers, microfilm 1712, 1713, 1818. Archives of American Art, Smithsonian Institution.

JULES ENGEL

Canemaker, John. "Animation Journal." *Millemeter* 3, No. 10 (October 1975): 34-35.

Clements, Grace. "Art." *Arts and Architecture* 62 (June 1945): 8,11.

Langsner, Jules. "Art News from Los Angeles." *Art News* 55, No. 10 (February 1957): 20.

Nordland, Gerald. *Jules Engel.* Paul Kantor Gallery, Beverly Hills, California, 1958.

Seuphor, Michel. *Jules Engel.* Esther Robles Gallery, Los Angeles, California, 1964.

LORSER FEITELSON

Dunham, Judith L. "Lorser Feitelson and Helen Lundeberg: Collaborative Lives, Individual Achievement." *Artweek* 11, No. 36 (1 November 1980): 1.

Feitelson, Lorser. Interview conducted by Betty Hoag, 12 May and 9 June 1964, 17 March 1965; microfilm 3419. Archives of American Art, Smithsonian Institution.

_____. Interview conducted by Fidel Danieli, 1974. Oral History Program, University of California at Los Angeles, California.

Langsner, Jules. "Permanence and Change in the Art of Lorser Feitelson." *Art International* 7, No. 7 (September 1963): 73-76.

Lorser Feitelson and Helen Lundeberg Papers, microfilm 1103-1104. Archives of American Art, Smithsonian Institution.

Los Angeles Municipal Art Gallery, Barnsdall Park, Los Angeles, California. *Lorser Feitelson, A Retrospective Exhibition.* 1972.

Moran, Diane Degasis. "On Lorser Feitelson." *Art International* 20, No. 5 (October/November 1977): 16-17, 35-41.

_____. "The Painting of Lorser Feitelson." Ph.D. dissertation, University of Virginia, 1979.

_____. "Post-Surrealism: The Art of Lorser Feitelson and Helen Lundeberg." *Arts* 57, No. 4 (December 1982): 124-128.

San Francisco Museum of Modern Art, San Francisco, California. *Lorser Feitelson and Helen Lundeberg: A Retrospective Exhibition.* 1980.

Seldis, Henry. "Lorser Feitelson." *Art International* 14, No. 5 (May 1970): 48-52.

Stofflet, Mary. "Double View: Helen Lundeberg and Lorser Feitelson." *Images and Issues* 1, No. 4 (Summer 1981): 16-17.

Tobey C. Moss Gallery, Los Angeles, California. *Lorser Feitelson 1898-1978.* 1988.

_____. *Lorser Feitelson: Magical Space Forms, Boulder Series.* 1987.

OSKAR FISCHINGER

Canemaker, John. "The Abstract Films of Oskar Fischinger." *Print* (March/April 1983): 66-70.

Fischinger, Elfriede. "Writing Light." *The Relay: Visual Music Alliance* 3, No. 2 (May 1984): 4-7.

Long Beach Museum of Art, Long Beach, California. *Bildmusik: The Art of Oskar Fischinger.* 1970.

Moritz, William. "The Films of Oskar Fischinger." *Film Culture*, Nos. 58, 59, 60 (1974). New York: H. Gantt, 37-188.

_____. "Fischinger at Disney, or Oskar in the Mousetrap." *Millemeter* 5, No. 2 (February 1977): 25-26, 28, 65-67.

_____. "You Can't Get Then From Now." *Los Angeles Institute of Contemporary Art Journal* 29 (Summer 1981): 28-34, 70-72.

Oskar Fischinger Papers, unfilmed. Archives of American Art, Smithsonian Institution.

609 Gallery, Denver, Colorado. *Fischinger: A Retrospective of Paintings and Films by Oskar Fischinger 1900-1967.* 1980.

Tobey C. Moss Gallery, Los Angeles, California. *Oskar Fischinger: A Retrospective.* 1988.

FREDERICK HAMMERSLEY

Ballatore, Sandy. "The Personal Abstract Language of Frederick Hammersley." *Art Space* 14, No. 1 (November-December 1989): 40-45.

Coke, Van Deren. *Frederick Hammersley: A Retrospective Exhibition.* University of New Mexico Art Museum, Albuquerque, New Mexico. 1975.

_____. *Frederick Hammersley.* L.A. Louver Gallery, Venice, California. 1978.

Frederick Hammersley Papers, microfilm 3962. Archives of American Art, Smithsonian Institution.

Hammersley, Frederick. "My Geometrical Paintings." *Leonardo* 3 (Great Britain: Pergamon Press, 1970): 181-184.

PETER KRASNOW

California Palace of the Legion of Honor, San Francisco, California. *Peter Krasnow.* 1931.

Danieli, Fidel. "Peter Krasnow: Pioneer Los Angeles Modernist." *Artweek* 6, No. 12 (22 March 1975): 5-6.

Ehrlich, Susan. "Peter Krasnow." *Forty Years of California Assemblage.* University of California, Los Angeles. Wight Art Gallery. 1989.

Hoffman, Joseph, and Nancy Berman. *Peter Krasnow: A Retrospective Exhibition of Paintings, Sculptures, and Graphics.* Judah Magnes Museum, Berkeley, California, and the Skirball Museum of the Hebrew Union College, Los Angeles, California, 1978-1979.

Los Angeles Municipal Art Gallery, Barnsdall Park, Los Angeles, California. *Peter Krasnow.* 1975.

Peter Krasnow Papers, microfilm 1712, 1713, 1818. Archives of American Art, Smithsonian Institution.

Price, Aimée Brown. "The Work of Peter Krasnow." *Humanities Working Paper* No. 26. California Institute of Technology, Pasadena, California. 1979.

Scripps College, Lang Art Galleries, Claremont, California. *The Work of Peter Krasnow.* 1965.

Tobey C. Moss Gallery, Los Angeles, California. *Peter Krasnow: California Modernist.* 1989.

RICO LEBRUN

Lebrun, Rico. Interview conducted by Paul Karlstrom with Constance Crown Lebrun/David Lebrun, 23 November 1974. Archives of American Art, Smithsonian Institution.

_____. *Rico Lebrun, Drawings.* Berkeley: University of California Press, 1968.

Los Angeles County Museum of Art, Los Angeles, California. *Rico Lebrun: Paintings and Drawings of the Crucifixion.* 1950.

_____. *Rico Lebrun (1900-1964).* 1967.

Rico Lebrun Papers, microfilm 2709-2714. Archives of American Art, Smithsonian Institution.

Syracuse University School of Art, Syracuse, New York. *Rico Lebrun: Transformations/Transfigurations.* 1983.

Yonker, Delores. "Rico Lebrun: From the Other Side of the Mirror." *Los Angeles Institute of Contemporary Art Journal* 5 (April-May 1975): 41-43.

HELEN LUNDEBERG

Carlson, Prudence. "Deep Space." *Art in America* 71, No. 2 (February 1983): 104-107.

Fort, Ilene Susan. "Helen Lundeberg." *Arts* 57, No. 5 (January 1983): 34-35.

_____. "Helen Lundeberg: An Appreciation." *A Birthday Salute to Helen Lundeberg.* American Art Council of the Los Angeles County Museum of Art, California. 1988.

Hagberg, Marilyn. "Poetic Mysteries." *Artweek* 3, No. 2 (8 January 1972): 1.

Hugo, Joan. "Determination of Vision." *Artweek* 10, No. 5 (3 February 1979): 1, 20.

Ianco-Starrels, Josine. *Helen Lundeberg.* Tobey C. Moss Gallery, Los Angeles, California. 1989.

La Jolla Museum of Contemporary Art, La Jolla, California. *Helen Lundeberg: A Retrospective Exhibition.* 1971.

Lorser Feitelson and Helen Lundeberg Papers, microfilm 1103-1104. Archives of American Art, Smithsonian Institution.

Los Angeles Municipal Art Gallery, Barnsdall Park, Los Angeles, California. *Helen Lundeberg: A Retrospective Exhibition.* 1979.

Lundeberg, Helen. Interview conducted by Betty Hoag. 17 March 1965. Archives of American Art, Smithsonian Institution.

_____. Interview conducted by Fidel Danieli, 1974. Oral History Program. University of California at Los Angeles, California.

_____. Interview conducted by Jan Butterfield, 29 August 1980. microfilm 3198. Archives of American Art, Smithsonian Institution.

_____. "New Classicism." *Post-Surrealist Exhibition.* 1935.

Moran, Diane Degasis. "Helen Lundeberg: The Sixties and Seventies." *Art International* 23, No. 2 (May 1979): 35-43.

Munro, Eleanor. "Helen Lundeberg." *Originals: American Women Artists.* New York: Simon and Schuster, 1979.

Palm Springs Desert Museum, Palm Springs, California. *Helen Lundeberg Since 1970.* 1983.

San Francisco Museum of Modern Art, San Francisco, California. *Lorser Feitelson and Helen Lundeberg: A Retrospective Exhibition.* 1980.

Young, Joseph. "Helen Lundeberg: An American Independent." *Art International* 15, No. 6 (September 1971): 46-53.

STANTON MACDONALD-WRIGHT

Agee, William. *Synchromism and Color Principles in American Painting 1910-1930.* New York: M. Knoedler and Company Inc., 1965.

Jan Stussy Papers, microfilm 2728. Archives of American Art, Smithsonian Institution.

Jean Macdonald-Wright Papers, microfilm 1266 (118 letters to Morgan Russell). Archives of American Art, Smithsonian Institution.

Los Angeles County Museum of Art, Los Angeles, California. *Stanton Macdonald-Wright.* 1956.

Macdonald-Wright. Interview conducted by Betty Hoag. 13 April-16 September 1964. Archives of American Art, Smithsonian Institution.

_____. Loan. LA5. Archives of American Art, Smithsonian Institution.

National Collection of Fine Arts, Smithsonian Institution. *The Art of Stanton Macdonald-Wright.* Washington, D.C.: The Smithsonian Press. 1967.

University of California at Los Angeles, California. *Stanton Macdonald-Wright: A Retrospective Exhibition: 1911-1970.* 1970.

Whitney Museum of American Art, New York. *Synchromism and American Color Abstraction 1910-1925.* 1984.

Whitney Museum Papers, N672. Archives of American Art, Smithsonian Institution.

JOHN MCLAUGHLIN

André Emmerich Gallery. *John McLaughlin: Paintings 1949-1975.* New York, 1979.

Danieli, Fidel. "John McLaughlin Retrospective." *Artweek* 6, No. 23 (4 October 1975): 2.

Figoten, Sheldon. "An Appreciation of John McLaughlin." *Archives of American Art Journal* 20, No. 4 (1980): 10-16.

John McLaughlin Papers, microfilm 1410-1413. Archives of American Art, Smithsonian Institution.

Larsen, Susan C. "John McLaughlin." *Art International* 24, (January 1978): 8-13.

McCallum, Donald. "The Painting of John McLaughlin." *Los Angeles Institute of Contemporary Art Journal* 11 (May-June 1976): 7-17.

McLaughlin, John. Interview conducted by Fidel Danieli, 1974. Oral History Program, University of California at Los Angeles, California.

_____. Interview conducted by Paul Karlstrom. 23 July 1974. Archives of American Art, Smithsonian Institution.

Pasadena Art Museum, Pasadena, California. *John McLaughlin, A Retrospective.* 1963.

KNUD MERRILD

Bertha Schaefer Gallery, New York. *Knud Merrild: Flux Paintings.* 1951.

Ehrlich, Susan. "Knud Merrild: To Be Transformed in the Flux." *Los Angeles Institute of Contemporary Art Journal* 39 (September - October 1981): 22-25.

_____. "Knud Merrild." *Forty Years of California Assemblage.* Wight Art Gallery, University of California, Los Angeles. 1989.

Fitzsimmons, James. "All is Flux." *Art Digest* 26, No. 12 (25 March 1952): 18.

Langsner, Jules. *Knud Merrild: 1894-1954.* Los Angeles County Museum of Art, Los Angeles, California. 1965.

Merrild, Knud. " A Statement on Flux Painting." *Contemporary American Painting.* University of Illinois, Urbana, Illinois, 1952.

LEE MULLICAN

Larsen, Susan C. "Lee Mullican." *Moderns in Mind: Gerome Kamrowski, Lee Mullican, Gordon Onslow-Ford.* Artists Space, New York City. 1986.

Lee Mullican Papers, unfilmed. Archives of American Art, Smithsonian Institution.

Los Angeles Municipal Art Gallery. Barnsdall Park, Los Angeles, California. *Lee Mullican: Selected Works, 1948-1980.* 1980.

Mullican, Lee. "Thoughts on the Dynaton." *DYNATON Re-Viewed.* Gallery Paule Anglim, San Francisco, California. 1977.

Mullican, Lee, and Merle Schipper. *Visions of Inner Space:Gestural Painting in Modern American Art.* Wight Art Gallery, University of California at Los Angeles, California. 1988.

San Francisco Museum of Art, San Francisco, California. *Dynaton.* 1951.

AGNES PELTON

Agnes Pelton Papers, microfilm 3426-3427. Archives of American Art, Smithsonian Institution. Raymond Jonson Papers, RJ4. Archives of American Art, Smithsonian Institution.

Stainer, Margaret. *Agnes Pelton.* Ohlone Art Gallery, Fremont, California. 1989.

_____. "Agnes Pelton." *Staying Visible.* Helen Euphrat Gallery, De Anza College, Cupertino, California. 1981.

Piper, Raymond F., and Lila K. *Cosmic Art.* New York City: Hawthorn Books, 1975.

HENRIETTA SHORE

Aikin, Roger, and Richard Lorenz. *Henrietta Shore: A Retrospective Exhibition: 1900-1963.* Monterey Peninsula Museum of Art, Monterey, California. 1986.

HOWARD WARSHAW

Howard Warshaw Papers, microfilm 2843. Archives of American Art, Smithsonian Institution.

"Nineteen Young American Artists." *Life* 18, No. 12 (20 March 1950): 83, 93.

Warshaw, Howard. *Drawings on Drawing: A Graphic Reflexion on the Language of Drawing.* Santa Barbara, California: Ross-Erikson Publications, 1981.

_____. Interview conducted by Mark Ferrer. 17 January-28 March 1974. Archives of American Art, Smithsonian Institution.

_____. Interview conducted by Susan Einstein, 1976. Oral History Program, University of California at Los Angeles, California.

JUNE WAYNE

Antreasian, Garo, and Clinton Adams. *The Tamarind Book of Lithography: Art and Techniques.* New York: Harry N. Abrams, Inc., 1971.

Baskett, Mary. *The Art of June Wayne.* New York: Harry N. Abrams, Inc., n.d.

Fresno Art Museum, Fresno, California. *June Wayne: The Djuna Set.* 1988.

June Wayne Papers, microfilm 2303-2314. Archives of American Art, Smithsonian Institution.

Langsner, Jules. "Creative Pursuit—June Wayne." *Arts and Architecture* 67 (March 1950): 30.

Santa Barbara Museum of Art, Santa Barbara, California. *June Wayne.* 1951.

Smith, Kathryn. "June Wayne: Breaking the Stereotype." *Currant* 2, No. 1 (May-June-July 1976): 8-13.

Wayne, June. "The Creative Process: Artists, Carpenters, and the Flat Earth Society." *Craft Horizons* (October 1976): 30-31, 64-67.

_____. Interview conducted by Betty Hoag, 14 June 1965. Archives of American Art, Smithsonian Institution.

_____. Interview conducted by Paul Cummings, 4-6 August 1970. Archives of American Art, Smithsonian Institution.

_____. "The Male Artist as Sterotypical Female." *Art Journal* 32, No. 4 (Summer 1973): 414-416.

Weisberg, Ruth. "June Wayne: A Life's Full Circle." *Artweek* 13, No. 17 (1 May 1982): 1.

Cover: Oskar Fischinger, *Circles, Triangles, and Squares* (detail), 1938, oil on canvas, 48⅛ x 36", National Museum of American Art, Smithsonian Institution. Gift of Mrs. Oskar Fischinger.

Published by the Santa Barbara Museum of Art
1130 State Street
Santa Barbara, California 93101

This publication and the exhibition which accompanies it are funded in part by the National Endowment for the Arts, a federal agency, and by Bente and Gerald E. Buck.

Exhibition Itinerary:
Laguna Art Museum, Laguna Beach, California
13 July to 16 September 1990

Oakland Museum, Oakland, California
13 October to 16 December 1900

Marion Koogler McNay Art Institute, San Antonio, Texas
6 January to 3 March 1991

Nora Eccles Harrison Art Museum, Utah State University, Logan, Utah
23 March to 16 May 1991

Santa Barbara Museum of Art, Santa Barbara, California
31 August to 27 October 1991

Palm Springs Desert Museum, Palm Springs, California
15 November 1991 to 20 January 1992

Design: Nancy Zaslavsky, Ultragraphics, Venice, California
Editors: Patricia Ruth and Cathy Pollock
Production artist: Jane Shibata
Typography: Paula M. Faatz, Ultragraphics, set in Bauer Bodoni and Univers; display type set in Modula Sans

Printed in an edition of 3,000 by Nissha Printing Co., Ltd., Kyoto, Japan

Library of Congress Cataloging-in-Publication Data
Karlstrom, Paul J.
  Turning the tide: early los angeles modernists, 1920-1956 / Paul Karlstrom and Susan Ehrlich.
    p. cm.
  Includes bibliographical references.
  ISBN 0-89951-076-0: $24.95
  1. Modernism (Art)—California—Los Angeles—Exhibitions.
  2. Painting, American—California—Los Angeles—Exhibitions.
  3. Painting, Modern—20th century—California—Los Angeles—Exhibitions.
  I. Ehrlich, Susan, 1942- . II. Santa Barbara Museum of Art. III. Title.
  ND235.L6K37 1990
  759.194'94'07479491—dc20   90-8332
                                                 CIP

Copyright © 1990 by Santa Barbara Museum of Art
All rights reserved. No part of the contents of this book may be reproduced without the written permission of the publisher.

Photography: Edward Albee: color pl. 44; Damian Andrus: color pl. 26, 52; The Buck Collection: color pl. 4, 20, 41, 50, 55; Columbus Museum of Art: color pl. 42; Detroit Institute of Arts: color pl. 43; André Emmerich Gallery: fig. 20, color pl. 46; Jules Engel: fig. 3,4, color pl. 13; Richard Fish: fig. 15, 17; Nora Eccles Harrison Art Museum: illus. 15, color pl. 3, 56; Solomon R. Guggenheim Museum: fig. 8; Long Beach Museum of Art: fig. 9, color pl. 1; Los Angeles County Museum of Art: illus. 16, fig. 7, 30, color pl. 29, 57; Judah L. Magnes Museum; fig. 10; Wayne McCall: illus. 12, 13, fig. 1, 19, 22, color pl. 14, 15, 16, 18, 22, 23, 24, 30, 31, 32, 58, 59; Lee Mullican: color pl. 51; Museum of Modern Art: fig. 20, color pl. 49; National Museum of American Art: illus. 22, color pl. 21, cover; Newport Harbor Art Museum: color pl. 52; Oakland Museum: illus. 25, fig. 11, 18, 23, 25, 26, color pl. 12, 48, 54; Palm Springs Desert Museum: color pl. 5; Herbert Palmer Gallery: fig. 27; Penny Perlmutter Gallery: fig. 29; Gordon Rosenblum: color pl. 25; Ed Ruscha: illus. 10; Jack Rutberg Gallery: illus. 17, fig. 2, color pl. 7, 8, 9, 10, 11; San Diego Museum of Fine Arts: fig. 28; San Francisco Museum of Modern Art: illus. 14, fig. 5, 6, 13, 14; 24; Sheldon Memorial Art Gallery; color pl. 36; Julius Shulman: illus. 1, 2, 3, 4, 5, 6, 7, 8, 9, 11; Skirball Museum of Hebrew Union College: fig. 11, color pl. 27; Syracuse University Art Collections: illus. 21, color pl. 34; June Wayne: fig. 31; Whitney Museum of American Art: fig. 16, color pl. 17